Luciana –
In all you do –
love,

MOUTH OF TRUTH:
BURIED SECRETS

Lillie

A NOVEL INSPIRED BY A TRUE STORY

Botorial Conference – 2018

LJ Bərəb...

ESSENTIAL PROSE SERIES 157

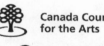

Guernica Editions Inc. acknowledges the support of the Canada Council
for the Arts and the Ontario Arts Council. The Ontario Arts Council
is an agency of the Government of Ontario.

We acknowledge the financial support of the Government of Canada.

MOUTH OF TRUTH: BURIED SECRETS

A NOVEL INSPIRED BY A TRUE STORY

Lillian Boraks-Nemetz

GUERNICA
TORONTO – BUFFALO – LANCASTER (U.K.)
2018

Michael Mirolla, editor
Cover image: Jocelyne Hallé
Guernica Editions Inc.
1569 Heritage Way, Oakville, (ON), Canada L6M 2Z7
2250 Military Road, Tonawanda, N.Y. 14150-6000 U.S.A.
www.guernicaeditions.com

Distributors:
University of Toronto Press Distribution
5201 Dufferin Street, Toronto (ON), Canada M3H 5T8
Gazelle Book Services, White Cross Mills
High Town, Lancaster LA1 4XS U.K.

Second edition.
Printed in Canada.

Legal Deposit – First Quarter
Library of Congress Catalog Card Number: 2017964470
Library and Archives Canada Cataloguing in Publication
Boraks-Nemetz, Lillian, 1933-, author
Mouth of truth : buried secrets / Lillian Boraks-Nemetz. -- Second edition.

(Essential prose ; 157)
Previously published as: Mouth of truth: a novel inspired by a true story.
Originally published: Victoria, British Columbia: Ekstasis Editions, 2017.
"A novel inspired by a true story".
Issued in print and electronic formats.
ISBN 978-1-77183-322-6 (softcover).--ISBN 978-1-77183-323-3 (EPUB).--
ISBN 978-1-77183-324-0 (Kindle)

I. Title. II. Series: Essential prose series ; 157

PS8553.O732M68 2018   C813'.54   C2018-900121-6
                                                        C2018-900122-4

To Jenn, Alex and Will,
And to my sister, Daeniela

I

Did you know that the stones of the road do not weep
that there is one word only for dread
one for anguish
Did you know that suffering is limitless
that horror cannot be circumscribed
Did you know this
You who know.

— Charlotte Delbo, *Auschwitz and After*

Chapter 1

She stands motionless in the walled garden. The sunflower heads have drooped, their golden crowns faded and withered in the pale sun. A crow shrieks as a sudden gust of wind chases the leaves off the big maple. It's the time of year when the past steals in and kidnaps her to the days when Papa was still alive. They'd celebrate his birthday and she'd write poetry about how much she loved him. On another day she and Papa would go to celebrate her birthday at Grandfather's villa in the country, where the sunflowers towered over her.

She was Batya then, before her identity was swapped for that of another girl. A threat of death bartered for the possibility of life. Can it be that she is now retreating to that place where Batya was hidden? Even now, each day she still arms herself to face the world as the new girl she had to become, Beata, the survivor. *Bee-atta*, she enunciates—a Polish name, so foreign to her then.

The wind turns into a gale, stealing her breath and almost knocking her off her feet. She soon overcomes her inertia and bolts for cover into the living room, sliding the doors shut with all her might to save herself, to escape from the world outside. The house is quiet but feels alien. Nothing here links her with the past. Not the glossy walls, the vaulted ceilings or the polished floors. At such times familiar memory flashes from afar pierce even the wall by which she has enclosed herself, leaving no exit. In the silence of this house the flashes blind her and burn her skin and leave her longing for a cool dark place where she had once felt safe. Where her father held her tight while bombs fell around them. She stops by a door and opens it. A steep set of stairs winds down to the cellar, where it is dark. There is something here of her father. Something she has put away and forgotten about. She moves carefully down the slippery steps and gropes for the light switch.

A bald light bulb illuminates an old trunk. She slowly lifts the lid. Breathing in the dust makes her cough. A smell of decay assaults her. It must reek like this when you open a coffin, she thinks. Rummaging through ancient clothes, misshapen hats and wrinkled fabrics, she finds the black shoebox. She hid it the day of her father's funeral, some thirty years before. She wanted so much to forget. But she opens the box. Inside lies a mix of photos, a bundle of typed notes rolled up and held by an elastic band, even the Polish passports with which they entered Canada. And a crumpled sheet of yellowed paper. She picks it up and smooths the wrinkles against her thigh. Her eyes strain to read the faded, typewritten words.

Name: Beata Bielicka
Born: Warsaw, Poland
Date: January 5, 1933
Mother: Magda Bielicka
Father: Pavel Bielicki
Religion: Catholic—Baptized at the Church of Three Crosses

Here it is—her false birth certificate and the new identity given her during the war. Her parents' aliases were different from hers now. Papa said he didn't want to put her in harm's way, in case he and Mother got caught. She could pass as their niece when out of the ghetto, where no one must know her real name. In the document, she became a Christian girl, Beata Bielicka. Soon Beata would become the voice in Batya's head telling her what to do. From the age of nine, Batya had to lie. Papa told her that lies might save them from death, but the truth might kill them. She didn't understand, because till then Papa had taught her always to tell the truth.

She unrolls the bundle of notes and reads the typewritten words on long sheets of paper. *I accuse*, it read, *Stefan Rogacki of blackmail.* Batya continues reading her father's accusation of the man who had been his best friend and who took in her little sister Tereska to protect her from the Nazis. She reads her father's testimony, as an indictment against Rogacki for blackmailing her father for his two properties in Warsaw. But it wasn't clear why the blackmail took place, except the next pages said that Papa lost his case because Rogacki appeared in court with a pack of lies against him.

This was news. She had known nothing of this and wondered how these papers got into her trunk. Rogacki took away their properties so small wonder they were poor when they came to Canada with nothing, only a suitcase each, their lives and their city in ruins. Papa, the once successful lawyer, started making a living by painting flowers on boxes and selling them to the local gift shop. She must ask her mother about this.

She examines the old black-and-white photos.

Papa lying in the grass between two young ladies. Were they his girl-friends?

A toddler, the name Tereska written below. She had almost forgotten what her sister looked like.

Papa and Batya in a forest before the war.

Back then the two of them would wander among the trees and ferns picking mushrooms and wild berries. Whenever they'd separate, Papa would whistle a tune to signal his whereabouts. With him by her side she had always felt confident and safe. During the war, Papa would guide her along dangerous streets, protecting her from the gun-toting Nazi soldiers. He would explain things she didn't know, things about the present and the past. He would tell her about the family's happy life before the war began and before she could remember.

How she longs for his words and his reassuring presence. She looks at the images glued to the black paper of the thin album, and fragments of life with her father flicker before her eyes like a silent black-and-white film.

Papa the lawyer reciting a speech for the court, walking back and forth in his study with hands behind his back like Napoleon.

Papa giving beggar children two *zlotys*.

Papa writing poetry and painting pictures.

Papa, who loved her and saved her life.

"Remember your past. Know who you are," Papa had told her when she was very young. If only he had told her more about himself. And now his secrets are buried in a grave.

She opens the envelope Mother handed her the day of Father's funeral and pulls out a piece of cardboard. Here is Papa's drawing of lilies of the valley, so real, the tips of her fingers can almost sense their silkiness as they trace the contours of the petals. "To my daughters, Batya and Tereska, hidden in a village," reads the inscription. Beneath it is Papa's poem, *about two sisters separated from their parents by a raging storm.* "Lilies of the valley, fragrant bells…" He promised *when the clouds passed and the sun returned, they would all be together again.*

But we were never really together again, were we? Batya puts the poem aside, tears rolling down her cheeks.

Papa's death, much too early, shut the door on that remote world where a part of her still lived. As he lay dying in the hospital, she felt as if she was dying with him. She sat beside his emaciated body, holding his hands—the hands that wrote poems and painted flowers; the hands whose fingers held that strange silver disk, turning it round and round; the hands that were now growing cold. She watched his parched lips forming words she could barely hear. Only his eyes spoke clearly, of physical pain and mental anguish. "I'm so unhappy," he murmured. She felt helpless. Her father, her fortress, was crumbling before her eyes.

Her mother, Marta, took her by the arm. "You have homework to do. Go home, Batya," she ordered, trying to pull her away from Papa's bedside. "Don't upset your father. Do you think he wants you to fail?"

She was an obedient daughter who usually did as she was told. Yet seeing Papa in pain, she rebelled and said no for the first time. But within an hour, under her mother's stern gaze and no longer able to bear the sight of her father lying there in the shadow of death, she gave in. As she was leaving the room she heard him whisper, "Forgive me, my child. Please forgive me."

Forgive him for what?

Mama returned to the apartment much later that night, her face greenish-white. "Papa is no longer with us," she said in a hollow voice and walked away. Numb and unable to cry, Batya sat on her bed thinking that her life, too, had ended.

During the burial, Batya stood beside the grave petrified, seeing nothing but the leafless branches of a willow tree, hearing only the thud of the earth against the casket as it was lowered into the frozen depths. *They are burying Papa alive, she thought. He is not dead. He is still around us—a ghost who will come in the night to haunt me. I have been a bad daughter.*

After the funeral, she stood by the window of their third-floor apartment, looking down at the faintly lit path. It was empty but she could still see, as she had a few days before his death, the stretcher that had carried Papa to an ambulance. His face was yellow and worn against the white sheet, his eyes reflecting pain but his lips attempting a smile as he looked up at her, standing there, waving goodbye. Soon he vanished inside the ambulance—just as that morning the casket had vanished into the grave. When friends came to pay their respects, Batya remained in her room. She lay on her bed till dark. She wanted to avoid the people crowding around her mother. Finally, she heard them leave.

She didn't know how long she had lain there when the door to her room opened. She sat up on the bed, startled. A figure stood on the threshold, bathed in the light of the street lamp streaming through the window. *It's Papa,* she thought again, rubbing her eyes. *He's come to punish me for wishing he would stop writhing in pain.* But as the room brightened, she saw it was her mother, regal and elegant in a black dress that emphasized her classic beauty and the deep sea-green of her eyes, now red from crying.

That was when her mother gave her the blue velvet pouch. "Papa also left you this," her mother said, placing it on Batya's desk. Batya already had the envelope with the poem inside. Now she understood that these two objects were all she had left of Papa.

Marta Lichtenberg's face revealed nothing. She turned to leave, closing the door behind her. Batya wanted the warmth of her mother's arms, yet she could not move. Instead she hugged the blanket Papa had so often used on his feet when they felt cold.

She feels a chill and shakes herself out of her memories. Still stooped over the trunk in the cellar, she finds the velvet pouch at the bottom of the shoebox. She takes out the silver disk, with its round face and sharp features, now tarnished black, like the moon during an eclipse. The face—half human, half mythological deity—seems to be staring at her, enraged.

The face looks much as it did when in Papa's possession: a polished disk with a vertical crack across the cheek and the elliptical mouth, splitting the lip and forming a narrow ravine to the chin. The mouth is open, as if ready to shout. The eyes, one round, the other narrowed into a small hollow, are menacing.

She turns it over and over, examining it for clues. On the back she can barely read the word *Cara*, meaning "darling" in Italian. Or is it the name of a woman? Below is an engraving—an image of some twisted logo—and another word she cannot decipher.

How did this ever come into Papa's possession?

Chapter 2

Strange, how a flight of stairs can transport you to the past and back again, she thinks, leaving the cold basement for the warmth of the kitchen. Hadn't Joseph told her to leave the past behind? Beata did just that when they married. For the past twenty years, she so wanted to please him that she promised to stop being a "Polack from the old country," as his friends called her. She just lived her life, as Beata.

As soon as they started dating, Batya's mother encouraged her daughter to keep company only with Joseph and no one else. Batya didn't understand what it was she felt for Joseph, but he seemed sweet to her and she would often kiss and hug him during their courtship. Although his response was cool, measured, she took this as shyness on his part and thought once they were married, he would soften towards her and open up.

When they met, she was not quite twenty, he four years older. She was intrigued by his grey-blue eyes. In those days he wore a long brown wool coat to school. She would watch him devour his many sandwiches at lunch and wonder why his eyes still looked hungry and searching. He seemed an angry young man, always ready to fight. Nevertheless, she felt attracted to his tall, lean, muscular body, his wide-shouldered frame. When he walked, he displayed confidence, as if he knew exactly who he was and where he was going.

They necked in the park after dark like many other couples along the beach at English Bay, yet always stopped just before things got out of hand, and then Joseph would quietly drive her home. She appreciated this, having been conditioned by her mother to fear men and sex. Joseph never forced himself on her and she felt safe. The Beata in her, liked that Joseph was a popular boy whose parents were well known in the community, and so she decided to hang on to him.

They started going steady and some months later, just before they became engaged, Joseph took her home to meet his family. The Batya part of her immediately loved his brothers and sisters and made fast friends with them. It was a miracle to have gained such a large family when so many of her relatives had perished during the war. She felt a special attachment to Joseph's mother, Dora, who seemed to understand Batya better than her own mother and soon became her friend and confidante.

Just before they married, Joseph graduated at the head of his class. On her wedding day, while dressing, she suddenly stopped and stared into the mirror. She saw someone strange in a white lace dress with stephanotis in her hair. *Who is she, this person marrying Joseph?*

Oh, get on with it, said Bea, in her usual brusque manner.

No, answered Batya. *I want to run away. This is wrong and I am scared.*

You're a coward, said Bea. *It's too late. They are all waiting.*

An uncertain Batya walked down the aisle of the synagogue, Bea urging her towards her future life. Split in mind and heart, it was as if both Batya and Bea joined Joseph underneath the *chuppah* to proclaim their vows. Joseph's face became soft and visibly moved as she arrived. It seemed then as if Bea and Batya integrated into a solemn and happy entity.

At the wedding, they ran out of food, either because her mother was a minimalist or the guests were unusually hungry, crowding the buffet table as if they hadn't eaten for days. Afterwards, Marta sent Batya on her way to her new life with a set of empty suitcases. Joseph received Papa's gold cufflinks and never wore them.

It was only after they were married that Batya discovered that she and Joseph were from two different worlds. She was an exile, a part of her left behind on the other side of the ocean. He was a Canadian, his feet firmly planted on the ground in the city where he had been born and raised, where he belonged.

Joseph was frugal, a character trait she didn't know about until after their wedding, when they moved into a studio apartment in East Vancouver and he furnished it with a second-hand sofa bed and barrels for tables. Though they didn't have much money in those days, they could have afforded better. Joseph cared nothing about the little things that made a difference to Batya like books, or holding her hand when they were walking across the street. She felt alone, on her own and often hurt by her husband's cool nature. But Bea, in her thicker skin, went about the business of daily living, taking the good, ignoring the bad, forgetting the past. For her it was simply a matter of survival. Bea, the survivor, didn't complain, but Batya missed having a protective arm to guide her. *When will you acquire some tough skin?* Barked Bea.

A few years later, they built a home on a hill, thanks to Joseph's hard work and successful construction business. On the city's west side, surrounded by posh residences, their house, with its large gallery on the second floor overlooking an expansive foyer, was perfect for entertaining, yet to Batya its modern design felt empty and cold. She longed to decorate the large rooms with elegant and comfortable furnishings. They argued. "You'll bankrupt me," Joseph said, still careful with his money, but agreed to get only the bare essentials. She gave in. Arguing was exhausting and got them nowhere so she retreated more and more into the dark hole of her childhood, where she would brood unnoticed. Bea made do with inexpensive and often gaudy objects here and there to brighten up the space.

A loud bang startles her, but it's only the laundry room door slammed shut by a gust of wind still raging outside.

Batya feels claustrophobic in this house, never free, connected as she is to Joseph by an umbilical cord of security and stability. Whenever she broods about being so completely dependent on her husband, Bea shrills in some part of Batya's head.

Stop feeling sorry for yourself! It's a new day and you've got to get on with it. Bea can be practical, at times a little vulgar, even offensive, a disturbing but strong creature Batya often summons to help her cope with a world gone mad. *C'mon, you screwed-up immigrant, you live in the past,* Bea would say. *Get your life together.*

Bea and Batya, the two forces inside her: one pushing her ahead and the other making her retreat. How can her children know what to make of her and which of her two personalities is real? Does Joseph know?

She senses their confusion. Like the time when she was reading poetry out loud, in front of her bedroom mirror, imagining that it was her Russian grandmother reciting lines from a poem by Pushkin. Suddenly she saw her daughter, Miriam, reflected in that same mirror, standing behind her, a puzzled expression on her face.

"What are you *doing,* Mom?" she said. "What language is that?"

When Batya told her it was Russian. Miriam exclaimed, "Mom, how weird can you get?" and left the room shaking her head.

What do you expect? screeched Bea inside Batya's head. *Your kid doesn't know who you really are and neither do you.*

On another occasion, the boisterous Bea put on a dinner party for friends and spoke and laughed so loud after a few drinks that Sam, who hated her drinking, came up and whispered in her ear, "Mom, you're drinking too much, and you don't look like my mom in that outfit."

Bea burst into laughter. "What can be wrong with my orange Japanese kimono?" she asked, swinging the tasselled sash in front of his nose. She turned her back on him and continued to burrow through the evening with a drink in each hand.

Chapter 3

It's almost dinner time. Joseph and the children will be home soon from school and their various activities and Batya will have to become Bea to survive the dinner crisis, Joseph's silence, and her children's need of her. The prospect gives her the jitters. Some unfounded or perhaps founded feeling of failure. Like the time her mother laughed at her when Batya botched up the sewing of a dress for a home economics course she detested. Bea shrugged it off, but Batya's deeply felt wound still stings. She ran into her room then and behind the closed door tore the dress to shreds shouting "I am a failure, a bloody failure." Then fell into a depression that Bea pulled out of soon enough. Rather, Bea conquered the oncoming waves and swam ashore, leaving Batya in the deeps fighting for survival.

The kitchen clock says it's too early for a drink. Maybe just a little one? Bea loves to drink for fun while Batya does it for oblivion. *What the heck!* She pours herself vodka on ice with a twist of lime. Depression lifts and she rises from her gloom into the light. Yet she knows these sensations won't last and the consequences of drinking are headaches and stomach aches, as well as having said and done things she was ashamed of.

The shrill ring of the phone cuts into her musings. It will surely be Mother, who calls every day to bombard her with trivial questions. Batya sips more of the vodka and picks up the phone, but it is not her mother's voice she hears.

"Batya, is that you?" asks Antonia.

"I hope so," Batya answers, not quite sure which of her two selves she might be today.

Antonia Horowitz Denner became her best and most trusted friend when Batya's family arrived in Toronto from Poland as poor immigrants in the forties. Their parents had struck up a friendship, and the two fourteen-year-old girls soon found common ground. She had grown to love Antonia and her parents, who had opened their home and hearts to her. The two girls shared an awakening interest in boys, marvelled at the flowering of their bodies and the allure of makeup. Batya admired her friend's science skills and ability to solve mathematical problems, but mostly she had envied how Antonia had jitterbugged with boys at school dances, while she, the wallflower, wilted in the corner of the gym. They had been apart for years, but after completing her counselling degree, Antonia had married a man from Vancouver and came here to live, and so their friendship resumed.

"Something's happened!" Antonia's voice intrudes. "To Andrew—" She breaks into a sob.

Andrew? Batya is shaken from her reverie. *Antonia's brother, the athletic golden boy, top of his class and her first teenage crush.*

"Andrew was charged with illegal possession of drugs," Antonia manages to say. "He was on his way to visit me. A flight attendant found some packages that fell out of his coat pocket while he was asleep on the plane."

"Oh, my God," whispers Batya.

"I have got to see him. Will you come with me?"

"Come where?"

"He's already been sentenced. He's in prison. He wants me to come. But I can't face it alone."

"Prison?" The word conjures up a brick wall wrapped in barbed wire.

"Batya? Are you still there? It's just a short drive." Antonia is pleading. "I'll pick you up on Saturday at nine, okay?"

"Yes, fine," Batya answers with difficulty. "Of course, I'll go with you." The certainty in her voice comes from the drink, from Bea, not Batya.

"Thanks for being there for me. You sure find out who your friends are at a time like this."

How could she not go? Poor Antonia, her dearest friend.

Antonia is the only person alive besides her mother who knew Batya's father. She felt even closer to Antonia's parents, who treated her like their own daughter. And she needed that, especially when her mother left Batya with the Horowitzes for three months after Shimon died. Marta had met a man she had known when still in Poland. They fell in love and were married in Vancouver, and Batya was to stay behind in Toronto with Antonia's family until her mother and stepfather asked her to come and live with them.

Mother could have waited and not married Max Stern so soon after Papa died. But Batya remembers her mother's weariness at that time, her impatience with everything and how she would toss at night and sigh. Batya and

Antonia reasoned that Marta Lichtenberg must have been very tired, having gone through the war, leaving her home country and then her husband's illness and death. And besides all that, there was the family's financial situation to consider.

Andrew, then a handsome and intelligent young boy appealed to Batya a lot. Something in the way he spoke and looked reminded Batya of her father, whom she missed terribly. Older by five years, Andrew treated her as if she were a little girl. Batya felt almost faint each time he swung by her waving a tennis racket under her nose. Andrew ignored her to the point of being rude and swept her aside when she got in his way. Nevertheless, her teenage heart kept on dreaming that someday this popular boy everyone admired would rescue her from being a foreigner, from being alone in the world.

But the unrequited crush soon waned as her life dramatically changed its course after her mother got married, and Batya went to live in Vancouver.

Chapter 4

Where is this prison? Batya wonders with no small amount of trepidation. She conjures up walls and barbed wire, those distant almost forgotten shards of memory. Besides, going away this Saturday with Antonia may be a problem. The word, *prison,* itself has sad connotations of fear, isolation, loneliness and hunger.

Once, on a Sunday afternoon outing with Joseph and the children, they drove past a large building on the city's outskirts, perched over a ravine. Intrigued, she had begged Joseph to stop in front of this prison-like structure with bars on the windows.

"What for?" he had said, sounding flabbergasted. "It's only Woodlands, the mental hospital."

She had scrutinized the place with a mixture of fear and fascination. She had never seen it before, but had heard that people thought ghosts roamed in the ravine below—spirits like her own perished family with whom Batya might commiserate. "There are ghosts here," she said. "Ghosts of unhappy people who died and were buried here."

Miriam and Sam were playing a word game in the back seat and seemed undisturbed. Joseph shook his head impatiently while she stared at the barred windows for a glimpse of the inmates behind them, women and children incarcerated inside a world gone mad, like hers in the past. That world was still alive in her, its brick walls squeezing her insides. That day at Woodlands, she heard the children's voices shouting, whining and wailing. She observed with compassion how they stretched out their arms through the bars as if seeking contact with the outside, as if wondering why this woman in the car staring up at them was free and they were not.

Free? She laughed bitterly.

"*Don't knock it*" sounded Bea.

All too clearly she remembers the time when her father took her to visit the orphanage in the ghetto, where she saw hundreds of children looking wistfully at her as she tightened her hold on her father's hand.

Before they came, Papa had told her about Dr. Janusz Korczak, the man who ran the orphanage in the Warsaw ghetto. He was devoted to the orphaned children and instituted a democratic court run by the children themselves, where there was only one adult present while the orphans aired their complaints.

Papa had said he believed in a democratic household, where children had rights that should be honoured and respected by adults. Her father was also a stickler for love, truth and justice. She wishes her mother had taken on these beliefs too. Instead, Marta expected obedience and forced behaviour for the sake of appearances. Freedom of being yourself was an elusive butterfly to Batya.

Her thoughts revert to the kitchen where she has been sitting for some time now reminiscing. She thinks about her own children. She tries to practise her father's teachings and pass on his philosophy to them. They have learned to voice their grievances, to be fair and to almost always tell the truth. How proud her father would be of his grand -children. Her children are well loved and live in peace, prosperity and freedom in a country that accepts them for who they are, and for that, Batya is thankful.

She looks forward to Sammy coming home from school. His presence calms and cheers her. They talk about friends, sports, their hopes, needs and wants, and about life's ups and downs. He understands her, warming her heart with the sparkle in his blue eyes and the wide grin that brightens everything around him. He is her one ally, so mature, uncommonly wise and intelligent for his age. Sam reminds Batya of her father: slim, of average height, with his head of light-brown hair and his nose strong and straight like Papa's. He has the personality to match, for he is kind, truthful and honourable. His grandfather's sharp sense of humour shows itself in the way he perceives people and can nail their foibles, and the way he questions religious, social and political dogmas, even when very young. She taught him, like her father taught her when she was little, that you must stand up for yourself—even though she herself often falters and lets the phoney Bea stand in for her.

One day when Sammy was eight years old he came home from school unhappy. He walked into her bedroom and sat in his special bean chair, where he would often vent his frustrations. He had tears in his eyes.

"This one boy, Mom," he said, "makes fun of me and tries to get the other kids not to play with me at recess. He pokes me every time I pass by."

"Do you know why?" Batya asked.

"He doesn't like me because the teacher made me a dancer and singer in *My Fair Lady*. I am Mr. Doolittle, and David thinks I am a sissy."

How predictable, Batya though then. Even among adults, you're immediately excluded from the flock if you dress differently or are artistic in some way they are not.

"Okay, Sam, if he does it again, you take him outside the school and punch him in the nose. Not too hard, mind."

Sammy looked at her wide-eyed. "But Mom, I don't believe in violence."

"Then solve it your own way," Batya said. "But I don't believe in going to his mother to complain. You must learn to stand up for yourself."

Sam walked away looking too serious for a little guy.

The next day he came home with a huge grin on his face.

"Guess what, Mom? I did what you said, and now we're friends. I didn't hit him too hard. At first, he cried and ran to the teacher, and she told me not to fight."

"Did you ask the teacher how she thinks you should have dealt with it?"

"I did. And she said I should have tried to talk it out first. And if that didn't work and David was still mean, then I should go to her."

Batya disagreed with the teacher but was pleased with what her son had done. She wanted him to learn to be independent and assertive. Not that she believed in an eye for an eye, but she had heard from other moms that David was a bully and picked on some of the kids. So, it was good for Sam to face up to this brat.

Her times spent with Miriam are different. They are good but could be better. Miriam is quieter and younger than Sam, and more introverted like Joseph. Batya sees in her a beautiful, artistic child, the promise of all she could be—of what she could never have been growing up during the war.

The day Miriam was born, Batya bounced with joy when the doctor announced "It's a girl." She almost danced on the delivery table thinking how great it was to have one of each, a boy and a girl. From the very beginning she had feared giving birth, but wanting to have children won out over the fear. Once Miriam arrived, she was glad that she was a mother of two and wouldn't have to go through childbearing again. The birth of her children was her greatest accomplishment after years and years of feeling a failure, never able to finish anything she started, first failing courses in school because of her poor English, then coping with relationships that went sour.

Miriam is an introverted young teen. Trying to draw her daughter out, Batya gets only one-word answers. Miriam is secretive and not about to let her mother know her thoughts. If only she had spent as much time with Miriam as she did with Sam, her first-born. Maybe then they would have come to know each other better. Maybe it is never too late.

In bringing up her own children, she tries not to emulate Marta's criticism and intrusiveness, so she lets Miriam make some of her own decisions and have her own opinions. She recalls how one day Miriam walked into her bedroom and handed her a piece of paper with a picture of a sunflower and squiggly writing that said "I love you, Mom."

"How beautiful," she said to Miriam. "Thank you, sweetie." But in retrospect she knows that she either didn't or couldn't respond wholeheartedly to Miriam, nor to Sam. As if a wall stood between her and them, as if her heart was frozen. At times she'd stand there longing to take her daughter in her arms and hold her. Instead, Bea seemed to be holding her back from *all that mush,* she'd say.

The front door opens and Miriam saunters into the kitchen. She pours herself a glass of milk from the fridge. "Hi, Mom," she says and kisses her mother lightly on the cheek.

Batya kisses her on both cheeks and embraces her trying with all her might to show her affection.

The girl stiffens and withdraws. "Mom," she complains, "why do you have to kiss me on both cheeks?"

One kiss for me and one for Bea, her invisible twin—*there is a comical element even in sad things,* Batya thinks to herself, almost smiling. Love is like quicksilver that escapes just as you think you've caught it.

Three years younger than Sammy, Miriam is slightly built and fair. She is tidy, and always busy drawing or doing something in some corner of the house. As usual, she observes her mother with big green eyes and a bottom lip that pouts when she sees something that displeases her.

"Where is Sammy?" Batya asks.

Her daughter's face brightens. "He'll be home soon, Mom."

Miri and Sam love each other and often protect one another from their parents' anger and frustration. They listen to music and play games, trying not to hear the nightly arguments in the bedroom or the harsh exchanges at the dinner table.

She knows that Joseph cares a lot for the children. He is fiercely proud and protective of them. Yet he never says so and is not demonstrative. Although she realizes that this is his nature, she keeps on hoping he will change. If she felt sure that he loved her, she might believe in her own happy future. But she sees no evidence of love. Always longing for a kind word or some sign of warmth and affection from her husband, she finds it hard to believe their marriage will ever become more for him than a convenient arrangement for managing a household and getting sex.

Enough of feeling sorry for yourself. Bea's soldierly voice returns. *The salad is made. Table set. Get a move on.*

She must take up the task at hand but can't help thinking again of going to that prison with Antonia. Besides hating the idea, she feels guilty about leaving the children on a Saturday. Even though they are now teenagers, she feels like a thief stealing her moments of freedom away from them. Weekends are family time, though on the one coming up, Miri and Sam are going roller skating with friends and then to a cousin's house for dinner and a sleepover. *How convenient!* shrieks Bea.

"Go away, you monster," Batya responds plugging her ears. Even Bea cannot efface the guilt.

There is still another kind of guilt she feels, often in the presence of her mother. Guilt about being alive, having survived the war, while her sister Tereska did not. Mother so loved the little girl when she was born that Batya had often felt invisible. Long ago, before her resolve to forget the past, she would ask herself, *Why did Tereska die and not me? What did I do?* Even today, Marta behaves as if she is carrying a secret about the war, some information Batya is not privy to. It feels as if Marta is forever blaming her for something.

Chapter 5

"So where are *you* off to?" Joseph asks on his way out..

Bea has an answer. *Out on the town with Antonia.* Meanwhile, Batya squirms, detecting a sound of suspicion in her husband's tvoice. Well, at least the answer is close to the truth.

It's Saturday morning and ten minutes after Joseph and the children leave, Batya hears a honk. Antonia is waiting outside in her Chevy convertible.

"The picnic is in the trunk," she announces.

"Picnic? Where are we going to have a picnic?"

"Andrew is at a prison where the inmates are allowed to visit on the grounds, and it's a nice day so we can eat outdoors."

"How can you think about food when we are going to a prison?"

Antonia laughs. "Don't sound so alarmed," she says, throwing her a sideways glance. "We still have to eat."

Batya grimaces and turns her face towards the window.

"What?" Antonia says.

"It probably has a wall and barbed wire around it."

"Don't all prisons have them? At least we won't be inside the building. How come you are so dolled up? And your skirt is up to your navel," she adds in a lighter tone.

Why is she being so critical? Batya knows her friend is trying not to show how upset she is. Antonia is wearing a black shirt over jeans and no makeup. Her dark hair styled in a pixie cut, the fringe accentuating her sparkling brown eyes.

"And your makeup is too visible," she presses on.

Antonia must have flipped. Even though she can be very candid at times, she has never been concerned about such things before. She shoots straight but rarely stands in judgment of others. She was always there for you when you were in need.

Antonia is the one person with whom Batya tries to be herself, as much as she can. At least she feels free to let go of her public persona in front of her, instead of parading it as she always does in front of others, even Joseph. Sometimes, when she is depressed about her life, she will talk to Antonia. Although Antonia, who has her own set of problems to face, often hides her feelings when talk turns to her personal life. Still, there is an unspoken pact between them—a pact of trust.

Batya is afraid even to trust her own mother. In the past, when she would open up, Marta would look at her as if she were a lunatic, daring to complain about her home and marriage. When Marta Lichtenberg married Max Stern, she stepped into a busy social life. She would shrug her elegant shoulders and shake off Batya's complaints, save to say that love and happiness in marriage are but an illusion, and that wives must grin and bear it for the sake of the children. "Look at yourself," she'd say. "You look awful. Angst ruins your skin. Look at your hair. Why don't you do something with it? You look so American with those streaks. And you could stand to lose a few pounds as well."

After such conversations, Batya would buy herself a huge piece of chocolate cake with ice cream, and end up with a headache and an urge to put even more streaks in her hair. What was the use? She so wanted her mother on her side, at least to offer some acknowledgement of their shared past, but Marta seemed blind to her daughter's troubles.

And now *Antonia* is also criticizing her looks. Batya pulls down the sun visor and looks into the mirror. In the morning light, the face that stares back acrimoniously is gaudy with makeup. She has painted dark lines over her own fair eyebrows and lined her eyes in black. Red blotches clown her cheeks and dark-red lipstick obscures the true shape of her lips. This is Bea, with gobs of makeup and flashy clothes. What could she have been thinking when she dressed this morning? Maybe her mother was right after all.

Antonia tries a gentler approach. "Don't you know that you are beautiful without makeup?"

Batya doesn't agree. She thinks of herself as plain, a bit pudgy and short, certainly not in her mother's league. Humbled by her friend's comments, she obediently begins to rub some of the paint off her face, going about it gingerly, as if afraid to reveal the Batya beneath the mask. She slips her long sweater over her mini skirt.

"That's better," Antonia says warmly. "Now you look perfect."

She appreciates her friend's compliment but doubts the "perfection" of her appearance. Papa always told her that it was the beauty of the soul that counted and that Batya had a beautiful soul. She casts off that memory, trying to brace herself for the dreaded visit to the prison.

They drive out of the city into the suburbs. She usually loves the ride on the country road along the Fraser River. There are no buildings on the way, only gnarled bushes, the infinite green of the firs and weeds poking out of dry wisps of grass, brightened by wildflowers on the roadside. Soon the road comes to an end, opening out onto a wide field with a watchtower at its centre. A guard is standing inside a walled-off area.

Batya sees the ten-foot wall that stood at the end of her street in the ghetto, imprisoning her and the other children, their parents and grandparents. She would peer through the holes made by pulled-out bricks and see the German guards' boots stomping back and forth. She'd hear the cracking sounds of guns shot at anyone daring to cross the checkpoint without a pass. She'd hear the strains of music from a carousel she could not see, but only imagine, its brightly painted horses going round and round, bouncing laughing children up and down on the other side of the wall.

Antonia stops the car at the gate to the compound.

Another guard steps out of a booth, demanding a visitor's permit. "Who is this?" inquires the officer gruffly, pointing at Batya.

"My cousin," replies Antonia.

Batya is taken aback by her friend's brazen lie and then struck by the bizarre notion of posing as Antonia's cousin. She shouldn't be surprised. Jews, during the war, had to switch identities to save their lives.

"Where's your ID?" barks the guard.

Batya hands him her driver's licence, and the guard scribbles something on a pad of paper before returning the documents.

"Open the trunk," he commands. Antonia pulls the lever, making a face at Batya. The guard pokes about, emptying the picnic basket onto the trunk floor, then searches the back seat and the glove compartment. He bangs a stamp onto Antonia's permit. "Go ahead," he says, finally opening the gate.

Antonia drives inside and pulls into a parking spot. Through the car window Batya takes in the gravel area blocked off by the cement wall and barbed wire. Beyond it, outlined against a blue horizon, stand rows of grey barracks. A snapping echoes in her head, as if a blackout window shade has suddenly rolled up, and in the dim light she sees a shabby room that stinks of excrement and disease. A taste of decay crawls along her throat into her mouth. She tries to control the urge to vomit by resting her head against the car window and breathing deeply. The sensation passes. She is thankful that her friend is busy tidying up the spilled picnic in the trunk, and does not notice.

Antonia calls out to her and the image vanishes. Taking a deep breath, she gets out of the car and joins her. They pass through another guarded gate and walk towards the lawn at the edge of the river, where a man stands underneath a fir tree.

"Well, hello," says Andrew, putting his arms around both women. Dressed in grey pants and shirt and with a shaved head, he really does look like a convict. "We have a reservation," he continues, pointing to the picnic table under the tree. The trees, flowers and emerald lawn beside the shimmering river suggest a sense of peace.

What irony, she thinks. Were it not for the military appearance of the barracks, the wall and the barbed-wire fence, this place would not seem like a prison at all.

With a sweeping gesture, Andrew motions them to the table. "I have invited another guest to join us. I hope you ladies don't mind."

Batya is more excited to see Andrew than she cares to admit but senses that he is putting on airs to camouflage his fallen status. She remembers him as being fairly serious. Not that he lacked a sense of humour. The combination had attracted her to him.

A short and chubby man with blond hair is walking towards them. He, too, is dressed in grey pants and shirt. "Ladies, meet Hans Schmidt."

Hans holds out his hand in greeting. His name strikes a chord. Batya has read a newspaper article about a playboy by that name, something to do with a big drug operation. *Like attracts like?* she wonders.

"May I offer you ladies a drink?" Andrew asks.

Antonia and Batya exchange looks.

"Voila!" Hans exclaims, lifting the lid off a tall tin garbage can next to the table. He reaches in and brings out a bottle of cognac.

The women look around nervously and sit down. Andrew laughs and assures his guests that the guards have been bribed with brandy and there is no one around. Hans pours the golden liquid into paper cups with the finesse of a butler.

The charade continues as Antonia brings out the egg and salmon sandwiches she has prepared for the picnic. Hans looks at them, turning up his nose. His arm bobs into the garbage can and emerges holding up a salami with a Star of David on the wrapper. "Made in Winnipeg," he announces with a wide grin.

The four sip their cognac, Andrew cracks jokes, and Batya, seated across from him, feels less nervous. She catches his grey eyes on her, once again feeling some of the old excitement surging through her.

Sex has always fascinated and frightened her. Often while making love with Joseph, vague images surface: a man hovering over her, playing with her in a way that makes her feel ashamed. She is not sure if this is a real memory or a nightmare. This, in addition to her mother's warnings, makes her fear sex even more.

Still, she has physical desires of her own, even if they go unfulfilled during lovemaking. She had never made love to another man before Joseph and often wondered if she was maimed in some way by her inability to meet his needs. Maybe she doesn't deserve satisfaction in lovemaking? Yet Bea spreads her legs wide and pretends, going through the motions purely for Joseph's sake.

"I am glad that you and Andrew are enjoying each other's company," murmurs Antonia. "He needs a bit of diversion right now. Hans and I are going for a short walk. Do you mind?"

"Not at all," says Batya. She turns to Andrew. "What do you do here all day long?"

"There is a good library. I've been reading a lot of Shakespeare, Kafka and Dostoyevsky," he replies, sitting close to her.

"That's wonderful!" His closeness is making her squirm.

"It makes being here almost bearable."

She didn't think Andrew had a bookish side to him. The cognac helps her muster enough courage to keep up a conversation. "So reading makes you a happy prisoner?" she says, trying to sound upbeat.

"Look, I read a lot but I also tend a garden here," he says, encompassing a large area with the sweep of an arm. "They have given me a free hand with landscaping. I find that being around nature, among trees and flowers, is liberating and inspiring. That way, the place doesn't feel so much a prison."

"I guess beauty and ugliness can exist side by side," she says. "Like love and indifference."

"I agree. I've changed, you know," he says, his face serious. "I hope you have forgiven me for ignoring you when we were young.

"You were not very nice. To me at least."

"Okay, so I wasn't. Nobody is perfect Your own father whom I remember you thought the world of wasn't perfect either, you know. Have you forgiven him?"

"Forgiven him for what? My father was a decent man."

"Yes, he loved the company of women. I often heard him at my parents' parties flirting with some of my mother's friends, and how they lapped it up!"

"So what?" Batya adds angrily, almost shouting, still unsure of what Andrew is driving at.

"*So what?* Apparently he was not so gallant with the ghetto Jews. There was more gossip about him when survivors started arriving from Poland."

His words send a sting into her heart. "What are you saying?" she asks, bewildered. "Don't you dare talk that way about my father. Certainly not you, Andrew. You can't dirty my memory of him."

"I am sorry, Batya. I am so sorry. I shouldn't have said anything."

She is sure he is just trying to trick her.

"You had better find out the truth from Antonia," he says, putting his arm around her protectively.

The Bea part of her likes the feel of him. Batya wants to run away. She pulls herself free and rushes over to where Antonia is sitting with Hans.

"Antonia?"

"Yes."

"It's time to go." Batya is exploding with the need to speak to her friend right away.

When they are back at the table, Andrew hands her a book. "I want to lend you this. It's Kafka's *Metamorphosis*. You can return it the next time you come."

She accepts it, not quite knowing what to say. She has no feelings for Andrew now, whatsoever and only hopes that he was bluffing about her father just to get a rise out of her. When they walk back towards the gate, Batya feels Andrew's eyes on her and wonders if the fascination she feels with him is hers or Bea's.

In the car, she says to Antonia, "We have to talk, now."

"Yes. Of course. What's wrong?"

"Can we stop?"

Antonia drives on until she finds a place to park. They sit in silence for a moment, then Batya tells her what Andrew had said. "I thought we had no secrets from each other," Batya says, accusingly.

Antonia shrugs. "I don't know what you are talking about."

"I've told you what your brother said about my father. It was he who told me to speak to you about it, and now you are denying it?" Batya is drenched in sweat.

Antonia looks away. "Oh, that. Really, I'd forgotten all about it. It happened so long ago. I meant to tell you sometime, but I didn't know how. I was afraid it would hurt you."

"Tell me what?" Batya asks. "Be straight with me as you always are, I beg you."

"Okay. But this isn't easy and I wish it could have been forgotten. I want to crucify my brother for this," says Antonia, her nervous fingers running up and down the steering wheel.

"A friend from Toronto and his mother visited us, some time ago. Both were survivors from the Warsaw ghetto. When they found out we knew your father, they told us some stories about him that my parents decided were best forgotten. Your father is dead. Why bring out his ghost from the grave?"

Batya winces. Papa might be dead but he still lived in her heart and memory.

Antonia leans forward, her face grim. "Andrew has become hard and bitter. He has forgotten what he promised our parents."

"What is it? Tell me!" Batya shouts. "Tell me."

"Did you ever know a Rebecca Karp?"

Batya sits up straight. "No. Never."

"I hope you don't think me cruel for telling you this now. Maybe I shouldn't..."

"Please, go on."

"This woman, Rebecca Karp," Antonia continues, "told many of the Jewish immigrants from Poland that your father was a traitor to his own people. That he helped Nazis round up Jews for deportation." Antonia stops as if afraid to go on, then continues. "My parents refused to believe this and forbade us to speak of it."

"I know nothing of this," Batya mumbles. "My God, it's a lie!" She leans back, trying to compose herself and not become hysterical, a trait she despises. She must defend her father. It is difficult to speak, but eventually the words come from her stiff lips.

"My father chose to become a policeman to save our lives and to keep order in the ghetto. That is all," she says. "I must straighten this out. How can I get in touch with this woman?"

"Mrs. Karp died, but I believe her son is still alive. Like you, he is a child survivor. But he is very bitter about the Jewish police. He lives in Toronto. If you want, I can get you his telephone number."

"I don't think I want to talk to him."

But why had her mother never spoken to her about this? Why her perpetual silence about their family's past? "I guess I must get in touch with him," she finally says.

"I always had good feelings about your father," Antonia says softly. "He was so nice to me when you and I were teenagers. Once, I remember, there was a party and everyone in the room was waltzing. Your father saw me sitting alone in a corner so he came up to me. When he found out that I didn't know how to dance the waltz, he offered to teach me."

Batya forces herself to answer. "That was so like him. He taught me many things," she says. She couldn't imagine Papa doing something wrong or immoral. "I will not think badly of him," she says. "He taught me to be honourable, honest and truthful. He never lied and always kept his word. He gave money to the poor and helped the homeless." The conversation is sapping her energy.

But there were a few things that had always puzzled her about her father. When he became a policeman in the ghetto, just before she left, he had changed. He was not the same person she had known before. He had lost some of his gentleness. Or is she imagining this now?

"I believe you," Antonia says. "I saw how he was with you, always gentle and loving."

"He could get irritable, but that was when he was already sick and dealing with pain. I was doing very badly in school. No matter how much he tried to help, the light wouldn't go on in my brain. He would get impatient with me." Batya shakes her head, as if trying to get rid of the nasty accusations buzzing in and around her head. "Before the war, when we went on vacations and to the theatre, he had loads of patience with me."

She looks at her friend. They have been sitting in the car by the side of the road for what seems like hours.

"Let's go," Antonia says in a low voice. "Thanks for coming with me. You are the only one who has stood by me through this."

Batya squeezes her friend's shoulder. She harbours no ill feelings towards Antonia and not even towards Andrew. She knows what the presence of a good friend can mean during a crisis.

"And I am grateful to you for telling me about Papa. Though I still don't believe all of it is true. Maybe someone told a pack of lies."

"Maybe. Check into it," replies Antonia. "Otherwise you will only end up torturing yourself."

They drive the rest of the way back to the city in silence, her father's last words echoing in her head, "Forgive me, my child."

At one point, suddenly, a cat runs in front of the car like a crazed thing and darts into a bush. Antonia brakes sharply.

"Thank goodness it's outside the car," Batya says, her skin crawling.

Chapter 6

The conversation with Antonia caws in her ears like a crow. What if those accusations are true? Surely a terrible mistake has been made by thoughtless gossip mongers. She must find proof to repudiate these accusations. But how and where? Maybe there is written evidence of the truth, in books or library archives.

Papa's study at home before the war had shelves and shelves of books, from floor to ceiling. All the wisdom and knowledge in them was destroyed when the Gestapo marched in, broke their spines and tore the pages. Papa had taught her to respect books and encouraged her to discover the worlds they offer. She will turn to books for information about the Jewish police. The university library must have records of the war, the Warsaw ghetto and the police force. But first she phones her mother.

"Mom, I need to know something," she says carefully. "Something about Papa."

"Yes? What?" Marta asks. Batya knows how much her mother hates to be asked questions about the war and her father.

"I spoke with Antonia Denner. You know her, my best friend."

"Of course, I know her," says Marta. "I knew her family well. What of it?"

"She told me something about Father—about when he was a policeman in the Warsaw ghetto. She said there was a woman in Toronto, Rebecca Karp, who spread gossip about him being involved in deportations."

"So?" Marta snaps.

"I want to know what really happened."

"What really happened? Your father wanted to save our lives. He worked as a guard in the German shop in the ghetto. What else could he have done? Given up and died? Everyone was dropping dead around us. You wouldn't be here today and neither would I if it weren't for him."

"But Mom, I want to know what else Papa did in the ghetto. Why haven't we ever talked about it? Rebecca Karp said that Father betrayed his people."

"He did no such thing!" Marta shouts into the phone. "I don't want to discuss it. And you should forget about it too. Criticism is cheap when the critics who know nothing about what happened to us sit in comfortable chairs and judge."

Batya has to agree, but Marta's defensiveness makes her sound as if she is hiding something. Her mother seldom tells the whole truth about anything and often alters facts to suit her purpose. Like the time Batya told her about the abusive old man in the village. When her mother didn't respond, Batya told her father. Later she heard Marta tell Papa that the old man was the kindest person she had ever met

"Mom, where did Papa get the silver disk?"

"I don't know, he never told me."

"And another thing," Batya presses on.

"What about Rogacki and the blackmail?"

"That is a discussion for another time, Batya,"

What is the use? Her mother would not speak about the war or Papa. "Okay, Mom. Thanks."

Feverish to know more about her family's past, Batya sets out for the library with a hopeful heart. To her amazement, the catalogue contains a large Holocaust bibliography. She jots down the call numbers. In the section where these books are shelved, she finds one titled *Notes from the Warsaw Ghetto*, by Emmanuel Ringelblum. The blurb about the book says that he recorded the events of the ghetto as they happened.

Hours go by and her eyes get blurry from reading. Her mind is confused and her fears are confirmed about the Jewish Ghetto Police. Yet in all the indexes of the many books written on the subject, she finds only one mention of her father, which says he was a lawyer in Warsaw who worked for the Judenrat.

She must get home in time to make supper. Later, at the table, she says nothing to the children or Joseph about her fears. After dinner when everyone is occupied with their own chores, she starts reading from the load of books she has brought home. Her research becomes an obsession as she reads during the day when everyone is out, then again at night. The more she reads, the hungrier she is for more information, growing more disenchanted with the Jewish police. The Holocaust diaries say masses about them. The unflattering images the writers create are so visual:

The greed of the Jewish Police was such that they'd take pennies from the smuggler boys for every potato or piece of bread the boy would smuggle. Then they took bribes for various favours and treated the people in an unnecessarily cruel manner. They'd beat them with their sticks and shout at the Jews who wouldn't comply with rules.

The diligence with which the Jewish Police performed their work was generated by fear and dilated into viciousness...

In another book she reads about how the Jewish police helped round up Jewish people, ordered them out of their homes and sent them to the Umschlagplatz—the deportation depot. Then they'd assist in loading the Jews into cattle cars. The ghetto diaries describe how the policemen took jewellery and diamonds in exchange for small favours, and how mean they were towards the Jews who resisted.

The reading nightmare continues when again, in another book on the Warsaw ghetto, again she finds her father's name in the index. On the page under deportations she reads the entry: "Shimon Lichtenberg, a lawyer, a Jewish policeman, involved in deportations."

So it is true. Papa was somehow involved in deportations, but how?. Is this the secret both her parents had kept from her? Resigned to this second-hand truth, though still uncertain, Batya makes notes and finally, unable to read any more, she returns the books to the library. Where to go from here?

She walks into a restaurant and orders a glass of wine. Either her father is guilty of criminal acts against his own people, or he is innocent and maybe he redeemed himself in some unknown way. Whatever the truth was, she must find it. But how?

Memories of Warsaw during the war, things she has not thought of for a long time, overtake her senses: the cold, shabby room where they lived, her nostrils filled with the smells of decay and the sick flesh of those dying from typhus, her ears attuned to their cries and at night the sound of bombs whistling as they hurled down from the heavens. It is still so alive in her mind.

* * * * *

It was 1941. They were imprisoned inside the wall of the ghetto. An air raid siren was shrieking and seven-year-old Batya ran half-asleep and barefoot into the cellar. People in the shelter said that the Russians were bombing Warsaw. Cold and afraid, she buried her face in her father's shoulder, her fingers digging into his arm while with the other he was shielding her mother and little Tereska. The neighbours huddled together. The whistling of a bomb above their heads sounded closer and closer to the earth. A sudden flash lit up the cellar, revealing the fear on people's faces before all heads bowed down towards the ground, hunching into their shoulder blades. They screamed, holding each other tight, and the children wept. A terrible boom was followed by the thunderous crash of a bomb falling on the next building. You could smell smoke because many buildings were already on fire. People inside them were being burned alive.

At last the siren's howl announced that the air raid was over, but the terror that gripped her body had turned her to stone. Father took her back to bed and stroked her hair. He told her a story about Little Red Riding Hood and the Big Bad Wolf and how, despite the treacherous wolf, Little Red Riding Hood survived. Listening to the voice of her beloved father, she fell asleep.

But fear menaced Batya's ability to sleep—the insomnia that emerged during those days would plague her nights for years to come. Later that night a sound awoke her, the scraping of a chair against the floor. She saw her father outlined in the faint light of a kerosene lamp. He was seated astride the chair, his hands over his face. Mother too was sitting there, her face pale like a ghost's. Batya sensed her father's despair in the line of his bowed head. He stayed like this a long time, while the two sisters lay in their beds, silent and weak from hunger. Later, she overheard her parents' say:

"People are dying of typhus and starvation," said her mother, her voice thick with fear. "We have no food. Tereska is coughing and there is no medication. Tuberculosis is spreading among our neighbours. What are we to do?"

"Nazis have started rounding up Jews for deportation to labour camps." Her father spoke quietly. "People's lives depend on their will to survive and sheer luck."

They sat in strained silence for a long time.

A few days later Papa came home wearing the uniform of a Jewish policeman: a grey jacket, a badge that resembled a star, a cap with the same badge, and a yellow armband, with a Jewish star, across which was written: *Jüdische Ghetto Polizei.*

Mother said that Father's new job might save their lives and possibly the lives of others. Batya didn't understand but she trusted her father completely. Soon Papa started bringing home a few pieces of bread and a bit of sugar he got somewhere. This was after their rations had run out that week. Papa said the police were not being paid but their job would exempt them and their families from deportations, for a time.

She and Tereska coveted their pieces of bread sprinkled with sugar. they tasted so good and gave them enough energy to get out of bed. The girls were allowed to go only as far as the courtyard because their building was quarantined for typhus. The streets were crowded with the dead and dying even in the courtyard. Batya saw sick people all around her. Bodies of small children, who had died from either hunger or typhus, were carried out on stretchers. She shivered at the thought that one day she might be the one. She'd close her eyes tight to blot out the horrible images of the partly decayed bodies of children beneath the rags and torn newspapers she'd seen in the streets when out with her father. Sometimes her meal of bread with sugar stuck in her throat.

Screaming and shooting were constant. A man on a wagon hitched to a horse collected the bodies off the streets and clopped away to "God knows where," Papa said. He also said there were long line-ups of desperate people on their way to the Umschlagplatz, where trains waited to take them to labour camps.

She didn't want to die and asked her father if this would happen to them. "Not if I can help it," Papa said. He was looking, he said, for a way to get them out of the ghetto before it was too late, before the next raid would round up the children for deportation. Despite their situation, Batya felt confident that the family would stay together no matter where they went and this calmed her.

One evening Papa came home, his face void of color. "I don't want to scare you, but we are in terrible danger. Even my uniform may not protect us from deportation. You girls will have to leave the ghetto."

"Will you come too?" Batya asked.

"I don't think so, dear child," replied Papa. "I don't think so."

The morning, when it was Batya's turn to leave, she woke up feeling sick and feverish. Surely they wouldn't send her away if she was sick, would they?

"She can't go today," her mother said. "We'll have to send Tereska instead."

"But no," Batya protested. "We all have to stay together."

By the time her little sister came to say goodbye, Batya was deep in delirium and pushed her away. In a few days, when she felt better, she realized what she had done but Tereska was gone. Papa sat her on his knee and said, "It is now your turn to leave."

"Papa, when will I see Tereska again?"

"When the war is over, dearest."

On that unforgettable day, Batya said goodbye to her mother, who seemed frozen as she kissed her daughter with cold lips. Papa led her close to a hole in the ghetto wall where the bricks were missing. He cut a piece of barbed wire that was in the way then handed her a piece of paper.

"This is your new name," he told her. "From now on you are no longer Batya Lichtenberg. You are Beata Bielicka. Remember this name on the other side, where you must survive as a Christian girl."

Batya promised to do what her father had instructed. Papa pushed her through the hole. Their hands parted suddenly as if some invisible force tore them apart. When she reached the other side of the wall, she could still feel her hand in Papa's, cut off as if she had left it behind. Feeling lost and abandoned, she walked away from the wall with a huge lump in her throat and the knowledge that she mustn't cry or draw attention to herself but act as this new person she had to become.

Someone grabbed her hand. "Hurry," the young woman shouted and pulled her away. Numb, Batya went with the stranger. All she could think of was why Papa had sent her away. Was it because she was too much trouble? At the station, they boarded a train for the countryside. The rhythm of the train made her drowsy, sounding a deep breath of relief as it sped through the peaceful forests. A feeling engulfed her, so different from the ghetto hell. This train taking her into the unknown felt strange, but safer.

After a few stops they got off, and walked a long way down a dirt road and through narrow streets until they arrived at a small wooden house with a garden full of trees. An elderly, hunched-over woman came out to greet them. She wore a big stained apron and a kerchief on her head.

The old couple, Lena and Bolek, later told her that to save herself she had to learn how to act as Beata, the Christian. In the meantime, the Jewish Batya cowered in the dark corners of the damp house, silent and obedient. Lena and Bolek eyed her with pity but without affection. How she longed for the warmth of her parents' arms around her, their love, her sister and her home.

"Laugh hearty and be merry," the old man told her as she languished like a mouse in a hole, trying to make herself invisible and anonymous. That was about the time when Bea began to surface, splitting Batya in two. Beata left Batya behind the ghetto wall and began the survival process. She giggled a lot and did nasty chores assigned to her by Bolek. She peeled potatoes and emptied bedpans with frozen fingers. She went to the country church on Sundays, partook of the body of Christ and drank of his blood. Beata performed all the necessary household tasks like a robot, while Batya sank more and more into a bog of apathy.

Miraculously, she found a few books in the attic of the tiny house and se-cretly buried herself in their grimy pages. In them she discovered another life that belonged to a Russian couple travelling through strange countries. She melted with pleasure absorbing the stories about Turkey and Spain, noting that the American tourists used the word "Okay" and ate oysters for breakfast. The Russian couple ate chocolates, something she craved, and oranges, which were unheard of in the village, and bread, which was scarce. Reading about these foods made her mouth water, for she was always hungry. But her apathy returned as soon as she left the pages of the book and re-entered real life.

It was Bea who laughed and ate boiled potato peels, acting as if she liked Bolek even when he asked her to pull down her pants so he could look up. Bea laughed and played. Batya felt ashamed and sick at heart. She hated and feared Bolek and ran to hide in the attic with the mice and rats and her beloved books. What if, she thought, Bolek reported her as a Jew to the Gestapo if she didn't do what he wanted?

Sometimes she longed to run away altogether but didn't dare. She was not allowed to wander from the house or cross the road lest some suspicious, meddling person noticed and reported her to the authorities.

Bolek's bald head had warts on it. He made horrible faces, the mean light in his eyes, repulsive. He'd bargain and offer her a piece of bread for being able to touch her. In response or whenever she could, she finally broke the rule and sneaked across the narrow road into a forest, where she hid behind a tree.

One such day, through the barren branches, she saw a man come up to the house and bang on the door. She heard him shout, "Where is he, where is Shimon Lichtenberg? I am going to report Batya to the Gestapo, and she will be tortured if you don't tell me where Shimon Lichtenberg is!"

After a moment, Lena opened the door. "The man you are looking for, Mr. Rogacki, is not here. He's in the next village." Batya thought she heard the old woman's false teeth clatter as she spoke. "Hiding in Antek Kozukh's barn."

The man, Rogacki, left in a huff. Batya wanted to run to the place where her parents might be hiding to warn them of the danger. But Bea—the self-preserving part of her—pulled her back. So she just sat there, rooted to the earth, frozen like a tree in winter. The only light that warmed her and gave her strength was the image of her parents coming to take her away.

Chapter 7

All is quiet at home with everyone asleep. She is sitting in the dark by the window, memories whirling about her mind like leaves in a gale.

More than a year has passed since that first visit to the prison and she has made a few more visits. She wanted nothing to do with Andrew and behaved indifferently. Her attraction to him was momentary. She has been able to get away with Antonia on those Saturdays, and although it was a tiring trip to make in one day, she has come to look forward to it as if it were, ironically, an escape to freedom. The prison awakened her slumbering memories sending her back to the dark planet where everything is bleak and Batya's voice calls out to her from its hiding place. Observing the convicts working around the property underlined her feeling of freedom.

She cringes at the sight of a cat that frequents their garden. It sometimes tries to crawl into the house, its meows like the cries of a distraught child.

Last night, when she couldn't sleep, an incident from her childhood came to haunt her. It happened the night just before the war began in Poland, when she was only five. She can still hear her father's reassuring voice saying, "Shush, my child. There is no cat in your room, my love."

"But Papa, I heard him meow!"

Batya knew that Nanny kept a cat in her room. A black one. She rarely let it out except on occasion to allow Batya's mother to play with it and stroke it. Batya feared the cat that would hiss at her.

That night there was a storm. She lay awake in a room next to her parents' bedroom. They were arguing. "You can't take her to the country," her mother cried. "I will not be left alone and I do not want to go to that hick place!"

Hick place? But Grandfather's villa was the most beautiful place on earth. The sunflower garden, the jasmine and the roses, the blueberry bushes, and the butterflies she tried to catch into a green net on a stick. Of course, there were wasps and creepy-crawly worms and schools of ants. But there were also the forests and the meadows. How she and Papa loved walking among the trees, singing Polish folk songs, picking mushrooms. The peasants would give them fresh black bread smeared with the world's best plum marmalade.

"But Kitten," her father tried to pacify Marta, his voice grave and patient. *Why did Papa call Mama "kitten?" why won't Mama let us go?* Batya despaired, before falling into a troubled sleep.

She woke up feeling a heavy weight pressing on her. What was it? The lightning flashed and in its blaze she saw the black cat lying on her chest. His eyes were wild, glowing with green fire. His claws hardened against her neck, choking her. The cat's jaws were wide open and his sharp teeth exposed as he shrieked like a wild thing.

She screamed, numb beneath the blankets, her body soaked in sweat and urine. Then Nanny crept in on bare feet, wearing the black leather gloves that she said protected her glycerined hands from drying out. Her face looked mean.

Batya hated Nanny, who was strict and beat her for wetting herself at night and then forbade her to tell her parents. She would slap Batya on the cheeks while washing her face and then push her onto the floor and kick her. Nanny tried to convert Batya into a Catholic and took her to church on Sundays. This and the black cat were to be secrets between them, she told Batya. Or else.

Papa appeared behind Nanny and walked up to Batya's bed. "Nanny's cat is here, Papa," Batya cried out. "He tried to kill me."

"Hush. There is no cat here, my love," said Papa, gently stroking her hair and covering her with a blanket. "Now go to sleep. Besides, cats aren't scary. They are cuddly pets."

She was comforted, though still scared. Later she heard Papa shout at Nanny, "I want you and your cat out by morning." Batya was overjoyed, but not for long.

On Sunday, Papa broke his promise to her for the first time ever and did not take her to her grandfather's villa in the country. He didn't tell her why, but she blamed her mother, though she dared not speak, as the atmosphere at home was tense. People with grim faces whispered in corners of rooms and on street corners as if something bad were about to happen. The next day Poland was attacked and their lives changed.

A siren wails in the distance banishing her midnight musings. Batya turns on the overhead light, which brings her back to the present. She goes into her study and re-reads the poems about the prison she had written and hidden away.

Lately Joseph has been eyeing her with suspicion. "Where do you go on Saturdays?"

"Out to get my hair done then out with Antonia," she lies.

Joseph shrugs his shoulders in disbelief. He is too smart not to suspect she is up to something. But he has no proof. Lately she has been neglecting the children as well as her husband. They seem far away in a world of their own. Her family is not a part of this strange life in which she is now living, as if the present formed her imprisonment, enclosed by the walls of her past.

In a haze, she makes sure the children's daily needs are met. Or rather, it is Bea who performs in Batya's stead, while Batya continues her quest to find meaning in her life. At the centre of her confusion, feelings for her father, accused of collaboration, loom over her.

Papa's truths have been blemished and her belief in the person she thought him to be lies shaken. Maybe Papa was both good and evil—just like Bolek, the old man in the village who was mean to her but at the same time protected her from the Nazis. Even Joseph, who could be cold and unkind to her, is able to show fondness towards their children. People aren't what they seem to be.

Joseph scorned the idea of her taking literature courses and refused to pay her tuition. "This whole going back to school is ridiculous. All our friends agree with me," he said from behind the newspaper. Following that discussion, she applied for a student loan.

Once, after supper, wanting to share her enthusiasm for her studies, she pleaded with her husband, "Can we go out for a walk and talk a bit?"

"I have to go back to the office. Another time," he replied and left her to an evening of study. Not that she minded. In truth, she was grateful for the free time to herself.

Yet the more displeased Joseph is, the more depressed Batya becomes. Meanwhile, as Bea, she puts on a show of good humour and fulfilling her daily chores, hopes that as long as dinner is on the table every day, Joseph will refrain from critical comments that hurt. After an argument with him, she refuses to have sex, infuriating Joseph and infusing herself with more guilt.

The Bea side of her continues to relish the material security Joseph provides, even though he makes her account each month for every cent she spends. Still, she doesn't have to worry about the roof over her head or her next piece of bread, and the children are well looked after. She consoles herself with the fact that Joseph is steadfast, a creature of habit if not love.

As time passes, Batya begins to hate Bea, who is also changing for the worse--wearing more makeup than ever, dressing in her most outlandish clothes and drinking like a pro. Batya longs to free herself from the shackles of Bea's life.

Desperate for some form of real communication, she purchases a book with blank pages and starts writing. Like someone sitting very far away from the stage where she can only see the spectacle through huge binoculars, Batya translates flashes of memories that appear in image fragments imprinted in her mind so long ago as photographs in grey or black and white. She spends hours filling the blank pages. In an attempt to write anything decent, she realizes that she has lost her written facility in the Polish language and had not yet gained mastery in English. While memories come pouring out she feels an impasse. Her childhood experience comes to her in Polish words which when translated into English sound flat. In despair at being always interrupted, she moves to another bedroom in their house, her excuse being a quiet study time. She puts a sign on the door "DO NOT DISTURB"

"You're crazy," concludes Joseph, hovering on the threshold to her new study. *Have you in fact gone mad?* says Bea. Batya is changing rapidly wondering whether in fact her behaviour is still normal.

She can't ever have a heart-to-heart talk with Joseph but for entering into an argument. If only she could harness a fraction of the feeling Joseph has for his children.

"You can't even figure out a simple detective story," he said to her one day in the car when they were on their way home from a movie. She didn't quite understand who had murdered whom because she hated those kinds of films. Her mind was elsewhere while the crime story went on and on, and the guns and the shooting reminded her of war.

"And you dress like a slob," she replied.

His face twisted with fury and he raised his hand as if to hit her, then withdrew it. Batya's whole body tensed like a violin string about to snap. Tears came instantly. They rode in silence and when they went to bed that night, she turned away from him.

Batya now feared her husband and soon began to avoid all emotional interaction with him and his critical friends. Frequent drinking bouts anaesthetized her, and she became more and more indifferent to her surroundings. She even began to spend nights in her study.

As fall darkens the days, so Batya's mood spirals downward. In the months that follow, she has nightmares of bomb explosions and shrapnel flying. She hears the pounding of black leather boots; she sees the green helmets of German soldiers. Swastikas appear from nowhere, resembling huge, crooked black crosses. She wants to confide in Joseph but fears he won't understand.

She wants to tell Antonia that she cannot visit the prison any more, but when the time for their regular visit grows near, she cannot stop herself. In the prison the hidden part of her reveals itself more and more, without any prompts from Bea. Batya realizes that she must face her childhood self now or live forever wearing the mask of Beata.

"What is wrong with you lately?" Antonia asks one day on the ride home from the prison. "You've changed."

More than ever before, Batya is aware of her own behaviour, her messy hair and red eyes.

"And you smell of alcohol," adds Antonia to complete the picture. "Have you been drinking?"

Yes. She was drinking the night before and had a sleepless night during which another nightmare had set in: a dream of her two personalities in the shape of two wild cats tearing each other apart made her wake up screaming. She tries to explain this to Antonia.

"Why is this happening to you now?" Antonia asks.

When they get to Batya's house, she invites her friend inside and shows her the dreams and episodes of her wartime childhood she has been recording in a notebook.

"Tell me more," Antonia says, sitting on the bed close to her and rubbing her back. "Let me help you," she begs. "You've never talked about the war."

Batya tells Antonia stories about her childhood, the few fragments she can remember and even shows her the diary. She talks about the problems between her and Joseph. Then she speaks of her bizarre behaviour of late and more about her being split between Bea and Batya. Words come in torrents. "My going out and drinking is making Joseph furious. Since I've gone back to school, he's become suspicious and thinks I'm fooling around with other men. But Antonia, I swear I'm being absolutely faithful to him."

"When did all this start?" Antonia asks.

"It's been happening ever since we started visiting the prison.

"Why should going to the prison bring all this out in you? Of course," Antonia hesitates, "the idea of prison and your concealed self may have something in common."

"Then you *do* understand. I started having the feelings I had forgotten. Like anger, fear, abandonment. Here is something I want you to see."

Batya takes a box out of her dresser drawer and shows Antonia her false document, in which she became Bea Bielicka. "This is how I became two people," she says.

"Small wonder you are confused and a mess," says Antonia, shaking her head. "I don't know what to say. How to help."

Batya opens her two closets. One is filled with clothing in muted shades of black, grey, red and white—semi-structured suits and plain dark dresses. The second closet contains garish clothing in see-through fabrics with exotic patterns in outlandish styles and screaming colours.

"Batya, you need help," whispers Antonia.

"I am confused but hopefully not crazy," Batya says in self-defence. "Clothes seem to underline my moods. When I am Bea the bohemian I wear different things from when I feel like Batya, the masked survivor. I know. I sound totally screwed up."

"Dear girl," says Antonia kindly, eyeing the clothes revealing the two different Batyas, "This is far from simple."

Batya falls onto the bed, exhausted. "I saw a shrink once," she tells Antonia, "but he really didn't understand. He didn't want to go back there where the real Batya lives, inside the ghetto prison. He insisted on interrogating me about my sex life and my relationship with my mother."

"But of course, you need to talk about the war. Get it all out," says Antonia.

Batya feels great affection for Antonia, who is making an effort to acknowledge her experience, unlike other people, who have told her to "let it go." Maybe it helps that Antonia has a background in psychology.

"After all, you are a witness, and child survivors surely are the last witnesses," says Antonia.

"I never thought of myself that way. Me? A witness?"

Chapter 8

Miri and Sam appear nervous when they greet her at the door. Something is wrong. Joseph is standing behind them, his face contorted with anger like the time he almost hit her in the car.

"Why have you been visiting someone in prison behind my back?" he shouts. "How dare you do this under my roof?"

"I'm sorry," she says feebly, though all she can think of is Joseph's reference to their home as only his. What has she been all these years, a tenant?

So what if you didn't tell him? Bea whispers inside her head. *It's not the first time you've lied to him!* It is true that she has lied on occasion to avoid Joseph's anger and subsequent fighting. But even if she had told him the truth, he would only have believed that she was doing something wrong that went against the grain of HIS society.

"Antonia is a friend and I could not leave her in her hour of need. That's all."

Joseph mimics her words and she feels cheap. She knows he never had much use for Antonia and thought her to be a bad influence. For a simple reason that she was her friend not his.

Squeezed between the forces of Joseph's anger and her guilt, she cannot concentrate on the scene in front of her. Unable to speak or move, she stares dumbly at her husband. He is so familiar and yet a stranger standing in front of her enraged. He moves closer to her holding his arm up in the air.

"Why must you be deceitful?" Joseph's words pound her brain. Batya cowers beneath his threatening arm as she did when a Nazi raised his baton over her head on the way to the ghetto. "Schnell," the soldier spat. She falls to the ground, her body shrinking like a ball of unravelling wool.

"I've called your mother," he says in a voice thick with anger. "Maybe *she* can talk some sense into you. You don't know what you are doing. You're drinking and now this prison and the university…" He dismisses her with a wave of a hand and walks away, his back a rigid wall between them.

Getting up with difficulty she walks unsteadily into the kitchen. She starts to prepare supper with shaking hands. Maybe this time Mother will see her misery and help her. But just as she is unsure of her role as a wife and mother, so she is insecure in her role as a daughter. Most times she feels more like a stepdaughter or a poor relative.

Somehow she manages to cook and serve dinner. While they all eat in silence she notices the children's furtive glances at each parent then each other. They eat quickly and escape to their rooms. Batya feels sorry for them, having to listen to their parents' fights now becoming more frequent. The two people who are the foundation of their lives have a crack in their relationship. She wonders how they must feel knowing this and whether because of it they aren't divided in themselves.

The pained look on Joseph's face informs her that her actions have hurt him deeply, yet she feels incapable of compassion, still smarting from their fight. The bell rings, Joseph opens the door, and the woman who walks in feels as remote and cryptic to Batya as the Sphinx. Despite her sixty-plus years, Marta is still beautiful in a cold sort of way. There is hardly a line on her cheeks, smoothed by richly applied day cream. Her green eyes are alert and bright, her brown hair coiffed into a French roll, and her tall, slim figure clad in a classic navy suit. She walks down the hall with her head up and her body stiff, as if one wrong move would crease her perfect attire. She enters the kitchen and sits down at the table with her usual grace and poise.

Batya has always admired her mother's looks and the charisma with which she easily charmed her friends. Marta functioned well on the outside but that veneer vanished at home. In private, Marta was often angry, sad and critical. She kept her difficult past well hidden from the public.

It has never occurred to Batya until now that perhaps her mother also has a hidden personality that helps her get through difficult situations, when she feels unable to cope as her true self. There were happier times before the war, when Marta Lichtenberg was more cheerful and more relaxed. Then they played together and Batya sat on her knee. But war changed all that and made Marta into a different person. In fact, it changed Papa too, When she saw her parents towards the end of the war they were different people, just as if they were wearing masks to hide their true selves, even in front of their daughter.

"Why would you want to visit people in prison?" Marta asks, her beautiful face grimacing, and Batya squirming beneath her mother's accusing stare.

"I did it for Antonia," she blurts out as she tries to push away the usual dose of blame streaming from her mother. She can also hear in Marta's voice her step-father Max's guilt-inducing words. Little do they know of her struggle and little do they care, she thinks, wondering why Bea has been silent.

She looks into her mother's eyes, begging for understanding. But they stare back at her like stones, her mother's lips clipped together as if she has eaten something sour.

"Regardless of Antonia and your sacrifice, Joseph and I feel," says her mother, "that you need to see a psychiatrist."

Joseph nods his head, his eyes lowered.

"Fine," Batya answers curtly.

With that, the interrogation is over. Her mother and Joseph, both sullen and wordless, leave her. Batya pours herself a vodka straight up. It overpowers her body with the delicious edge of a drug, killing the depression and arousing excitement. Two more drinks, she hopes, will stave off the poison her mother and husband have planted inside her gut. In her dark study she sits, trying to forget this day. Later, in the bedroom, she tries to sleep but the alcohol pulsates in her blood. Eventually the drug leaves her throbbing body and makes way for a nightmare.

Walls are crumbling. Brick torsos with barbed-wire arms are moving towards her so close now that she cannot breathe. She sees a cluster of dust and, through it, her body transforming into a worm. She is no longer of use to her family. Bea appears in a red dress, dancing, mocking her, as Batya crouches in fear trying to crawl away.

In the early morning, she turns to Joseph lying beside her and touches his shoulder, longing for some measure of comfort and affection. He takes it as an invitation to sex and crushes her body with his. For Joseph it is over in minutes. He turns on his side and dozes off. Here, in bed with her husband, the image of another man insinuates itself. The old dirty man in a Polish village. A bile of revulsion rises to her throat. She slips out of bed and goes to sleep in her study.

The next day, she makes an appointment to see a psychiatrist.

* * * * *

Dr. Mack listens patiently to her story and the recent feelings of terror brought on by her childhood memories. She talks about her life in the ghetto.

"What about your sex life?" he counters.

She gives him a fragment about Bolek and the last episode with Joseph.

"Do you climax when you and your husband make love?"

"No," she replies.

"Well, there are many other ways to make love."

"I don't know about them," she admits, feeling embarrassed.

"Get a book and read it. There are many on the topic. It's up to the woman to show her husband what she needs."

"My mother and husband think that there is something wrong with me because I visit a friend in prison."

The psychiatrist's glasses slip well down his nose.

"Now why do you need to do that?'

Because I am helping my best friend with the visitations which are difficult for her because the inmate is her brother."

"I see nothing wrong with that as long as you don't get involved in something that may be unhealthy."

She tells him about her emerging nightmares and childhood memories,"

"You might have to confront these," he says, "in order to eventually be at peace with yourself. Maybe you need some time to yourself to evaluate all this?"

Batya shrugs off the last statement. How could she find time to be by herself?

"As for all the other problems you spoke of," he adds, gesturing with his long arm pointing towards the door, "Our time is up but you'll need to work out this problem plus the abuse you experienced as a child. Please make another appointment with the receptionist on your way out."

Batya leaves with an empty feeling on the one hand, glad that there seemed to be nothing wrong in her visiting the prison, on the other that she was able to open up a little. She won't come back though, she decides. The psychiatrist exhibited a kind of a chilly indifference towards her at the end.

When she tells Joseph and her mother what the psychiatrist said, they are not pleased. "We feel that you are doing an immoral thing by associating with convicts and lying about it," they tell her almost in unison.

Tired of their criticism and their lack of understanding, Batya turns more and more to studying, to the bottle and to her diary. She drinks practically every night now to kill the pain. Batya and Bea are in conflict. She feels as if she were being pulled apart in a bizarre way and it's scary. She must get rid of Bea somehow but she feels weak..

Finally, no longer able to stand the suffocating atmosphere at home, she remembers the psychiatrist's words. Maybe she and Joseph need to separate for a while. Late one evening just before the Christmas holidays, she finds the courage to confront Joseph, who is parked in front of the television. How can she tell him that she longs for freedom even if it is for a week.

"I need to talk to you," she starts timidly. "Lately when we have been having sex, I don't feel good." She tells Joseph about the man in the village.

"That was a long time ago," he replies unsympathetically. "I have been to see a counsellor about you, and he said that you are probably frigid and that it's your problem."

Frigid? Is that what she is? Maybe the sexual act frightens her, but she has feelings. What does he mean by frigid?

"I need time to figure this out." She takes a sip of her vodka on ice. It is distractingly soothing. "We need to give each other space," she continues. "Maybe we could have a temporary separation, just to get our bearings."

"What are you suggesting?" Joseph asks icily.

"I could go away for a while or you could stay away temporarily. I would stay here with the children." With each word, she is wading deeper and deeper into a cesspool. These options seem preposterous even to her as she hears herself uttering them. She wishes she had planned what to say.

Joseph grins. "Wouldn't you like that?" he jeers. "You want the house and the kids, and freedom. Everything for yourself."

It's not true. She hears a voice in her head, no longer knowing whose it is. *But am I not deserving even of our children? Maybe I'm not. I feel worthless here.*

"So, I'll go away for a little while. I am choking and need to breathe," she cries out.

"On your own?" Joseph snaps. "You'll only end up in the gutter."

Now she knows what he really thinks of her. The conversation is over. He stares at the TV screen, concentrating on the football game. She envies his self-composure. And what can she do? Nothing has been resolved; only her feeling of worthlessness deepens.

Her false world of pretence has collapsed. Her relationship with Joseph is at an end. She wants to leave but can't bring herself to hurt him and the children. Yet how can she live a lie while the only reality she knows is crumbling like the wall in her dream?

The only place where she can still achieve a degree of privacy is her car.

The December wind whips the branches of trees by the roadside and rain pelts the windshield as she speeds along the poorly lit beach road. She slows down to drink from the flask she had filled with vodka. In front of her, frantic tree branches thrash in the wind and thoughts, horrible thoughts invade her brain.

Can an immigrant ever completely adapt to a foreign land? *Will I ever feel native to Canada, like my children have and their children will? Or will these trees always remind me of Polish trees and these gardens of Polish country gardens, and these homes, the poorer ones, of the houses in the Polish villages? Even the rain falls differently here,* she thinks, taking another gulp of vodka.

The worst of it is that there is a story inside me bursting to be told, but who will listen or understand? She stops the car. Didn't Antonia say that I am a witness? I should give my own testimony, but to whom? Maybe the only reason I survived was because Papa was a policeman. And now everyone says he was not a good man. Now I will be punished for his actions as well. But surely not everything he taught me was bad or wrong. Papa once said that survival is the strongest human instinct, not just of the body but of the mind, of the soul. And when you feel your soul dying, then what?

Where is the hope that burned in survivors at the end of the war? They were sure they would give birth to a truth that would set them free. But instead, the truth was destroyed by the secrets and lies that ran rampant during and after the Holocaust.

Don't talk about yourself or your past!
Trust in no one! said Mother.
Put on a happy face.
Don't wear your heart on your sleeve!
Stiff upper lip! said the English friends.
You'll just end up in the gutter, said Joseph.
Will she never be free?

She tilts the flask again, hoping more vodka will ease the tension she is feeling, then she starts the car and drives, slowly at first then faster and faster. Her mind is so tired, she doesn't care where she is headed. Her vision is blurred and the edges of the road ahead are invisible through the rain cascading down the windshield. She lifts the flask to her lips again and, finding it empty, powers down the window and flings it out into the wet dark night. Rain slants into the car. A gigantic wave of hopelessness overtakes her and she feels a headache squeezing her forehead like an iron band.

Suddenly, to her right, a tall brick wall emerges from the darkness. It is moving towards her. She must confront it now! This damn wall from the past that is holding her captive.

Crush it and exorcize it from your life once and for all. "Get it over with!"

she shouts out the open window into the fog as the steel vice of pain squeezes her head tighter and tighter. *I'll kill both Bea and Batya right now. I hate them both!* She drives even faster now, tears and rain mingling into a watery curtain between her and the outside world. She can't see the road but no longer cares. She holds the steering wheel tight and aims. There is a screech and a hollow bang as the car slams into the wall. A scream tears out of her body and hurtles into space as she falls deeper and deeper into blackness.

Chapter 9

"She's awake," says a faraway voice. A hand props her head up against something hard. Footsteps recede, voices fade. Batya lies on the wet grass with one arm tight against her chest as if she is holding someone very close to her. Behind her closed lids, a light flickers in a dreary room in the ghetto. Little Batya is holding her two-year-old sister, Tereska, in her arms. There is a commotion by the front door. Mother runs into the room, crying. "Father has been arrested."

Batya knows what that means. She might never see her father again. He might die. "Dress Tereska!" her mother says. "We must all go now. They found a little black book on him with notes about the ghetto."

The three, Tereska still in Batya's arms, run down the street. Mother knocks on the door of an apartment and a man opens the door. He is half naked and there is a completely naked woman skulking behind him. Mother begs him to get Father out of the Pawiak prison.

"I'll see what I can do," says the man in a gruff voice, practically pushing them out and slamming the door.

Two miserable days later, Father appears. He is limping and tells them that a German soldier hit him on the leg and back where the kidneys are, for disobeying orders and for certain names in his notebook.

"The ghetto has become a disease-infested hellhole and we are living in a death camp," says an old lady through an open door of the next room. Batya hangs on to her mother for dear life.

The next morning, Batya goes down to the end of the street where the wall is. It looms there in front of her and she can't go any farther. It is very high and Batya puts her hand on the barbed wire and feels it tearing her skin. She must get away from it somehow. How she envies the thin, hungry, little boys who searching for food on the other side, slither like herrings underneath the wall where the bricks have been pulled out. But she dares not follow them. She stands there facing the impenetrable barrier as if it were her greatest foe. Suddenly, the street she is on and the wall disintegrate inside a deep black well.

* * * * *

Everything is white. Where is she?

"A man walking his dog saw her driving," says a voice through a fog. "She deliberately turned and crashed into the brick wall."

The voice wants to know her name and address.

Batya sees a vague outline of a man in a police uniform. She hears him ask questions of someone in a white coat. "There is a sizeable hole in the wall her car made when it crashed," the policeman says.

A hole, she thinks crazily. Like the one she had crawled through as a child. Only that hole was already there waiting for her.

"I had to go through it to save myself," she mumbles into the air. Her vision gradually clears and she sees Joseph shaking his head at what she had done.

If only Papa was here.

Joseph comes closer. "They are confiscating your licence," he informs her grimly. *Why isn't he her friend at a time like this?*

"I am Dr. Brown, Mrs. Lichtenberg-Mintz," says the man in white. "I'm glad to see you awake. You have a slight concussion and you'll need to stay here a few days because your head wound must heal."

She feels something tight above her left eye—it's a bandage. Maybe she can go home soon. But where is home? She doesn't want to return home. Joseph will be cold to her. And she can't stay with her mother, who even if she wanted to help, fears her husband's disapproval. Max Stern can be as critical as Joseph.

Mother and Joseph are standing at the foot of the bed. *Why are they always together? Why did I come out of this alive? Why did I survive the war?*

The psychiatrist comes to see her in the hospital and asks all sorts of questions. "Do you want to go back home?"

"No!" she says without hesitation.

She hears Dr. Mack tell Joseph and Marta that it would be better if Batya stayed elsewhere for the time being.

"Batya has been suffering from post-traumatic stress due to her war experiences. She should have been to therapy long before this. I told her to make another appointment but she didn't."

"But Batya was a mere child during the war. What did she know?" her mother says.

"Mere children…." The doctor looked directly at Marta. "suffer the most. They don't have the mechanisms of coping that adults do. And adults who suffered trauma as children experience lingering effects in later life. I think that through this accident, Batya suffered a crisis that has been building for years, a crisis from which she may now begin to heal. But first she needs to take the time to face herself. She will need time to herself. And she will need psychiatric sessions and perhaps some medication to quiet her nerves. She can only heal by facing her past, not by running from it."

In her confused mind, Batya feels grateful to the doctor for his words to Joseph and Mother. Maybe now they will know why she is the way she is. Maybe even Sam and Miri will understand. Maybe it is not all her fault. Maybe everything will be okay.

Exhausted, she drifts into a fitful sleep. She dreams again of her little sister. Tereska is lost. Batya is looking for her. She sees a little girl on the road ahead and calls to her, but the girl hurries away. When she finally catches up and turns to embrace her, the girl has the unrecognizable features of an old woman.

In the afternoon, Antonia comes to visit and Batya tells her what the psychiatrist said. "Could this affliction, this traumatic disorder explain my split personality, I wonder?"

"It is not an affliction, dear girl," says Antonia, frowning at the thought. "In my counselling practice I've met many people who have post-traumatic stress disorders. People who have suffered trauma in childhood—even in adulthood—and have done nothing to heal themselves. Some don't even know they have it. In fact, until recently North American psychiatry didn't know how to treat war trauma."

"Why is that?"

"There has been little war experience here in North America. The actual wars take place elsewhere."

"Is that why no one here is ever interested in what happened in Europe during the war?" says Batya.

Antonia hugs her. "Don't worry about this so much," she says.

When Joseph and Marta return to the hospital, they ask the doctor when Batya can go home. "As soon as she is steady on her feet," the doctor tells them. "She is still pretty weak."

"I want to stay somewhere else for a few days, not with either of you." Batya finds her voice and wonders whether these words came out of her or some other person. Bea's voice has been totally absent from her head. Maybe the accident silenced her, just as Batya had intended.

Joseph shakes his head in resignation. Mother looks bewildered.

"I want to see my children," Batya says as firmly as she can.

Mother and Joseph leave without a word.

Poor Joseph, she thinks. *How can I describe my feelings for him now? Never has my soul betrayed him, even though I know he would not believe it. If only I had not felt so damn alone in this marriage. If only I had not been damaged by the war.*

Antonia is standing in the doorway. "I'm here for you," she says, walking up to the bed. "You can come to stay with me for as long as you need," she continues, rubbing Batya's arm with affection. "As soon as you can leave, I will come get you," she adds, bending down to kiss her bewildered friend.

"Antonia, dearest, what a blessing to have you for my friend," Batya says and bursts into tears. She feels as if a link on a chain that has held her life together till the car crash has suddenly broken. She listens for Bea's voice again but no longer hears its drone. Can it be that she is just Batya now?

* * * * *

The next day, Sam and Miriam come to visit, carrying sprigs of large purple orchids tied with a white ribbon. At the sight of them, Batya feels joy. Here are her babies, her own flesh and blood, and here she is, their mother, running away from them instead of towards them. She stretches out her arms, and Sam takes her hand while Miriam pats her on the shoulder.

"Dad said you had an accident, Mom," says a frowning Sam.

Miriam sits down in the chair close to the bed.

What can she do to make them understand? And understand what? That she is all screwed up?

"Yes, my darlings. I simply didn't see that wall," she lies. How can she tell the children that she no longer wanted to live? Thoughts cluster in her head like locusts, but just seeing Sam and Miri lifts her spirit.

"It is hard to explain what happened to me. I want you to know that I love you both very much but am not well enough yet, in my heart and soul, and to heal I may have to stay away from home for a while."

"Where will you stay, Mom?" asks Miriam quietly. Batya hears a note of disappointment and sees Sam's face grow pale.

"I am going to Antonia's for a while," Batya murmurs and sits up in bed, stretching out her arms again to embrace her children. The three cling together as if to keep out the bad spirit that is tearing them apart.

"Everything will be okay. You'll see," she says, wishing she were as sure of herself as she sounds. "I just need time to heal."

"From what?" asks Miriam.

"From the demons of my childhood. You know a little, but not the whole story. Someday I will tell you. Someday." She wants to do everything in her power to make them feel her love. But that bit of wall still exists between her and her children. Those ruins she must clear away from her mind once and for all.

The children are silent. Though teenagers, they still need their mom. She knows this only too well.

"We will talk again, my darlings. We'll be together as soon as I get out of here," she says, but her words sound weak.

Miriam and Sam get up to leave. The white chill of the hospital room grips her as she watches them walk away. Sam's usually cheerful eyes are downcast, Miriam's face inscrutable. What are they feeling and thinking? Batya wonders, falling back onto the pillows.

Dr. Brown discharges her two days later and Antonia comes to take her home.

"You went mad that night," says Antonia, accusingly at first after they got to her place and Batya was comfortably seated in a big living-room chair. "What happened to you?" she continues in a gentle voice. "I have been so worried since I heard how you crashed into the wall. I phoned Joseph and he told me. I don't think the poor man knows what really happened."

"I don't know. That night I felt that living had become intolerable and I lost myself. I couldn't help it. It was as if some powerful hand at the wheel drove me towards that wall."

"You were being ruthless. But maybe that is good. Sometimes you have to destroy in order to rebuild."

"But how can I rebuild? I don't think my children can be happy with me as I am now, and maybe they never will be, not unless I change."

"Don't worry, dear girl. Your children will understand you one day and all will be well again."

Batya bows her head, as Antonia puts tea and cakes on the coffee table. "The kids are probably the most hurt by your not returning home. Your mother and Joseph don't understand and haven't been very supportive," she continues.

"What you're saying is true. I feel it," Batya says. "But how can I explain to them why all this happened?"

"I am sorry to have to put it in such a crude way. Have you thought of telling them a simple truth? Children can be forgiving if they feel loved and included, and I know you love them. But have they been included in any of this? Why not ask them to come over here and have a talk with them?" Antonia suggests.

"I tried in the hospital," Batya says, recounting their conversation to Antonia. "I can't possibly make them understand why I am leaving our home with them in it."

"Explain that it isn't them you are leaving."

That sounds easy in theory, she thinks. In Miriam's life, Batya was a stranger, as she saw one day in her daughter's drawing. Of the four figures, three were pierced by an arrow, while the fourth one—from whom the arrow came—stood behind, isolated and different from the others. She'd forgotten that drawing, realizing only now how perceptive her daughter is.

And Sammy, whose eyes would lose their shine when he saw her either stoned out of her mind or brooding. What must he have been thinking then of his mother? Antonia is right. Tomorrow, she will ask them to come to visit her.

"About Andrew," Batya says. "What has happened to him?"

"He's gone back to Montreal. He has friends there and wants to start his life all over again."

How commendable, Batya thinks. As if it were that easy.

The next day, when Sam and Miriam arrive at Antonia's, there is concern on both their faces.

"Mom, when are you really coming home?" Miri asks.

"I told you that I need some time to get my mind straight" is all Batya manages to say. There are no words she can add that will make sense.

"Mom, don't you love us and Daddy anymore?" asks Miri.

"But I do. I love you and Sam more than anything in the world. But I have to be right in myself to be there for you," she said. "I have not left because of you, but because of my own problems. Please, please believe this."

Sammy puts his arm around her. "I believe you, Mom."

They sit in an awkward silence until Batya serves cookies and tea and the conversation continues about everyday events. Finally, Miriam taps Sam on the shoulder, saying it is time to go home.

Why don't I want to go back home? Batya asks herself, watching them walk slowly towards the car.

"Wait," she shouts, "Come back!"

They stop.

"I want to show you something."

Batya runs to her room and brings the silver disk outside.

"This is something my father gave me," she explains, breathless. "He never told me who gave it to him except that he got it in the ghetto where we were imprisoned during the war."

Sammy takes the silver disk from his mother's hands and Miriam looks on with interest. The now polished disk glows in the sunlight.

"What a strange face," says Sam.

"I don't know where it came from," Batya explains. "I feel that in some strange way it connects me to my father, when he worked as a policeman in the ghetto."

They look at her with puzzlement. She has never mentioned that part of her past. They sit on the steps to the house and Batya explains the origins of this object or as much as she knows about it.

The first day she saw the disk was after the ghetto had burned down. She was standing by the window in the house of the old couple where she was hiding when she saw her parents walking up the road. She wanted to run to them but froze as she had been conditioned to do, lest she draw the attention of suspicious neighbours.

Batya looks at her children. She is telling them things about her life they have never heard before. "My parents had tears in their eyes when they told me the news. They said my little sister, Tereska, had been taken away by the Gestapo after a neighbour informed on her. You see, we children were sent away from the ghetto to people who were supposed to keep us safe. They snuck us out. But not together. They separated us. 'We don't know what really happened to her,' my parents said."

The children remained silent while Batya sat there, remembering. The old woman, Lena, had served tea, and Batya had vanished inside her little room and, falling to her knees, fervently prayed to God. She prayed for her parents to stay with her and for her sister to be saved. Later, when she sat on her father's knee, he showed her that silver object: a face whose stern expression frightened and intrigued her when a sunbeam filtering through the window filled the disk's hollow eyes with strange light.

"That day, my father showed me this silver disk. When I asked him where he got it, all he would say is 'It is a bit of a mystery.' I thought someday he would tell me. But he never did.

"And after that," says Batya, "I said goodbye to my parents again. It hurt so much, but they had to return to their hiding place."

"That is very sad, Mom. I never knew about your sister," says Sam.

"But where did your father get this object? What does it have to do with your sister? What happened to her? And what does it mean that your father was a ghetto policeman?" asks Miriam. "Who was he working for?"

"I am not sure. Papa didn't talk about it. But he was a good man, your grandfather. And you see, like you, I have all these questions. Now I need to find out what really happened there, and maybe this object will lead me to the truth."

"So what do you have to do, Mom? Can we help?"

How sweet they are. If only they could help me, Batya thinks.

"I have to get information about this and other matters. People kept many secrets in the war, just to stay alive. And there are reasons for my staying away that I can't explain right now. But they have nothing to do with you two."

Sammy looks disappointed. "I wish you luck, Mom, but I also wish you would come back home."

She wonders if the torment of returning home to a damaged relationship would be any worse than the torment she feels right now. The children depart again, leaving Batya to consider whether sharing her past has helped them understand what she is trying to do, even when she herself doesn't know what that is.

Later on, after work, Antonia arrives with a book on post-traumatic stress disorder and they skim through the contents together. Many things fall into place: the nightmares, the flashbacks, the depression, the drinking and the confusion. Maybe Antonia is right. Maybe to heal this trauma, she must re-visit the dark planet where she was hurt. Maybe there she'll find the blueprint with which to rebuild what had been destroyed.

At Antonia's everything except Antonia is unfamiliar. Although Batya feels safe here, there are problems. Antonia's menagerie consists of her two teenage boys, a husband and three creeping cats. Michael, Antonia's husband, is an ivory-tower scientist who looks down with polite scorn on "ordinary, non-scientific beings" like Batya and even his wife, except when he wants his whims fulfilled. He is a workaholic who practically lives inside his lab where, Antonia says, he has a room with a couch, a closet, a table and chairs. The boys are away a lot at school and at sporting events. But the cats are a constant menace.

When Batya is downstairs and the cats are nearby, her skin creeps in response. They brush by her legs and she flinches. She watches them, their sharp claws, their arched bodies tensed to jump at any moment. One is black as ebony, one is a pink-grey angora with thick fur that makes her sneeze, and the last one, a marmalade cat called Orlando, has the wildest green eyes. She tries not to show her fear in front of Antonia, whose kindness towards her is limitless.

Batya reciprocates by buying groceries and cooking meals and even cleaning house while Antonia is out. She knows she cannot stay much longer. A month has passed, a new year has begun, and it is time for her to live on her own. Just as Bea found self-confidence within the boundaries of her marital and financial status, so Batya must find herself in this sudden freedom, even at the price of deserting her family. *But where to go from here?*

Chapter 10

Antonia insists on a talk.

"You may or may not agree, but all I want to do is help. You need to get away, and I've found a place and maybe a reason for getting away for a while."

Batya shakes her head in protest. "How can I leave Vancouver? Where can I go without money or some kind of job? I don't know how to function on my own!"

"Don't panic," says Antonia. "You remember from our teenage days the old apartment my parents had when they were in Toronto? We still have it. You can stay there. I warn you, it's dirty and will need cleaning, but you can have it for as long as you need. No rent."

"I couldn't take any more advantage of you."

"Don't be silly. If you move in and clean it up, at least I'll know it's liveable. You'd be doing me a favour." Antonia continues, ignoring her friend's misgivings. "I also thought you could contact Julian Karp, son of the woman who gossiped about your father. Maybe some clues from him can help you deal with it."

"But what about my children?" Batya asks, while remembering that she has already told them she'll be away without knowing where and how.
"It would only be for a while. They can stay with Joseph and I'll look in on them. Don't worry."

Batya smiles at the irony in what her friend is saying. Antonia, who bases her ideology of life on the family unit, is now encouraging her to leave hers behind. Yet Batya trusts Antonia's intuition. If only she could trust her own. Maybe leaving Vancouver for a while is just what she needs.

"I'm not going to call this stranger," she protests. "Why would he want to help me?"

"I know him," says Antonia. "Take his number, just in case."

Batya reluctantly writes the contact information for Julian Karp into her address book.

The next morning she telephones Miri and Sam, asking them to come after school. She will tell them about her plans to leave for Toronto and assure them that they mean the world to her.

As the time of their visit nears, she paces the living-room floor, stopping every so often to look through the window onto the street. What sense will the truth make to two teenagers who love their parents and want their home intact?

She pours a shot of vodka to fortify herself. She knows she shouldn't, but it is her only tonic now, so long as she doesn't overdo it. The warmth of the liquid electrifies her as it always does at first, giving her the illusion of strength. There they are now. Sammy is parking the car in front of the house. She flings the door open with enthusiasm inspired by the drink. They come up the path to the door and, on seeing her, Sam's face lights up as he grins.

Tears come to her eyes for no reason. *How maudlin I have become,* she thinks, wiping her cheek trying to appear as if she were brushing away a strand of hair. Sam walks in first, handing her a bouquet of red roses. She puts them up to her face. The red brilliance of the flowers and their perfume seem out of step with the smell of alcohol and the dark purpose of this meeting. Through the silky blossoms, she sees Miriam behind Sam, serious and unsmiling.

"Come into the kitchen," Batya says, walking ahead and placing the flowers inside a glass pitcher, then filling it with water. They sit at the table. Sammy, who loves animals, starts petting the black cat that has invaded the kitchen. Batya takes another sip of vodka, forgetting she promised herself not to drink in front of the children. She hopes the other cats will stay away. Antonia has been keeping them mostly in the basement during Batya's stay but today they have appeared upstairs.

She serves pie and ice cream, making small talk. Sam and Miriam talk about school and friends while she listens, hungry for details of their lives. It feels so good to be with them again and for a moment it seems like old times. Sam pulls Miriam's hair and she squeals, moving away, and now she too is smiling.

Surely now is the time for the real conversation she should have had with them when they came over last. About her and Joseph and the war. How to begin? She is not going to talk to them about suicide, unhappiness and the past. But what can she say to make them understand? She feels the old numbness returning, the inability to face reality. If she could have more vodka, it might help. No. It would make things worse. As it is, she has had too much.

"Look," she starts. "I wanted to explain why things that you may not understand have been happening. As I have told you before, I have been failing to cope with the simplest of issues. And…" She can't continue. Emotion chokes her and she feels tears again on her face. She catches Sam's questioning gaze. And Miriam, she notices, is concentrating on her fork as it slides in and out of the pie.

"Don't start that, Mom," says Miriam sharply. "I am tired of you always acting the victim."

What is she saying? Batya feels as if she is shrinking into herself. Sam looks at his sister in horror.

"I didn't know you felt that way, Miri," Batya says, faking composure. And Sam, does he also think of her as a victim? She has not thought of herself that way. She is a survivor. Do they think she is just feeling sorry for herself? Do her children respect her at all?

"I can only tell you what has been going on," she manages. "Things fell apart between me and your father, and we haven't been able to patch them up."

"I thought it was about that silver disk. Where does that fit in?" asks Sam.

"It's a mystery. I have to go away for a while to find out more about it and your grandfather's life during the war. I may have to search out some people in Europe who can give me information."

She tells them more of what she has found out about her father. What has been said about him.

Sam listens intently, while Miriam seems distracted.

"I need to get to the bottom of these accusations, and I don't think I can do it here in Vancouver."

The explanation sounds dry, even to her. Her children stare at her without any significant change of expression. What can her father, a Jewish policeman in the Warsaw ghetto, possibly mean to these young people? Has she failed by not telling them the whole story? Did they learn anything about the Holocaust in school? Maybe it was just ancient history to them. Perhaps the only way anyone could understand what happened to her family during the war was to have lived through the horror themselves. But she would never wish that on anyone.

The kids are silent. Sammy nods like an old wizard, but seems puzzled by her words. Miri avoids Batya's eyes. She is young, and her mother is leaving for a reason that has nothing to do with her.

Sam breaks the awkward silence. "Mom, maybe you and Dad should give it another try."

"Maybe we should, but right now is not the time."

"We have to go, Mom," says Sam, shaking his head in resignation and gently hugging her. Miriam kisses her on the cheek.

"Dad is taking us to visit Auntie Mona. She is sick. I'll phone you," says Sam.

Does he speak a little too quickly, and is Miriam too anxious to get some fresh air away from her? She hugs and kisses her children and doesn't want to part from them. They are the only real happiness she has known in her adult life. *At least Joseph will be good to them*, she thinks.

Miriam glances at her mother before she leaves. Her blue eyes cast a sharp light. It is a look of inordinate perception that pierces Batya's conscience. The look that says "What is Mom up to now?"

"Please," she says, putting her arms around her children. "Please tell dad, that I never wanted to hurt him. Much of all this is my fault. It's because of my past that this has happened." She can't tell them how afraid she would be to come home, to once again reach the point of wanting to do away with herself.

The children draw closer for a moment as if intuiting their mother's angst, then start to leave.

"I'll talk to you soon, my darlings," she mutters on the verge of tears, splinters in her heart. But she hangs on till the door closes. *What a wimp I am. What moves me?* she despairs, watching Sam's car drive away back to a secure life with Joseph.

Later when Antonia comes home from work they sit down over a cup of tea.

"Well, at least you have a place to go to think things out," says Antonia. "How are your finances?"

Batya shakes her head. She hasn't a cent of her own and no bank account either. What little she has in her purse will tide her over for a few days till she gets a job. But then there is the matter of airfare, and she doesn't even have a credit card in her name.

As if reading her mind, Antonia reaches for her handbag and pulls out a cheque and a pen. "Here is a loan."

"No, Antonia, please." Batya tries to stop her from writing but Antonia pushes ahead.

"To be paid back when you have the money," she announces. "If you need more, don't hesitate to ask."

"But I have no way of repaying you," Batya cries.

"Take it, take it," Antonia urges. "You will find a way, I know you will." She looks at her watch and knits her eyebrows together, just as she used to do when she was a young girl. "I have to grocery shop now," she says, handing Batya the cheque. Antonia's purse is wide open and Batya can't help but spot a stash of chocolate bars and wrinkled gold wrappers.

"That's my secret antidote to my frustrations," Antonia says, laughing. Both burst into laughter and it feels good.

Antonia always seems so composed, so able to deal with problems at hand. One day Batya must ask her friend what her frustrations are.

That same evening, Joseph phones, having heard from the children that she is leaving for Toronto. "You had better come home now or someone else will move in to take your place," he shouts into the phone.

"Look," she says, "I need time to think. To be on my own, to try to find out how I feel. Can you understand that?"

"No. I don't understand a mother who leaves her husband and children. Neither does your mother understand and most certainly not our friends."

"Can I come and see you at the office tomorrow afternoon?" she asks.

"Suit yourself," says Joseph.

* * * * *

The next day, once more fortified by a couple of shots of vodka, Batya walks into the building where Joseph presides as head of his company. The door to his office is open but she hesitates on the threshold.

Joseph, dressed in a grey wool suit, leans forward at his desk, writing something. When he sees her, his handsome face assumes an angry twist around the mouth and his nose wrinkles in disgust. But in the steel-grey depths of his eyes she sees the same wounded puzzlement she saw in the eyes of her children. She doesn't blame him for all that has happened. *He is as much a victim of these circumstances as I am,* she thinks.

Seating herself across from his desk, she attempts to tell him of her unhappiness and what drove her to want to kill herself. As she speaks, she knows how ridiculous her rationale sounds to her practical husband. Her words come out confused and her manner is that of a fumbling child.

He raises his arm in dismissal, as if what she is saying is nonsense. "You weren't suicidal," he says quietly. "You were drunk. Are you drunk now?"

"It's also about my father," she tries to explain. "I'm leaving Vancouver because I have a responsibility to clear his name."

"At the expense of abandoning me and the children?" Joseph's voice cracks and he looks as if he is about to cry.

His show of emotion surprises and moves her, and she is unsure how to respond. Up till now she has only seen his feelings in the form of anger. *Yes, I am always the guilty one*, she thinks in panic. But she says, "I'm truly sorry for all this…" And without finishing the sentence, she rushes out of the office.

This, she knows, has been her conditioning—to escape, to run away. *Poor Joseph, how I have hurt him.*

Back at Antonia's, she takes the silver disk out of its pouch. *What the hell,* she thinks, *there is no cure for this except vodka.* She reaches for the bottle.

More and more she begins to understand the nature of her father's cancer. She is convinced he didn't really survive the Genocide. He betrayed his people and so he died of sorrow, of guilt and regret. The cancer grew in his stomach as an ugly reminder. It could become her cancer too, if she doesn't find herself and the truth she seeks.

It is dark outside, the bottle is empty. Still holding the silver disk, she runs out into the street, tripping and falling over people's lawns, the thorny rose bushes slashing her skin. The ground is wet beneath her feet. She looks at the silver disk through the glittering curtain of rain. Its fierce expression gleams out of the darkness, staring into her, its eyes filled with questions. This creature is like her—a maimed survivor with a wound in her soul, beyond repair, beyond redemption.

The street is empty and she is drunk.

She joins a few passers-by seeking shelter from the ambush of rain under the overhang of a closed shop. In the dark she can barely make out their faces. She imagines telling them her story. Her mind plays back her childhood. She hears someone whisper, "Can't you see she's drunk?" She hears a laughter that insults. The kind she heard once from the locals before, when the ghetto was burning and the sky was red over Warsaw. All these years she has been silent about her past because no one wanted to hear. Not even her mother. Now, even Bea is silent. *But drunk or not, I, Batya, will not remain silent.* And challenging the jeering stares of strangers, she walks away in the pouring rain.

Let me not grope in vain in the dark
But keep my mind still in the faith
That the day will break
And truth will appear
In its simplicity

— Rabindranath Tagore, "Fireflies"

Chapter 11

Toronto, January 1982

The fetid smell in the Horowitz apartment repulses on entry. Dingy, chilly rooms and the odour of decay makes nausea well up in her throat. This smell, a powerful trigger for memory, is what Batya had first experienced in their ghetto apartment in Warsaw in 1940, after Nazis ordered all Jews to live behind a ten- foot wall. The mouldy stench of rotten vegetables wafted from the kitchen, where pots and pans stacked on top of a dirty stove, reeked of old food. The grey stench of poverty and neglect, its hunger and shabbiness engulfed her new world.

In the Horowitz apartment the furniture stands covered in dust. Yet she remembers well when the family lived here and she was staying with them, how neat and clean-smelling the place was then. It became her home soon after her father's death and her mother's departure to marry another man.

Rooms are bereft of doors, except one to the bathroom with a broken lock. The tub has yellowed and the toilet rusted. Throughout, the dirty windows let in little light but make visible the scratched-up tables and the faded upholstery.

The Horowitz children seemed to have forgotten this place after their parents' deaths. Antonia, who has only been once since, warned her. Such as it is, Batya feels comforted. This is where she had her first crush on Andrew and dreamed of romantic love, and where the family treated her as their own daughter.

She opens the windows then sets to work with cleanser and rags. Before long, the place brightens and smells better. She will buy flowers later. There is a washer and dryer at the end of the corridor where she launders the yellowed bedding and the towels scattered about. Next, she scrubs the kitchen, the pots and pans with a scouring pad.

Afterwards, she lies down on a clean bed. This is the second time in her life she has escaped from her family. The first was when she left her parents in the ghetto. Her children must be feeling the pain she had felt when she kissed Mama goodbye and let go of Papa's hand at the wall. Except that Miriam and Sam still had their father who would be good to them.

There is a brown envelope lying on the bedside table addressed to her, care of Antonia. She tears it open, recognizing the unexpected scrawl of her mother's handwriting.

My Dear Daughter,

I am sad that we parted so coldly at the hospital. But I felt that you wanted no part of either me or Max. You didn't even phone us to say goodbye.

We think and talk about you a lot and have come to the conclusion that you are not yourself and are in many ways conflicted about our past and your father. I had always thought that because you were a mere child when all that happened to us, it would not touch you. Could I have been wrong?

I cannot discuss this matter with you as anything about the Holocaust sticks in my throat. I have chosen to forget the past and start a new life. I don't want to go back there either. I choose not to disturb the memories which, according to the doctor, have surfaced for you.

I have had one change of mind. After the war your father started writing a book about his life in Warsaw. He was very secretive about his writing and never spoke to me of it. I just left it in a file and put it away in a drawer, All I am willing to do now, and I have talked this over with Max, who has kept your father's papers under lock and key and which on my orders were not to be disturbed, is to send his notes to you.

He had someone translate what he wrote into English, but I never wanted to read it in either language. I was too busy trying to find work and cope with your father's illness. Make of it what you will. I think that it covers your father's younger years. I hope that being away from Vancouver will clear your head. Try to drink less and think more of your children.

Love,

Your Mama

How typical of Mama to make her feel guilty, to be critical. Who is she to talk about drinking? And to think that just because she was a mere child Mama thought she didn't suffer?

How could she think this?

Batya has seen her mother on many occasions come home from parties inebriated. On the other hand, mom is trying to reach out to her by sending Papa's notes, which Batya never knew existed. She saw him on many occasions typing with two fingers on an old typewriter. But her father was always writing something, so no one in the household ever questioned it.

Excitement surges through her as she yanks the elastic band off the package of typewritten pages. The title at the top of the first page is "Testimony." This is what she has longed for—a glimpse into her father's life.

As soon as she starts to read, she feels a transformation taking place like a current buzzing in her ears, as if through the words on the page she can hear her father's voice speak to her.

Chapter 12

Testimony of Shimon Lichtenberg

Toronto, 1947

I wish to tell you of the time before, during and after the Scourge, when my mental and physical deterioration began. Although the struggle to save myself and my family from the horror of the Scourge feels too immense to explain in mere words, I will, for lack of a better method, channel my testimony through that medium.

Once a rich and a happy man, I will die poor with nothing to leave behind except the truth of my experiences. My loved ones will have to discover this truth in their own hearts and minds, not only about me, as a father and a husband, but also about themselves. And this shall be their inheritance.

Ani ma'amin be-emunah shelemah—I am a Jew never before religious, who now has faith that one day our souls may be freed from death's terminal clasp, as was prophesied in the Holy Book: "And many of those whose bodies lie dead and buried will rise up, some to everlasting life and some to shame and everlasting contempt" (Daniel 12:2).

Through suffering and repentance, the soul ascends to higher levels, they say, therefore, I ask forgiveness of God and man in hope that there will be healing for both my soul and the soul of my child, Batya, and all other children whom the horrors of war have damaged, and who, because of this, are doomed to struggle with the legacy left them by the Scourge, by their families and by society.

I once had compassion and felt deeply for those who were suffering, helping whenever I could, no matter that the less fortunate were of a different faith or nationality. I revered children and like the old doctor, Janusz Korczak, respected their right to love and justice, food and shelter, good education and loving care, I believed in honour and truth and love. That is the man I was or thought I was before I was to die, although I continued to live. Life changed me into another, someone I no longer knew. Now the man I once was returns to tell his tale.

The change in me for the worse was gradual and started when I read *Mein Kampf*. I found anger and doubt eating at the marrow of my Jewishness. This was a book everyone around me, even in Poland, was reading. Its influence on the minds of some readers was undoubtedly considerable, because it confirmed their own beliefs about the Jews. However, I will not speak generally as I am certain that at least a few of the more intelligent, fair minds balked at many of the unreasonable deductions made by a madman.

Hitler's writings on Jews made me ashamed to the point of my becoming wary of monetary transactions with people of Aryan background. Yet I started analysing both the Jewish and Polish methods of making money, and discovered that they weren't as far apart as the Madman would have everyone think. Money meant survival in both Jewish and Christian quarters, where buying and selling was just another means to livelihood. This widely read book did nothing to make me feel proud of being a Jew. I had often felt that if I had a real Jewish upbringing in the home of my parents, I would have known who I truly was and would have felt great satisfaction in being a Jew, despite the negativity all around me.

Self-hate seems to me a disease, a rot that multiplies and festers in your system, eventually destroying what is good in you. How did I come to this?

I presume to relate my story from the very beginning. By the beginning I don't mean my sojourn in my mother's womb or my exit from her body, but that moment of awareness in which one begins to perceive human sounds and voices as distinct from those of animals, or from the splashing of bathwater in a nursery, or the frightening thunder of summer storms.

As a child, I recognized the difference between the soothing atmosphere of love created by my mother and the sounds of hate sizzling inside my parents' bedroom. I heard my mother scream and I heard the lash of the whip, followed by a female wail of submission, followed in turn by relative peace for the nine months of my brother's gestation.

Do the roots of disenchantment with oneself grow from one's family home, or do they creep into one's mind from an intolerant society? I wondered then, but I know now that the constant criticism, the blame and intolerance coupled with competition and jealousy between two married people are surely the first germs of dissatisfaction with oneself.

My father was a difficult man—a stingy man, not only with the money but also with his feelings. Good-looking and intelligent, he was match--made with my mother, a daughter of a wealthy Russian merchant who equipped her for marriage with a huge dowry. I loved both my parents and stood between them waving a white flag of truce. I was ineffectual. They separated when I was a teenager. The shouting matches were now only between my father and myself, and the older I got the more acid flowed into my stomach from these verbal and, eventually, physical altercations.

Mother was a gentle woman who suffered in silence. With her I tiptoed on eggshells. I fought with Father for her material well-being. His stinginess extended to the point of harming our everyday life. In those days a woman's dowry was passed on to the man, who disposed of it as he pleased.

At the point of their separation I felt a split in myself. On the one side I tried to be the principled, honourable and kind person my mother wished to make of me; on the other I became an angry warrior, fighting an invisible foe to prove myself worthy of my disapproving father.

It was only when my schooling began in Russian Poland that I became aware of the seeds of hate for Jews that were sprouting in the fabric of Polish society. They took root in my mind, already affected by the dissension at home. In pre-war Poland, and elsewhere in Europe, we were thought of as undesirable foreigners. The unfairness of this seeped into me slur by slur. I tried to understand why we were so detested. I didn't feel foreign because I loved all things Polish and Russian, spoke both languages, roamed the rich Polish forests, skied the Tatras and rested in the golden wheat fields. Before I married, I admired and kept company with beautiful Polish women with their round faces, their hair the colour of wheat, and gorgeous legs.

My family had assimilated into Polish society, but there was a street in the old part of Warsaw that haunted me, in a quarter where poor religious Jews lived. I would sneak up there after school, hide behind a fence or a wall of a building, and observe the street and its people. Gentile children would sometimes follow me and hide behind me. If they didn't know I was a Jew because of my fair features, they soon found out.

The street had cracked cobblestones and garbage strewn all over. The sharp, pungent smells of fish and garlic saturated the air. Chickens ran in the streets, cackling, their feathers flying everywhere, except for where women sat on low stools in front of the decrepit buildings, cleaning decapitated birds. There were other women, with painted faces and dresses that showed off their bulging bosoms, stopping men on the street. The occasional horse and cart with vegetables and fish passed through, driven by an old vendor.

One time, several children in worn clothes approached me and my schoolmates. In their faces, smeared with food and soot, I saw sweetness. I wanted to take them with me, feed and clothe them. Yet there they were laughing merrily at us, while we clung, terrified, to a wooden gate behind which we tried to hide.

We froze when two men stepped out of a house and started walking towards our hiding place. The men wore long black coats and black hats, had long beards and held prayer books. Their bearing, I thought, was proud and holy.

The children who had followed me ran away crying. "Scarecrows, scarecrows," they wailed, while I remained as if my feet were nailed to the cobblestone road. These men stirred a kind of reverence in me. Yet I wasn't one of them.

I went back to my secular life—my fine, clean home in a well-kept part of the city, where our large apartment glistened with crystal and silver. When asked, my mother explained that we were assimilated Jews, the rising middle class who preferred to live in comfort and coexist with Christians. I felt this was a betrayal, an injustice. Surely, we were a part of those people on the other side of town, who undoubtedly needed the support of the wealthier Jews? But as a mere child, I could do nothing about it. I liked my room and its luxuries.

I didn't realize that it wasn't only a question of wealth but also a question of faith in one's religion and traditions. Men in black with long beards frightened the Gentile children. The men in black with beards were religious Jews, proud and certain of their beliefs. The men in black with beards and prayer books were my people. Already then I began to feel the dichotomy in my personality and the pretence that went with it.

One day about this time, my mother took me somewhere outside of Warsaw by train. Through the window I saw a crowd of people and a cortège of men on horses. Someone said that Tsar Nicholas was riding through the town. I was glued to that window when, suddenly, I saw him. He sat on a black stallion in front of a military unit, tall and proud in a red velvet Cossack jacket with many medals pinned to his chest. As he rode by the train window, I caught his eye and he smiled at me. The light from that smile illuminated a sense of pride in me.

The next day at school, the children who had laughed and run away from the Jewish street the week before clustered around the teacher, rowdily explaining what had happened in the Jewish district, pointing their fingers at me. I stood proud and tall, feeling like the Tsar on his horse. When the Latin lesson began and the teacher called on me for answers and I gave them correctly, he jeered, "How can a Jew know Latin as well as you?"

All the injustice I felt that day in the Jewish quarter suddenly welled up in me. An unthinking force compelled my hand to grab the bottle of ink perched on my desk and throw it at the teacher's face. Ink ran down his cheeks. He strapped my hands over and over again till I no longer felt them. I was taken by the collar and hurled into the hallway, after which I was expelled. The light that the Tsar's smile had kindled in me soon went out. I learned that I had a potential for ruthlessness beneath my seemingly peaceful exterior, or so my mother told me.

With the help of a great deal of money and persuasion from people of note, my parents enrolled me in another school, where I managed to get by despite continuing anti-Semitic slurs. I was then ten years old. It was 1912.

In those days I struggled with the question of how I fit into the Judeo-Christian equation. I got on with my Polish colleagues well. We'd study together and help each other work out academic problems. I'd often walk around the city observing the many churches and their holy architecture and then I'd pass by the Great Synagogue. It resembled a palace, with a central building and wings on the sides and in the back. Its facade was graced by Roman pillars and two tall candelabras standing on each side of the entrance. The roof was crowned by a sphere, the colour of celadon.

Once, the door was open and I crept inside. There I saw a long, large hall with a vaulted ceiling and rows of benches on either side. At the end of the long aisle was a podium which, I later found out, was called the Bimah. When I saw a rabbi walking towards the door, I fled, feeling ignorant about the Jewish faith, even though my mother had taught me about our one indivisible God.

Chapter 13

Batya felt as if she had held her breath through the entire reading, so absorbed in it she was. How difficult and conflicted her father's childhood had been. Like hers in a way. And now Miriam and Sam's. Maybe her father's words are sending her a message that she must return home to her children and help them cope with their broken home. She puts the thought away together with the memoir into a drawer by her bedside table and closes it tightly as if never wanting to re-open that part of her life again.

She tosses all night in the strange bed, dreams and thoughts mingling, memories snaking out of the night's dark well. Her children's faces appear and fade inside the turbulent whirlpool of sleep. As soon as the morning light trickles in through the window, Batya telephones Sam and Miriam to give them her phone number in case they need to reach her.

"I love you both so very much," she tells them, her heart pounding with guilt and longing.

"We love you too, Mom. We're always here for you," says Sammy, his voice serious.

"I miss you, Mom," adds Miriam in a small voice, as if she were forcing herself not to cry.

I don't deserve their love, Batya thinks. *They are there for me, but I am not there for them.* She thinks about her own mother and how indifferent she seemed when they said goodbye at the hospital. Yet her conscience moved her to send Papa's papers. *Marta is right: I must hurry back to the children, but first I must find connections to Papa's life in the ghetto or I can't live with the doubts.*

Her thoughts drift to Julian Karp. All she knows about him is that his mother hated her father for being a Jewish policeman. She finds her address book and opens it at the page where she has written down Karp's number. She stares at it blankly for a few minutes. The sooner she completes this task, the better.

She needs something to steady her nerves and indulges in a sip of vodka. Several drinks later, she dials the number.

"Karp speaking." The voice that answers is deep and strong.

"This is Batya Lichtenberg," she says quickly, trying to sound normal and composed.

"Yes. How can I help you?"

"Do you remember my father, Shimon Lichtenberg?"

"Yes," replies Karp sharply. " Of course I do."

"Could we meet? I would like to talk to you about something of great importance to me," she rattles off, scarcely breathing between words.

"I don't quite see the point of meeting, but if you insist. I am going out of town for two days, but when I return on Wednesday I can meet you at the Union Station. Would three o'clock do?"

"Union Station. Three o'clock on Wednesday," she agrees.

"There is a small bistro there, on the lower level. You can't miss it."

"How will I know you?" she asks.

"I'll be wearing a black leather jacket and a red tie," he says and hangs up.

How unpleasant he is! How can I handle this? She panics, still holding the phone to her ear.

On Wednesday, at the appointed time, she rides the subway to Union Station. She finds the bistro and, with no small amount of anxiety, enters it. Searching through the crowd of diners, she sees a man sitting alone at a table wearing a black leather jacket and a red tie. She walks over, weak in the knees.

"Hello," she says hesitantly, "I am Batya."

"Julian Karp." The man rises from his chair. He is slim and of medium height. There is a bottle of wine on the table, but only one glass, half full. She could use some, she thinks, smelling the evergreen scent of cologne wafting from him. They sit down.

"Do you live here?" he asks.

"No, I live in Vancouver, at least I did until recently." Her voice is flat. Her eyes gravitate to Karp's wine glass. She feels his eyes following hers and immediately he motions the waitress to bring another glass. He is saying something but she can't make out what it is, as the restaurant is noisy. The glass arrives and he pours the wine. She takes a sip and then another. The heady liquid strengthens her resolve to pose a question.

"What about you? What do you do in Toronto?"

"I teach sociology and history. My recent interest is the study of long-term effects of war on children and adult survivors. Myself, I survived the Warsaw ghetto."

"I wish I could understand these long-term effects," Batya says, surprised at his candour. "I am a child survivor myself."

"Yes, I thought as much. Where did you survive?"

"Also in the Warsaw ghetto, then in villages."

They avoid each other's eyes, as if trying to escape the awkwardness of this meeting and even of the past that unites them. She feels a curious excitement. He is the first child survivor she has met on this continent.

"What do you think happens to child survivors as they get older?" she asks.

"I think their experiences have a critical impact on them when the memories start to surface. Have they come to haunt you?"

She recalls what the psychiatrist told her about post-traumatic stress disorder.

"They have lately. What about yours?" she says, not quite knowing where this conversation is leading.

Suddenly, their eyes meet. She sees his face as if for the first time and feels his brown eyes scrutinizing her. Although he is gaunt, his cheeks hollow, and there is a large gap between his Adam's apple and the knot of his red tie, he is pleasant to look at. The collar of his shirt seems much too big for his rather scrawny neck. Yet she finds him attractive.

"They have come to haunt me as well. That is why I became interested in the studies being done now."

"What studies? Who is doing them?"

"Scholars and psychiatrists, are investigating the adult personalities of child survivors who have experienced war and suffered trauma in childhood."

Her respect for him increases. He is a scholar. But she remembers that he is also her father's critic. How should she begin to speak of her father with this stranger?

"My father—" she attempts.

He stops her with a movement of his hand. "Now I know what this is about." There is an irritated edge in his voice. "Your father worked as a policeman in the Warsaw ghetto."

She senses the anger in him percolating.

"Do you know that there were charges against your father for being a Nazi collaborator? This was documented in the post-war Polish court."

"Please," Batya whispers, shaken by this abrupt turn of the conversation, "you are quite mistaken. It is not what you think."

"Why did he not leave my mother be, when she begged him to?" says Karp, raising his voice. "He ordered us out of the apartment and into the courtyard to have her identity card checked by a Nazi officer. He held a baton over our heads. Luckily, because my mother had a work permit, we were sent into a line that went to another part of the ghetto, and not to Umschlagplatz where the cattle cars were waiting." Karp's face has gone pale as he speaks.

How can she know if these accusations are true?

He says more things and his tone of voice grows angrier, but she tunes him out. She focuses on his cheeks growing more cavernous as he speaks and the widening gap between his neck and his shirt collar. She feels the lash of guilt, for having survived and for her father's sins. And yet she still cannot believe that her beloved father would have done this to other Jews without good reason.

After a short while, she finds her tongue. "People said that those who had identity cards from German shops were exempt from deportations. My father would have known you were safe and that is why he did what he did. His own life was also at stake if he didn't do what they commanded."

"A feeble excuse! He should have left us alone," thunders Karp, and she feels beaten by his bitterness and the hate he harbours.

She tries again. "As I understand it, a Nazi gendarme nearby would surely have killed my father and his family if he disobeyed." Her voice thins into a wail. But how can she be sure what she is saying is true?

"I'm not blaming you personally," Karp declares in a calmer voice. "I was a kid like you, and scared. But I have been trying to work out how men like your father, some of them intelligent and educated, could have done what I see as criminal acts against their own people. And you, who are biased in favour of your father, naturally do not see or want to see the wrong he did."

He might as well have thrown acid in her face. "My father was not wilfully doing anything against his people. He just wanted us to live."

"Aha…he had a will, but he used it to survive at the expense of other lives," he interrupts. "What infuriates me are your excuses for his crimes."

"Are you saying that better I should have died than someone else?"

He glares at her like an animal at its prey, not quite ready for the kill. "Let us not get personal," he says, pulling back. "I am not a religious man, but in Judaism we talk about an individual considering the well-being of the community before his own."

"But my mother, my sister and I also were a part of that community!" Batya exclaims. "I don't believe in altruism," she continues. "One has a responsibility to oneself first because, if you are not responsible for yourself, for your own life, then who is? Unless you believe in God, of course, and make Him responsible," she mutters, feeling drained. "Do you believe in the power of God?" she adds.

Karp looks away as if at a loss for words.

"And," she continues, determined to defend her father, "wasn't it better to have someone like my father get you out of your apartment than a Nazi policeman who might have shot you on the spot had you resisted?"

"Your father," he says quietly, and she knows he is now practising self-control, "helped Nazis send Jews to the trains. They all did it. All of the Jewish police. They even took bribes for promises they made but never kept. They would agree to help someone, take their money, and then not follow through on what they had promised."

"Not all, surely," she says. "My father worked most of the time as a guard in the streets and German shops, warning the workers of the approaching Nazis, and he didn't take money for this. Why do you assume the worst?"

"Because he was seen at Umschlagplatz during deportations. You've been lied to."

"When was this?" she asks, refusing to believe.

"In July of 1942. Don't you know that the courts of Israel indicted the entire Jewish Police Force in the Warsaw ghetto as an evil entity?"

"Maybe they did but they are unjust. You have to consider individual acts of kindness, and I am sure there were some. How dare they judge every policeman as evil?"

She would like to hit him, to hurl her glass at his head, though it is not in her nature to be violent, at least not until now. Most of all she feels frustration with her parents, their silence about the war as if they were keeping a secret. She had no knowledge of her father's activities after she left the ghetto in June of 1942 and not before that either. Papa never spoke of his job as a policeman.

Why did she have to come to this bistro in a strange city to find out the horrors in the closet of her family's history? Now she is determined more than ever to get the whole story.

"But who was it that charged my father with Nazi collaboration?"

"I understood that it was his 'best' friend." Karp puts an ironic emphasis on the word "best."

"Rogacki? How do you know of him? He was a collaborator himself and a liar," she shouts. Her mother had always said that he was, even though he had taken in her little sister after she left the Ghetto.

Karp is silent.

She has had enough. The bitterness of the conversation churns in her stomach. She springs out of her chair and heads for the exit. She hates Karp with all of her being and does not wish him to witness her anguish. She has always despised hysterics.

"Wait!" Karp calls, running after her. "Don't go. Please, come back and sit down." He takes her arm almost forcefully and steers her back to the table.

"I know you are tormented. Who wouldn't be in your place? These are not simple issues. No one knows what motivates humans to do what they do. Of course, I know that not all Jewish police could have been bad. Occasionally they helped if they could, but most ended up with bad reputations."

Batya looks down at the tablecloth and after a minute stops sobbing. She must look pathetic, sitting there bowed over in the chair looking like the victim her daughter had accused her of being.

"I don't condone your father's choice of how to survive in that world," Karp says, more softly now, "but I can understand it, if I really try."

"Look," she forces herself to speak. "My father was a good man. I saw many things he did that shaped my respect for him. I remember him taking me to Korczak's orphanage and how he looked at those orphans with love and compassion. He despaired for the children dying in the streets, and he sacrificed himself for his family." She gulps down the rest of her wine.

For a second she sees a kinder light in Karp's eyes. "Yes," he answers. "I, too, remember children lying in the streets dying. I was one of the starving ones." Then the kindness goes out of his eyes, his face becoming harsh beneath the bright light above their table "One day, in desperation, I slid under the brick wall to go and get bread for my parents, who were ill from starvation. A kind Pole on the other side threw me a loaf of bread. Not all Poles were bad. Many helped us. When I slid back into the ghetto, a Jewish policeman took the bread away from me, telling me it was a dangerous practice in case Nazi soldiers at the nearest checkpoint saw us or their police caught me."

"But not all Jewish police were like that. You said so yourself."

He doesn't answer but she begins to feel empathy for this child, now a man, who had suffered as she and many other ghetto children did.

"What happened to your father?" she asks. "Obviously your mother survived."

"He first had typhus and then was shot by a Nazi," says Karp. "Look, I know I seem bitter," he continues, "but recently I have looked quite seriously into the legacy left us, child survivors. And because of that, what happened between our parents should not affect you and me, should it?" He pulls his wallet out of his jacket pocket. "Here is my card at work. I do hope we'll meet again. We should not part as enemies. After all, we have a mutual friend in Antonia and an interest in the past."

She likes the way he put those last few words, though she might have heard a note of sarcasm in them.

"Thank you," she says, taking the card. "I too am bitter about the war."

"After all these years, you are still that hidden child, as I am," says Karp. "If you really are interested in how the war affected survivors, you could come to some of the lectures here at the university."

"Yes, I would like that," she says, feeling more relaxed.

"I don't know exactly when, because the lecture series is still in the planning stages. Can you give me your telephone number?" Karp stands up and pays the bill. She offers but he refuses her money. She hands him her telephone number she has written down on a napkin, which he takes from her carefully sliding it into his wallet, then starts walking towards the exit door.

She remembers the silver disk she put in her purse thinking that maybe by some miracle he might know something about it.

"Wait," she calls after him.

He stops. She takes the silver disk out of her purse and shows it to him.

He examines it, his hands sliding along its polished surface. When he finally looks at her, his mouth is set in a firm line of stubbornness. "Where did you get this and why are you showing it to me?" His words border on impatience.

She hates his manner all over again. "I inherited it from my father," she explains. "He said he got it in the ghetto but never told me from whom or why. I am showing it to you because I am looking for answers. I need to find out how my father came by it in the ghetto." She hesitates, seeing his frowning face. "But I won't bother you with it anymore."

"Don't you know where he got it? I am sure it wasn't a birthday present." *He must know that his sarcasm verges on cruelty,* she thinks. Karp looks at his watch. "I am sorry but I have a class this evening I still have to prepare for," he says in a gentler tone.

They walk into the dark street.

"What did you mean by saying that it was not a birthday present?"

"Don't be naive. I am sure it was a bribe—what else? Some poor Jew wanted to be left in the ghetto instead of dying in a cattle car on his way to

Treblinka."

She snatches the disk from his hands then turns her back to him and leaves.

His arm stops her. "Don't go off in a huff. I shouldn't have said that."

"Goodbye then and thanks for the wine," she says drily. She walks away despite his attempt to stop her.

She can't and won't believe his theory. The disk remains a mystery until such time as she can prove him wrong. In the meantime she knows all too well that she and her father are both on trial: she for desertion, he for betrayal.

Tired from the meeting, Batya stops at a small park on the University of Toronto grounds and sits down on a frozen bench, but she doesn't feel the cold. The silver disk is still in her hand. The look of anger on its face reflects her feelings. It could be her anger with Karp or with Papa for dying and leaving her alone in this silence. Papa, who wore the hats of a poet, an artist, a lawyer and a policeman. But most of all, he was a caring father, the kindest being she had ever known, and his love for her has been the light of her existence.

Karp's accusations have hardened her against him, but when the initial anger leaves her, she feels a certain bond of having shared a treacherous past. Their meeting has stirred in her an even deeper need to find out more about her father. It has given her new energy and the motivation to prove Karp wrong.

She gets up from the bench and walks among snow-laden trees through icy streets back to the apartment. The November wind howls, its sharp teeth gnawing at her skin through her thin coat. She wraps the wide woollen scarf around her shoulders and steps carefully along the slippery sidewalk. It was on a wintry day like this in Warsaw when she walked with her father and asked him about the meaning of memory.

"Sometimes, when you smell a flower or taste a food, hear a song, or hold in your hands a photograph or an object that has meaning, you remember through these things what connects you to a person, a place or an event," he had said.

The silver disk must somehow connect me to Papa and to the life we shared, she thinks. A crazy notion enters her mind. Maybe she should visit some of the Toronto jewellery stores tomorrow, to seek information about who might have made this piece. But now back to her new home base, to read Papa's remaining pages.

Chapter 14

Testimony of Shimon Lichtenberg

Toronto, 1948

World War I had ended. By 1918 the Tsar was dead. Poland had regained its independence. Then the war between the Poles and the Soviets began. I fought only briefly because I was wounded in the leg and dismissed from the army to the hospital. By the time my leg had healed, the war was over. I was twenty years old with a soldier's uniform and a rifle hanging on the wall of my experience. And I was ready for college, a time during which I began to sow my oats.

While still attending gymnasium, now known as high school, I had formed a close friendship with Jan Rogacki, a Gentile boy who was much less privileged than I. He never had enough to eat or enough money to buy even a glass of milk. I would take him home, feed him and often lend him a few *zlotys*. I never asked to be repaid. I would fund most of our ventures together, for which he appeared grateful. I thought nothing of it as it meant helping a friend.

I felt his reciprocity in that he was always by my side and on my side. Our friendship continued well into our lives as grown men. As we romped around Warsaw and nearby towns and villages, Jan Rogacki, with his wit, apparent honesty and frankness, was a great companion. He did have one fault, however. Although he was a quiet man, he didn't mince words when it came to criticizing and even bullying men or women passers-by, especially those who appeared different in dress and looks. At such times, I would feel embarrassed, both for him and for myself. I might have coached him on looking for human similarities rather than differences, reminding him that one ought to base one's judgment of a person on their inner being and not their appearance, but for some reason I stopped myself.

We both enjoyed adventure and sport, riding horses and hunting. After college, motivated by a desire for justice and tolerance, I took up law. I had an idealistic notion that I would build a bridge of communication between Polish Jews and Polish Christians.

Jan accompanied me in my escapades with beautiful women, of whom there was no shortage. When it came to women, I would occasionally detect a certain bitterness in the cracks he made about my financial means, which were more than adequate, while he was not able to afford courtship of women, gifts and restaurants. I felt sad about this and kept on offering him money, not really expecting to ever get it back. We continued to explore nightclubs, brothels, foreign cities and countries, all at my expense. Our female conquests were many and successful. Theatre, restaurants and cafés—that was the life.

My mother would sometimes warn me that Jan wasn't all he appeared to be and that I was too trusting for my own good. I strongly disagreed. Maybe there was a grain of truth in what she said. Maybe he even resented all my help; certainly at times his remarks revealed that he was somewhat jealous of my position. Our friendship was no doubt, I once told my mother, to his advantage. But the good feelings I had for him overcame any doubts about his character.

Then I graduated, became a lawyer and opened my own office. Work was plentiful and there was no shortage of people, both Jewish and Christian, needing my help. My friendship with Jan continued but I became busy. I still lent him money while he struggled in small jobs that he never held on to for long. Though not as frequently, we continued to have great times together, until one night in the winter of 1929, when my wild life as I had known it abruptly ended.

I had been invited to a friend's house, where I wandered around a large drawing room filled with all sorts of people, drink in one hand, cigarette in the other. Oh, I was a proper dilettante, bored with the crowd, noise and idle conversation. Suddenly, I stopped short.

Right in front of me, next to a marble table with a statue of a Greek goddess, stood a real beauty, the likes of whom I had not seen even among my most stunning girlfriends. She had the face of an angel, with blonde-brown hair pinned back at the nape of her white neck. Her eyes, I was certain, were the colour of olives, with a special sheen that matched her silky dress. I stood there mesmerized until the hostess took my arm and introduced me to Marta Berdicki, whose sudden smile lit up my heart. Was this woman real? I wondered. We chatted for a while, then she excused herself and I didn't see her again until, on my way out, I found her standing at the front door, waiting either for a ride or for the pouring rain to stop. I told Jan to go home by himself and embarked on my usual pursuit.

"May I have the honour of escorting you home?" I asked the young green-eyed beauty. She shrugged her shoulders indifferently and turned away.

"How will you get home in this rain?" I persisted.

"I will walk," she replied proudly, holding her head high under the umbrella, but not moving from the entrance that partly sheltered her.

Getting wetter by the second, I suggested, "How about taking a taxi with me?"

"I left my money at home."

The wind and rain were really getting to me, and to her as well, I thought. I wasn't sure if her changed posture and the slight grimace on her gorgeous face were meant for me or the weather.

Once again I offered to take her home, on the condition that she would pay me back. I looked down at her shoes and could see they were soaked. Marta lowered her eyelids and conceded.

Ours was a six-month courtship: stolen moments in cafés and movie theatres, walks in the moonlight and other romantic rendezvous punctuated by Marta's lilting voice singing "J'ai deux amours" and other popular love songs of that happy era.

Despite all this, I was getting nowhere with Marta, who was determined to keep her virginity intact. However, she did introduce me to her rather large family. When parading through the crowd of older relatives, she was caressed and catered to like a favourite pet. More and more I began to notice that when I spoke to her she seemed to be somewhere else, not really listening. I started testing her intelligence and found that she could be street-smart and shrewd, even though she couldn't concentrate on the moment. I believed all that would change, and I was not going to let small things stand in the way of our union. I also believed that her cool exterior would vanish with familiarity.

My mother warned me against her and said that Marta knew nothing about love. I, in turn, told my mother that Marta was fun to be with, easy going and energetic. Mother reminded me that there was a ten-year gap between our ages, me being older, of course.

Her family were poor Jews, all living in that part of Warsaw where the people had always seemed mysterious and sacred to me.

Marta was ambivalent about her religion. This suited me well since I was not religiously inclined, but I had to have her no matter what. I was beguiled.

One sunny afternoon in Warsaw's Stare Miasto (the Old Town), we were standing on the banks of the river Vistula. The sky was a cloudless blue, reflecting in the calm surface of the legendary Polish river. The September air was still and warm. I had been carrying a box with a ring in my pocket for two weeks, unsure if she would have me and also not sure whether I was ready for marriage. But if not now, I asked myself, when?

Looking at her I felt the same deep feeling I had that first night I met her. Without a moment's hesitation, my hand reached into my pocket and produced the box containing the ring. She looked at me, her cat-green eyes luminous in the sunlight, and took the box. On opening it she fingered the ring with reverence and, after a silence that seemed eternal, shyly nodded a yes. The rest was ritual.

The year was 1931, when the city of Warsaw was pulsing with so much life that it was nicknamed "Little Paris." Life was good. I was doing well. We got a big apartment in a quiet part of the city. Marta became a lady of leisure, with servants and clothes that enhanced her beauty. I stopped seeing Rogacki as often as before, but we still invited him to the house for dinner and to the theatre. I noticed that he was flirting with Marta and that she liked the attention. Though I doubted anything further would develop, I couldn't help feeling a little jealous and thinking that he was trying to take something that wasn't his.

My fears were short-lived. Soon after my marriage to Marta, Jan began courting a young lady with a handsome dowry. We made a nice foursome, and not long afterwards, Jan proposed. They were married with us in attendance and started their married life in a villa in a small town near Warsaw. Jan was now well-heeled as his wife came from a wealthy family, and so he acquired a new sense of self-confidence. He joined the army and became a colonel, with a decent salary. Despite this, we still found time to get together as two old buddies, though our activities were much tamer then when we had been single. Marta and Jan's wife, Maria, became friends.

In 1932, Marta announced that she was pregnant and not too happy about it, worrying about her figure and a change in our lifestyle, in which she rejoiced. I, on the other hand, was thrilled and hoped for a son. In 1933, as fate would have it, a baby girl was born. Batya was such a beautiful little girl that people on the street would stop to admire her lying in her carriage—her head of golden curls, eyes like her mother's, and a sweet disposition. She soon became the love of my life. Life returned to normal after we hired a nanny and a cook. Marta, for her part, received Batya into the world with a certain detachment which I ascribed to her being very young, all of twenty-two.

As a young boy I had observed the Jewish community with curiosity. Now this world was open to me. Although my respect for religious rituals deepened as I began to understand the whys and wherefores of the practices and prayers, I was not able to participate as a full believer. Still, I secretly became proud of my Jewish heritage. I kept this newly evolved feeling hidden while in my public life I considered myself a Pole, a citizen of Europe influenced by German, French and Russian cultures.

In the meantime, next door in Germany, Hitler and the Nazi Party came to power. We heard rumours about how Jews were treated in Germany. I feared the Scourge would soon come to Poland and argued with my father that we should all get out before it was too late. "It'll never happen here," he said categorically. So we stayed and, in 1938, another daughter, Tereska, was born. Strange, I thought at the time, that one daughter was born on the eve of Hitler's rise to power, while the other on the eve of the night of broken glass, Kristallnacht.

Soon 1939 approached and with it the Blitzkrieg. I suddenly became a man standing on the surface of ice that was cracking beneath my feet. Weeks after Poland lost the war and one week into the Occupation, Jews lost their human rights. Jewish shops, businesses and offices were closed with signs on their doors: *JUDEN VERBOTEN*. Professionals were let go from their places of work. One of my best friends, Dr. Levin, came to my office one afternoon with tears in his eyes. The hospital had let him go and got rid of other Jewish doctors as well.

"Watch out, Shimon," he warned. "You may be next." And sure enough, one morning I came to my office and was barred from entering by a two by four nailed across the door. A sign said *VERBOTEN*. It was one of the most painful moments I had experienced in my life, though many more were to come. In the meantime I had lost my right to do what I loved, to practice law.

Children of dear friends were barred from school because they were Jewish. Tereska was too young to go to school, but Batya would have started in grade one that very September. Instead we kept her home and my father volunteered to teach her to read and write. When the moment came for me to wear a white band with a blue Star of David on my arm to identify myself as a Jew, I was forced to accept that our previously bright and free lives were gone. Gloom descended.

No Jew was allowed inside a restaurant, park or streetcar. "We're branded now," said a colleague from work, "like cattle."

With the invaders came the curse of racism and persecution, growing like an infectious sore on the flesh of our society. I walked the streets of Warsaw, a Jew, considered by the Nazis a creature as despicable as vermin in the new order that I now inhabited. This was a place no longer a part of the world I knew and loved, studied and revelled in as a young man. In this new world, Jews were worse off than cats and rats, who could always find something to kill and eat.

More than once I was handed a shovel and told to dig a ditch. I stood in the ditch I had dug, staring at the polished boots of an SS man. I philosophized even then that as long as I continued to live a virtuous life, I would be a happy man. Did it matter what I did for a living? I, an ardent student of Plato and Aristotle, a once happy man, father of two beautiful girls and husband of a wife I cherished, was standing in thick mud smelling of dung, looking out of a ditch at a polished German boot, my stomach heaving from hunger and nausea, my pockets empty, my new armband already soiled. My hands were black with mud, my soul kicked by the black boot of a racist. Could self-hate get any deeper than being stuck inside a bottomless ditch and forced to clean the boots of our torturers?

The process of dehumanisation had began

Chapter 15

Batya has reached the last page of the memoir. She had entered a world she had not known, the world of an adult during the war, the world of her beloved father. So submerged in his world she had become, that she could hardly recognise the contours of her apartment. With this new knowledge, she becomes more aware of how deeply she lives in two worlds. No longer as the Bea/Batya split, but as a child of war and an adult in peace time coping with the inner turmoil inside her that the war had caused. The experience of her father's anguish has now also crept into that chaos.

His words revealed a side of a father she never knew. *Who was this man so full of angst and anger and scorn? Why did he stop here? Is this all?* she wonders, fumbling through the pages. *What happened that he stopped writing?* There was so much more to his life, especially during the war. What came after or during the "process of dehumanisation?"

Her hunger to know more is insatiable. From reading her father's words she begins to understand her uneasy relationship with Judaism. She, like many, had to deny being a Jew in order to survive. *How can you love yourself if the society around you hates you?*

She must phone her mother. Or should she write to her? No, she can't wait that long. She dials Marta's number even though it is almost midnight in Vancouver.

"Hello, Mom."

"Batya. What's wrong? Don't you know how late it is?"

"Yes, sorry, Mom," she says.

"Didn't you get my letter?"

"Yes, I did. That's what I am calling about—Papa's notes. Is there more?"

There is a prolonged silence at Marta's end. "I don't know," she says finally. "Max keeps your father's files in his filing cabinet. But I am sure there is no more."

Batya detects a false note. She is well versed in what lying sounds like, especially from her mother.

"Be happy with the information about your father's youth."

So she did read them, but said she hadn't.

"But Mom, I need to have them all."

"There are no more, I tell you," Marta says with a feeble finality.

Disappointed and angry, Batya bids her mother a hasty goodbye and practically slams the phone down. There *must* be more to her father's story. Why else would he call it his testimony? How cruel of Mother to withhold it. If she can't get any more info from her, she will damn well discover it for herself. She will begin with the silver disk. *It is a wild card, but who knows?*

* * * * *

Early the next morning, Batya makes her way down a wintry street in Yorkville. Snow-laden trees bow towards the ground. The usually cheerful and quaint buildings with pointed roofs now stand steeped in winter, icicles hanging over the doorways of shops. Cars resembling white tents move slowly through the pelting snow.

She walks into the first jewellery store on her list. A well-dressed man standing at the counter smiles, welcoming his first customer of the day. She walks up timidly and, as she is about to place the velvet pouch on the countertop, the silver disk slides out and drops onto the glass with a clatter. The man picks it up immediately, protectively wiping the place where it has fallen with a felt rag, his smile morphing into a deep frown.

"I am so sorry. I hate to bother you," Batya says, "but would you have a clue as to what is engraved on the back of this piece?"

The man looks at the silver disk without enthusiasm. "Sorry, I have no idea what these symbols and words mean. Perhaps you can try another shop. We don't carry things like this here," he says, pompous in his rejection.

So much for this store, she thinks, and walks out into the cold wind. She passes a number of elegant shops that carry pedestrian-looking jewellery and is reluctant to enter them. None seem the type where anyone would know anything about her obscure silver disk. Maybe she needs to find a shop with unusual objects and jewellery.

Several blocks down she sees one. This shop is not on her list, but its window display shows a few graceful vases and some glass jewellery. A sign on the door says *VENETIAN GLASS*. Inside it's dingy and cold, not at all like the previous store. The dimly lit showcases display various pins, earrings, necklaces made of glass beads. Antique clocks in diverse sizes and styles hang on the wall.

Batya shows the silver disk to the grey-haired sales clerk.

"Sorry, we don't sell estate jewellery," says the woman firmly. She has a slight accent and Batya thinks it might be Italian.

"I wonder if I may ask you a question," she says.

The woman first looks at Batya as if she is trying to figure out who this intruder is, and then looks at the silver disk again more carefully.

"What an interesting piece!" she exclaims. "It resembles *Bocca della Verità* in Rome," she adds. "Mouth of Truth. It is a replica of a Roman drain tile, a famous one." Her demeanour has changed from suspicious to intrigued. "Where did you get this?"

"My story about this piece is rather long. But can you tell me what the engraving on the back of it might mean and what are the funny letters below the word *Cara?*"

The woman picks up a magnifying glass lying on the counter. She turns over the disk and examines it.

"Strange," she mumbles and starts writing something on a pad, then hands the piece of paper to Batya. The words on the paper say "Mano Cornuto by Cornicelli."

"What does this mean?"

"The object engraved into the silver at the back is a horn, meaning *mano cornuto* in Italian. The horn is meant to defeat the evil eye and bring good luck. It seems to be the logo of an Italian jewellery store in Venice, known as Cornicelli."

Elated, Batya thanks the woman and asks her if she knows how to find the address of this jewellery shop.

"We have a list that includes some of the jewellery shops in Italy," the woman says. "Wait here."

Batya is bursting with impatience, glad there are no customers in the shop to distract this kind woman. Maybe this will help to put her on the path to the creator of her father's mysterious object.

A few minutes later the clerk returns with another piece of paper. "I found it," she says. "The Cornicelli address is in Venice, Italy. The owner's name is Carlo Moller. Good luck," she adds. "I hope the shop is still there."

Batya thanks the woman and rushes home to write a letter to Italy, practically dancing for joy all the way. Yet the task at hand may seem easier than it really is. How does one write to a stranger out of the blue, asking about a strange object from a strange land, and get the facts she seeks? She has no choice, she reasons, but to write the letter. It might be her only chance to get any information about the silver disk. After several false starts, a letter materializes.

She waits for what seems an eternity to hear back. Each day she runs to the mailbox with bated breath, only to walk away disappointed. Two weeks pass and, just when she has almost given up, a letter arrives from Italy, written in excellent English.

My Dear Lady

What wonderful news!

Your letter came to me as a complete shock. I thought that Shimon Lichtenberg and his family had not survived the war. We have much to discuss, as I knew your father. However, this is not a discussion to have over the telephone or by mail. Due to my deteriorating health, it would be advisable to communicate with you in person, and since I cannot come to you, perhaps you can come to me.

As to your query about Mouth of Truth, there are only two pieces like this that I made myself. One piece was made for an antique shop here in Italy, a copy of a copy. The original, which I had made for my wife's birthday so many years ago, is in your possession. This is a part of a longer story we need to discuss. Please bring it with you when you come.

Just by the way of precaution and before we proceed further, can you snap a photo of *Bocca* and send it to me together with a photo of your father? I shall then be assured of this being the real thing.

My deepest respects,

Carlo Moller

He needs proof. He doesn't believe me, Batya concludes. Although she is impatient to find out what he knows, she understands his concern. She takes pictures of the *Bocca* and finds a photo of her father of which she makes a copy. Then, when all is done, she sends them off to Moller, hoping fervently to hear from him soon.

Another two weeks pass, then a letter arrives.

My Dear Batya,

I was delighted to have received the picture of my mini *Bocca* and your father's photo. Now you simply must come. I will put you up at a nearby hotel here in Venice.

I would suggest a stopover in Rome so that you may see the real *Bocca della Verità*, the large version of the miniature you now have.

Please let me know of your decision. I am enclosing my telephone number and address.

As well I am enclosing the address and telephone number of a lady in Rome, Madame Berent, a friend from Warsaw. (She is Polish but more French than Italian.) Please contact her. I will forewarn her of your coming. She, too, knew your father.

With warmest affection and respect,
Carlo Moller

Madame Berent, who knew her father? Oh joy! Where had Batya encountered this name? Somewhere in the maze of names she had overheard her parents mention in their many post-war discussions with friends, the name Berent.

She must ask her mother. Batya has never been to Italy or anywhere else in Europe since they left Poland. The very notion of returning grips her with more excitement than she can bear. The feeling when reading the letter from this man swells to exhilaration. He knew Papa! And she, as her father's daughter, is welcome to come see him. Maybe she is finally onto something. Though the desire to find out all she can about her father prevails, it doesn't feel right to accept a hotel invitation from this stranger. She must have a plan of action. She must get a job immediately, any job, so she can earn enough money to go to Italy.

She phones her mother, with whom she has not spoken since she hung up on her.

"How are you, Batya?" asks Marta. "It wasn't nice of you to hang up on me."

"I was angry with you, Mom. I am sorry. Don't I deserve to know all that is in Papa's file?"

"There is nothing more there, I tell you." Marta sounds angry.

"There must be more! Papa wouldn't have stopped writing just like that.

He must have intended to go on. Maybe it's the negative information about him you want to withhold?"

"There is no more. Leave it alone."

Lies and more lies, Batya thinks, resenting her mother's attitude.

"If you are prepared to listen, Batya, I have something to tell you," says Marta.

"What?" says Batya with impatience.

"Max has filed papers on our behalf with the German government to seek wartime reparation for the persecution we suffered in the ghetto and while we were in hiding. If we win the claim, you may get some money. But you need a letter from someone who knew you in the ghetto to certify your claim."

Batya had never heard about this before. She doesn't want payment for having suffered as a child. She wants compassion and understanding from her mother, not money.

"You were there. Why can't you be my witness?"

"It is my claim too, my dear. It needs to be someone else."

"But I don't know anyone who could write me this letter."

"There are some people living in Europe who may do this for you. I found someone here who knew me in the ghetto, who can support my claim, but this was after you were gone. I'll try to find somebody for you. I'll let you know."

Batya is growing more impatient by the second. It's not as if a cheque will ease the pain she is feeling. "You do whatever works for you, Mom. I am planning to go to Rome and Venice in connection with the silver disk. I found someone who knew Papa, and there is this woman in Rome whose name is Berent."

Batya holds her breath, believing this will come as a huge shock to her mother.

"Berent? Yes, of course," Marta replies. "She lived with us in the ghetto and she could write the letter. I don't know where she lives now. But why are you going away so far? What will you use for money? Are you never going to assume your responsibilities to your family?"

There she goes again, Batya thinks. She refuses to reply to what she feels is emotional blackmail.

She hears her mother sigh. "All right then, I will ask someone here for Berent's telephone number and I will call her."

"Mom, I already have Madame Berent's telephone number from the man who made the Mouth of Truth. Do you really want it?"

"Of course I do. Give it to me," Marta says, sounding resigned. "You take care, Batya. The children miss you."

"I miss them too, you know," Batya says, on the verge of tears. She gives Marta the Berent number.

"Don't forget your obligations. You should have known better than to leave your home. There are people here who think very badly of you, including Max."

Batya remains silent.

"But we all miss you," Marta adds charitably and hangs up.

Batya sits by the phone, exhausted by the conversation. Despite her mother's finally relenting to send her Papa's notes and agreeing to phone Madame Berent, she still sounds angry with Batya. It seems as if Marta has a strange need to abuse her, to make her the scapegoat for problems not of her own making. And she certainly prefers to keep her in the dark about things that matter.

Batya quickly brushes off these thoughts. Bea is still there, but only as a distant memory and a name in a false document. She is no longer Bea who puts up a front and she is no longer Batya who cowers. She picks up her long neglected diary and starts to write sounding as Batya and not Bea. *But who is this new Batya?* She wonders.

* * * * *

Within a few weeks Batya has found a part-time job as a clerk at a home furnishing store. Soon she will gather enough money for a plane ticket and modest accommodations in Rome and Venice. She must also repay what she owes Antonia.

In the meantime, she enrols in night classes at George Brown College to get her certificate in ESL. She has just enough money to cover the cost of the course. When her job ends, she will at least have some other training for future work.

Days at work seem endless and the classes at night are difficult but interesting. She is learning about the culture of many countries, their customs, each language and its specific characteristics that show up in an immigrant's English pronunciation. She likes the idea of learning about immigrants, having been one herself. But all the while she is feverish with longing for the moment she can leave for Europe.

Busy night and day, she hasn't spoken to Sam and Miriam but longs to hear their voices. Now that she is planning a trip to Italy, she dreads having to tell them of yet another trip that will take her even farther away than Toronto. But it must be done. She calls on Sunday night, hoping the children will be home. Miriam answers the phone.

"Hi, Mom. How are you?" Miriam says, sounding cheerful.

"I am fine. And how are you, sweetie?"

"She would like her mother around," butts in Joseph. He must have picked up the other receiver. She cringes at the unexpected sound of his voice.

"My boyfriend Tom is over, Mom," says Miriam with enthusiasm. "Wish you could meet him."

There is a note of happiness Batya had never before heard in her daughter's voice. Her curiosity is mingled with shock. Her fifteen-year-old already has a boyfriend.

"And you think it's quite all right for Miriam to have a boyfriend?" Joseph pipes up again.

"Dad, get off the phone," she hears Sam say in the background.

Joseph hangs up the phone before Batya has a chance to respond. If only he showed some kindness. He might even have asked if she needed anything.

"Don't listen to Dad, Mom. All my friends have boyfriends. You don't have a problem with that, do you?"

What should she tell her daughter? Certainly not what her mother told her about all men being pigs out for just one thing. Who is she to tell her daughter what to do? In some respect Marta was right to warn her about foolish mistakes a young girl can make in a moment of passion. Except that Batya has never felt passion. But maybe Miri is different and she should warn her.

"Miri, you be careful now." Batya tells her daughter.

"Aw, Mom, don't worry. I'm on the pill."

She is on the pill? Her baby on a birth control pill at such a young age!

"Do you want to speak to Sam?"

"Okay. But I want to discuss this boyfriend business further."

"No, Mom. There is nothing more to say. Here is Sam. Goodbye."

Batya hears echoes of her conversations with her own mother, except that she has never been as assertive as Miri. She hears Sam pick up the phone.

"Hi, Sammy darling. How are you?"

"I am good, Mom. Doing the usual stuff…"

"Do *you* have a girlfriend, Sammy?"

"Oh, Mom … of course not," replies Sam seriously.

"Well, please look out for Miriam. I don't know about this pill."

"The doctor says it's safe. Don't worry. Tom is a nice boy."

"I love you, Sammy."

"I love you too, Mom."

"Sammy, I have to go to Europe to get information about my father. It will only be for a few weeks. Please understand and be patient with me."

"Okay. But what about Miriam? She really needs someone to help her with her girl problems, you know, like boyfriends, clothes."

Yes, Miri needs a mother. Joseph is right.

"Please tell Miri about my trip to Europe, Sam. Tell her that I will call her and will return as soon as I can. That's all I can do right now. Please believe me." She knows she sounds desperate and hates herself for it.

"Love you. Please look out for Miri," she adds.

"I promise. Love you too. Bye, Mom."

She puts the receiver down slowly. Except for the sound of her children's sweet voices still ringing in her ears, the room is overwhelmingly silent.

Batya reaches for a bottle of vodka, the only thing she knows that will dull the painful gnaw of guilt, besides getting into her pages to spill out the angst she feels.

Chapter 16

Rome, Late Summer 1982

"Bella Roma, bella, si signora?" says the driver, smiling at her through the rear-view mirror. *Bella, that's for sure.* Batya's excitement mounts at each turn of the car into another street, at the sights that appear around each corner and on the horizon. It is almost the end of daylight and the beginning of dusk. As the taxi speeds through the streets of Rome, electric lights are turning the ancient ruins to gold. How splendid they are, she marvels, looking through the window. This city lives with its past just as she does. Imagine the mysteries that lie behind these stone facades and the ghosts that live among the massive columns, the ruins of Caesar's palaces and the temples to the gods. Above all, she wonders what awaits her at the site of *Bocca della Verità.*

At the hotel, the porter brings the suitcase to her room, opens the rooftop balcony doors and points to a structure in the distance glowing like the others she'd seen along the way, rising golden against the midnight-blue sky. "The Spanish Steps," he explains.

She lingers on the balcony, breathing in air pungent with flowers. The hotel room overlooks a church bell tower and other rooftops, crowned by the distant Spanish Steps. She stays outside until extreme tiredness overtakes her. *Tomorrow cannot come too soon,* she thinks, lying in bed. She examines the wallpaper patterned all over with cupids and trumpets as if about to announce some momentous event. Finally, the balmy night air envelops her and sleep comes.

In the morning, a taxi carries her to Santa Maria in Cosmedin, an eighth-century church that, according to her guide, was in ancient times a distribution centre for bread. *How strange,* she thinks, *that this was once a house of bread and now it's a house of worship.* Or maybe it isn't strange at all. Bread was so scarce during the war that it was as holy as a prayer.

Bocca della Verità stands at the end of the long narrow portico adjoining the church. The silver disk in her hand is but a speck alongside the visage of its gigantic parent. Her breath falters. She has read the tourist literature about the history of Mouth of Truth. Now here, at last, she comes face to face with the marble enigma whose open circular mouth is big enough to accommodate a liar's hand and bite off its fingers—so says the legend.

Visitors stand in line ahead of her, each slowly inserting their hand into the mouth then quickly withdrawing it, giggling as if surprised to see the hand emerge from the mouth intact. She longs to be alone with the oracle that personifies the idea of truth. She wants to examine its mysterious bearing up close; fathom the hollow depths of its eyes; touch its face; to divine, perhaps, how a miniature replica of this stone found its way to the Warsaw ghetto and into her father's hand.

Finally, her turn comes. Up close, she feels tiny in front of the gargantuan orb. The sun is casting a glow into the hollow eyes, filling them with that peculiar light she first saw in the replica her father revealed to her in a Polish village.

Harsh daylight exposes the bearer of truth to be neither gentle nor kind. She will not put her hand into the open mouth. She is guilty of too many lies. Most of her life she has been lying; Bea, lying to Joseph, lying to herself, lying about not being a Jew during the war and afterwards. She dares not tempt fate, nor ape the gestures of the laughing tourists. She has a reverence for this anonymous creature with the power to judge true or false. She imagines her father as he became before he died, taking his secrets with him to the grave, leaving them as ghosts for her to chase after. She shakes her head to dispel her thoughts and, making room for the next would-be teller of truth or a lie, backs away from Mouth of Truth holding her own miniature version close to her heart.

She steps into the murky interior of the church, its walls a greyish white stone encasing a chilly dampness and a pungent smell of incense. Beneath a window stands a graceful statue of a lady. Her benevolent face is much like the one in a village church she attended with the old woman. Lena, who took in Batya/ Beata, during the war, taught her to pray before the statue of the Holy Mother, whose flowing robes of stone were partially submerged in a pool of floating lilies and flickering candles. She seemed so beautiful then, like a kind fairy.

In the distance Batya can hear a choir. She pictures little boys in long white smocks chanting the Sunday prayers and, for the first time in a long while, she hears Beata's voice, reciting the Lord's Prayer.

Beata had to learn how to cross herself and how to be a good Christian girl, while in the folds of her white Confirmation dress hid the little Jewish Batya, always hungry for a piece of bread. After church, she and Lena would line up with other village folk to be given a loaf that was to last them for almost a week. Here, beneath the cloud of incense, Batya smells the sour scent of yeast in the rising dough; she can almost taste the coveted bread, so crisp and fresh from the oven.

Needing air and daylight, Batya leaves the church. She casts a backward glance at *Bocca della Verità* and walks out into a sunny square, promising herself to return another day. In the meantime, where should she go next? What other important sights should she see? She walks a while without purpose or destination, then stops for a cappuccino at a corner bistro and sits down at an outdoor table.

Beauty abounds everywhere. The sun is shining, the air is warm, the trees and flowers are blossoming, and much as she would like to linger here a while and not have to face the tourist crowds, she must see the ruins. She wants to understand how the old lives side by side with the new in this city, in a place where the past does not have to lie buried but can be kept alive for the sake of posterity. At another table not far from hers sit a man and a woman, laughing and holding hands and drinking red wine. How she envies them their camaraderie.

She finishes her coffee and walks until fatigue overtakes her. A lone taxi stops at the curb. She asks the driver to take her to see the ruins of Rome. The driver's amused smile says it all. She is a typical tourist, overwhelmed by the splendour of a city where she doesn't know her way. After a few minutes, the Colosseum appears just as she has seen it so many times on film and in postcards. She asks the driver to stop, pays him, then walks towards the massive structure.

On entering the cool interior, she finds a stone slab to sit on. All around are the ruins of what was once a theatre for the sport of killing. She has read many stories about ancient Rome. Her imagination conjures up the spectacles that must have once taken place long ago in this arena of life and death.

She imagines spectators, with their disdain for the underprivileged, entertaining themselves and relishing the sport of killing those they felt were beneath them. They were the judges, deciding who was to live and who was to die. And now the grey ruins signal a fallen city, an empire that fell in its greed for power that squandered lives, cities, a country and a people. She can almost hear the cries of the dying slaves and animals echo through the ramparts, their suffering ignored by abusive rulers. These parallels to the life in the Warsaw ghetto distort her capacity for appreciating the complex architecture of this giant.

People scatter about, lingering in the archways. A faint sound at her back draws closer and closer. She turns around. An enormous black cat creeps forward, its wild green eyes fixed on her. Gaunt and predatory, it suddenly shrieks and lunges into the space beside her, she makes a frantic effort to stand up, her own scream shredding her throat. She runs towards the exit, tripping over the stone slabs. The echo of the cat's cry follows her as she flies through the gate and falls breathless onto the grass where it is quiet and brighter.

Once her breathing has calmed, she rises and starts her walk back to the hotel. Rome has so many associations for her, all of them linked to the past. She has read about the Roman ghetto and what happened there during the war, but that is a visit for another day.

It is time to phone Madame Berent, whom she is anxious to meet. According to her mother, this lady lived with them in the Warsaw ghetto. Batya tries to place her in their crowded ghetto apartment. She would have been one of the mothers who tended their sick children, combing their hair to rid them of the lice crawling over their bodies and clothing, because lice carried typhus. These mothers were young like Batya's mother; their married lives were just beginning when the horror came. They continually probed their children's heads and clothing, squishing whatever they found between their thumbnails.

Back at the hotel, she dials Madame Berent's number. As the phone starts to ring at the other end, she feels the sharp pressure of her mother's comb moving along her skull. In the apartment, where more than twenty-five people lived in crowded quarters, long dirty sheets surrounded the beds. She heard the dying adults and the children moaning from behind the hanging rags. Covered bodies were carried out daily. A little girl she had played with several days before was among them. Following the stretcher was the girl's weeping mother. There were many others like that woman. Could one of them have been Madame Berent?

"No lice," her mother announced, finishing the combing and braiding her daughter's hair. "No need to cut it off."

"Hello?" a voice finally answers.

"Madame Berent?" Batya isn't sure how to address this lady. Carlo Moller called her Madame, and apparently she speaks Polish.

"Yes, this is she. Who is calling?"

"This is Batya Lichtenberg, Madame. Do you remember Shimon and Marta, my mother and father?"

"But of course. How could I ever forget them after all that we went through together?" says Madame Berent in Polish. "Your mother phoned to tell me you were coming. We must meet."

"I would very much like to see you," Batya answers in her rusty Polish.

"How about tomorrow at 2:30 then? It is Via Poli 11, apartment 8."

"Thank you, Madame. I'll be there."

* * * * *

Inside the apartment building on Via Poli, Batya avoids the narrow elevator with its claustrophobic interior. She pushes a button in the dark entry hall and when the light goes on, she quickly runs upstairs before it goes out. There is a card tacked onto the door bearing Madame Berent's name. Batya feels self-conscious as she nervously presses the bell. Her beige travelling skirt is creased and the blue blouse needs rinsing. Not like her at all, but surrounded by the magic of this city, she has forgotten all about clothes.

A girl in a black-and-white uniform greets her at the door. She follows the maid down the corridor into a room reminiscent of the room in her pre-war Warsaw home that her mother called "the salon." It is large and bright, furnished with French Provincial couches covered in a flowery print. The air smells of lemon. A woman, presumably Madame Berent, reclines on a chaise lounge at a low table near a fireplace. She wears a long, loose black dress. Her white hair is swept away from her face and done up in a classic French roll. Batya notices a younger man with a swarthy complexion and jet-black hair sitting next to her.

"Little Batya! You've grown into a lovely woman. Welcome," Madame Berent says in Polish. Batya takes in the lady's features. Her nose is long and thin; her watery grey eyes beneath the drooping lids show interest at the sight of her guest. She puts down a deck of cards to greet Batya, who clasps the older woman's outstretched hand.

"Meet Grigori, my nephew. He prefers to be called Grisha. We were about to play another hand of rummy. I was getting bored with losing, so you are just in time."

"Dobry dhen," Grisha greets her in Russian, lifting a thick eyebrow, his eyes looking her over. Batya notes a look of scepticism on his face, which appears weary and heavily lined despite his seemingly strong physique.

"Grisha came from Russia several years ago and dreams of going to Canada," says Madame Berent.

The man smiles, exposing two gold teeth. His face has a deep scar on the left cheek. His dark eyes are intense. Standing in front of him, Batya becomes more aware of this man than she would care to admit. It's as if the air has become matter, closing in around them.

"Please, please sit down, here, near me," says Madame Berent, patting the seat of the chair next to her. Batya does as she is told, while Madame shakes a white porcelain bell and the maid reappears. "This is Anushka," she says, "my dear housekeeper." Anushka smiles at her mistress and spreads an embroidered cloth on the round table. Soon she brings a tray with a small samovar, a dish with lemon slices and a cake. Madame Berent slices the fresh-looking yellow cake, Batya recognises as the Polish *babka*, while Grisha pours the tea with the awkwardness of a bear. His movements are rough and hasty in contrast to his aunt's refined and delicate gestures. The two seem to complement one another like mother and son. Like her and Sam.

Grisha hands Batya a napkin, then a piece of the *babka*. The familiar taste of almonds comforts her and takes her back to her family home in Warsaw, where this, her favourite of all cakes, was often served. Papa used to pick it up at a bakery and bring it home for supper. The table, set for tea in the library, gleamed with a silver tea service. She so remembers the elegant Polish *babka*, tall and yellow, sprinkled with yummy vanilla-flavoured powdered sugar. Inside, the raisins were plump and sweet like candy. How happy were their lives then.

Batya lowers her face towards the teacup and tries to fight the onset of unexpected emotion.

"What is wrong, my dear?" asks Madame Berent.

The sudden kindness unnerves her. She must compose herself in front of these strangers. She looks up, attempting a smile.

"You went through so much, my child. It leaves its scars in later years," says Madame kindly. "I know how it was. We lived in the same building in the ghetto as you and your parents. My daughter died there of typhus."

"I am so sorry." Batya speaks in a whisper.

"After our escape from the ghetto," Madame continues, "I was in hiding not far from where your parents were also hidden. We were all helped by the same man, a man your father later sued for blackmail. I knew where you were hidden as well, and the threats made against you by our so-called rescuer."

"So you knew my father," Batya manages to say.

"Yes. I remember him. Your father was a witty, creative man. And very smart." Madame smiles at Batya. "He was with the Jewish police," she adds.

Batya flinches and almost chokes on her mouthful of cake.

"That so-called rescuer had no heart," Madame continues. "Rogacki took all our money and, when we had no more, threatened to hand us over to the Gestapo."

"What happened then?"

"We all ran away to other hiding places. This was after Rogacki threatened to inform on you if the people who were hiding you didn't reveal your father's whereabouts."

What Madame was saying seemed to back up Batya's mother's opinion of Rogacki. "But wasn't he my father's best friend?" asked Batya, remembering her father's notes.

"Maybe at one time they were friends. But war changes people. I heard that after the war, in response to your father's lawsuit, Rogacki reported in a Polish court that you father was a Nazi sympathizer."

Batya feels as if she is about to fall off the edge of a precipice. If only her father had told her these things himself, instead of her having to hear them from strangers, years later.

Gathering her nerve, she asks, "Why would he do that? What proof did he have? Do you believe this accusation?"

"We believed that Rogacki decided to defame your father's reputation as a reaction to your father's lawsuit against him,"

Batya winces. "But it is hard to know what to believe. My father was a Jewish policeman, and they were disliked by the people in the ghetto."

"Don't judge him for that," Madame replies sharply. "I know what they said about the Jewish police. But desperate people did desperate things in order to survive. Jews in the Warsaw Ghetto were dehumanized." *That's what papa had said in his memoir.* "Your father was a fine, honourable man."

These were also her mother's very words. She wants to ask Madame many more questions but is afraid that she will lose her composure again.

"Madame," she says finally. "I have come for another reason."

"Yes, your mother told me all about it. I will gladly write you the letter," Madame says without hesitation. "Your mother and I were good friends. The war made us very close, but living so far from one another now, we have lost contact.

"I was there when your father sent you out of the ghetto. We all had false papers in order to survive on the other side. I left the ghetto shortly after you did."

Batya looks at Madame Berent. She seems to have a comfortable life. Batya wonders what she had to go through before she found peace.

"Would you be so kind and tell me how I could go about getting my reparation?" Madame adds.

Batya copies the name and address of her mother's lawyer, from a piece paper she keeps in her purse.

"Your letter should be ready in several days, my dear. I'll telephone you," says Madame Berent, a weary look now settling on her face.

It is time to leave. Batya reaches over to hug Madame's slight form.

Grisha, who has remained silent throughout the conversation, gets up. He comes up to Batya and when he takes her arm, she feels an uncommon current flowing between them. He escorts her to the narrow elevator and as she is about to enter it, he bends towards her and plants a kiss on her cheek.

"May I phone you?" he asks.

Startled, she moves away and quickly enters the elevator. On the ride down, electrified by his kiss, she peers into the mirror on the wall, her fingers retracing the imaginary outline of his lips on her cheek.

Chapter 17

The visit to Madame Berent left an enduring impression—not only of the woman and the way she spoke of Papa but of her obvious respect for him. Madame didn't seem the type to be either trifled with or be taken in by just anybody. She seemed a generous sort of person. One could tell this by her attitude towards Anushka and Grisha, and her kindness towards Batya. She has to admit that Grisha had also left an imprint on her imagination as well as on her cheek..

Several days later, Madame Berent calls in the morning to say that the promised letter is ready and to please come for tea. In the afternoon Batya returns to the lady's home with a bouquet of red roses, anxious to receive the letter but also to see Madame Berent and Grisha again. In the short time she has known them, they have become an anchor for her here in Rome.

Grisha greets her at the door and this time kisses her on both cheeks. The strong floral scent of his cologne wafts into her nostrils, and excitement surges through her as it did by the elevator when he first kissed her.

"Who is there?" calls out Madame Berent from another room.

"Come, Batiusha," Grisha says softly, taking her hand. "My aunt has been waiting for you. We have missed you. I even asked my aunt for your phone number, but she told me to leave you alone."

"But why?" she asks, feeling the warmth of his hand on hers.

"Because it's dangerous. Because you are still married."

"True. I am married, but at this moment we are separated. And besides, you and I have not done anything bad." She should have added "yet."

They walk into the salon, where Madame Berent is reclining on the chaise lounge. The table is laid out for tea with the samovar, china teacups, cookies and cakes. Madame is wearing the same clothes she wore the previous visit and looks as if she has not moved since Batya was last there. The entire scene, in fact, is identical, except for the addition of a bald-headed man in a striped suit, seated on the sofa.

"How glad I am to see you, my dear," Madame says warmly. "Batya Lichtenberg, this is Monsieur Voltari, my lawyer. He has come to witness our signatures." The lawyer nods in greeting.

Batya offers the flowers to madame.

Berent takes the bouquet and breathes in their scent. "I thank *you*," she murmurs, giving the bouquet to Anushka. "Have a drink, some cookies, and don't let Grisha seduce you. He has been after me about you." She leans forward and whispers, "Very impressed by you, you see."

Monsieur Voltari gives Batya a pen to sign a letter in which Madame Berent affirms having known Batya throughout the war years in the ghetto and in hiding. This acknowledgement means more to Batya than the letter of support for the reparation claim. It signifies that finally, after all the years of silence and secrecy about her past, she has a witness to her true history.

Then the lawyer passes the letter to Madame for her signature. He promises to send the document to Marta's lawyer in London, bows to Batya and Grisha, kisses Madame's hand and leaves.

Grisha pours Fra Angelico into three crystal liqueur glasses, handing one to Batya. The hazelnut and vanilla–infused nectar slides down her throat, calming her nerves. They chat for a while, while Madame Berent dozes off.

"I could use some air," Batya says to Grisha quietly.

"Come with me," he says.

In the kitchen, Grisha puts a few brown paper packages into a knapsack and announces that he has planned a picnic. Anushka eyes the two of them suspiciously, staring from one to the other then back again.

"Allez-y!" she says, adding cookies to the picnic pack.

They walk out of the building into the sunny street bustling with people and restaurants. "The Spanish Steps are only minutes from here," says Grisha. "Have you seen them yet?"

Batya shakes her head, "only from my hotel room." That's exactly where she wants to go right now, putting aside for the moment, the real purpose of her visit

They stroll along the Via Condotti, passing by elegant boutiques and cafés, till they reach Piazza di Spagna at the foot of the Spanish Steps, swarming with tourists and locals. She follows Grisha's tall, muscular body as he pushes through the crowd, making way for her. He takes her hand and clasps it tightly while they climb the regal steps. They pass the multi-level garden bright with azaleas and other flowers that glisten like jewels in the sunlight, warming her heart and mind. At the top the two, stand side by side still as trees. From here, she sees a city that is intact, its integrity unquestionable. Here, the old and the dead live side by side in accord with the new and the living.

When they reach the Villa Borghese Park, she realizes she has lost track of time. The park's wide pathways lined with trees have the scope of Warsaw's Lazienki Park. Batya and Grisha hold hands in the shade of the trees, silent, as if spellbound by each other and the surroundings. In the Giardino del Lago there is a temple on the water dedicated to Aescalpius, god of medicine and healing. Life here seems to move in slow motion. On the lake, boats and birds glide past the naked statues of men and women, some beheaded, and of birds and animals with ferocious wide-open jaws. They sit down on a bench beneath a willow tree, its green hair drooping towards the earth. All of a sudden, Grisha moves closer to her and kisses her deeply, his tongue penetrating her mouth. At first she tenses and becomes inert as if paralyzed, then her mouth softens as she succumbs to the kiss.

"Why don't we come back here another day?" he suggests, his breath hot against her face. "I need to eat something."

What a curious thing to say at a time like this, she thinks. Though she is mesmerized by this place and would like to linger, she acquiesces. Walking next to Grisha, she is aware of her step being lighter and quicker than it has been in a long time. The real world is all but forgotten for a moment. Everything about this man seems romantic and exciting. She has never before felt such sensations. Grisha puts his arm around her as they walk her body molding to his.

In front of her hotel the old anxiety sets in as reality catapults her back to earth. This is not what she came for. Besides which, she is wary of an impending physical encounter with Grisha, to whom she is terribly attracted. Surely this attraction she has for him is exactly the opposite to her so called frigidity that Joseph spoke of. Her moral will at this moment is weaker than her need to find out if she is indeed, as Joseph thinks her to be, frigid.

Then the predictable happens. Fear of closeness gives her a jolt and pulls her away from him. "I must go in now." She hears her voice as if coming from a distance, then turns away abruptly and walks into the hotel. When the glass door closes behind her, she looks back and sees Grisha standing there with a perplexed look on his face.

Back in her room she hurls herself onto the bed and curls up like a foetus. She falls into a state of inertia, becoming Batya, the frightened, hidden child, who ran away escaping the sexual advances of an old man.

At night, in disturbed sleep, male figures circle around her, their arms reaching out to touch her. She recoils, afraid of their animalistic lunges, their naked bodies writhing in front of a flame that burns through her. From one side she sees a man with dark eyes nearing her, his arm reaching out to touch her. She awakes with a start, drenched in sweat but with an aching need to be loved. She can almost smell Grisha's presence, his cigarettes and his cheap cologne. But all there is of him is the memory of the previous day, when she left him standing on the street.

She wants to see him and yet … she tries to shake off the disturbing dream and her confused feelings, by arguing with herself that Grisha is not after all that old man. She must be resolute. It would be best to go out and explore before she has to leave for Venice, which is very soon.

In the lobby the clerk hands her a note. "A man delivered it this morning, signora."

> My Dear Batiusha,
> Please forgive me for scaring you so. I cannot deny the fact that I want you.
> I know you want me too. Let me prove to you that I am not some kind of a werewolf. Let me explain. Please meet me at the Spanish Steps where we were yesterday at eight o'clock tonight. I promise, I won't touch you until you say so. I will be there waiting.
> Your Grisha

My Grisha? she thinks with disbelief. But this is too soon. Yet, it was caring of him to have brought this letter. There is something gentle about this but there is also something ferocious about the man. What should she do?

As the day wears on, tired of endless walking, she finds herself at Piazza di Spagna, as if her feet directed her there. She has known all along that the encounter with Grisha must happen, even if only to prove Joseph wrong.

There he is now walking towards her with a single red rose. *How romantic*, she thinks cynically. Who was it who told her - *trust your intuition, it is usually on target.* Was it her mother, who taught her nothing about life beyond obedience to parents, marriage and children?

At the sight of Grisha, the expected warmth and excitement return.

"A drink?" he suggests, regarding her with uncertainty.

They sit down in a café with a carafe of wine on the table between them.

Grisha appears secretive. She longs for him to touch her now, but he is distant. Her psyche is performing tricks on her. *Is this how he operates to ensure her final submission? Or is he being honest and simply respectful of her confused feelings? Can she trust him—and her own feelings?*

After an hour of small talk, with excitement gathering momentum between them, she rises from her chair. "Walk me to my hotel," she tells him. Still wary of each other, they walk several feet apart. He seems to be sticking to his promise, while she misses their closeness of the day before.

This time, the sight of the hotel doesn't make her cringe. After all, he has promised not to touch her.

"Can I come in with you?" he asks carefully as she opens the door. "I still have the picnic from yesterday, a little soggy but it may be all right."

She lets him into her room, where he produces a bottle of wine from his bag.

"Just a little?" he says.

She nods.

After a few moments of small talk and sips of wine, he gets up from his chair and sweeps her into his arms.

"My little *golubka*," he mumbles in Russian. "I will never hurt you." He holds her so close, she feels the pounding of his heart. His tenderness melts all fear and doubt within her. No one has ever been this tender with her. Then he kisses her for a long time with a passion she has never known, until, unable to contain their longing for each other, they begin to strip off their clothes.

Naked and vulnerable, she is drawn to his muscular body and the soft bristle of the thick hair on his chest. She lies down next to him inhaling his animal smell, his sweat mixed with cologne. He draws her closer to him and his hands, gentle at first, gradually become rougher in their urgency. Sensations she had never known existed consume her body. Still she holds on, like the time when she was learning to swim but afraid to drown and hung on with one toe touching the bottom, then finally she let go, abandoning herself to the current.

Long afterwards, she is aware that her fear of sex has abated, that such an intimacy can feel effortless and natural. They fall asleep holding each other and when they return to consciousness, it is already dark and she realizes that the image of the old Bolek had not come to haunt her this time.

"Now I am really hungry!" Grisha announces, jumping out of bed. He lights the candle on the table and lays out the Russian food he has brought with him: kielbasa, smoked fish, onion, cucumbers, tomatoes, black bread and vodka.

She watches him with a childlike fascination as he sits down at the small table in his underwear: his hair a black halo of wiry curls, the tanned skin of his bare torso, his face and his eyes glistening in the candle's flame. One side of his mouth where the scar is, tightens into a ferocious twist as he attempts to cut the bread with a penknife, holding the loaf against his chest, Russian style. Having accomplished this, he smiles, exposing the gold teeth.

To her, on this fiery night, he is the vision of a fearless, wild gypsy. She will remember this always.

"Come. Eat," he commands in his gruff, husky voice. He takes a cassette recorder out of his bag and turns it on. A song she has never heard sounds all around them. They feast to this music and when they are done, she asks him to play the song again.

"'*Violino Tzigano*.' It is an old Italian tango," he says, pulling her up and leading her in a dance. The song, romantic and sentimental, flows straight into her soul. They whirl like two dervishes in the forest by the fire. When the song ends they collapse onto the bed.

Lying in the dark with only the faint light from a candle, she snuggles up to him, feeling that if the world were to end this very instant, her happiness would be complete. *But no one thing endures in its perfect state,* she thinks, her lids becoming heavy with sleep.

Grisha's voice breaks into their warm cocoon. "I must catch the last metro home," he says. "My aunt will be worried. She has been kind enough to take me in, and I can't have her waiting up so late," he tells her, turning on the light. "I loved being with you," she hears him say. He is already dressed and kissing her forehead.

As the door closes behind him, loneliness overcomes her, and before falling asleep again, she counts the imaginary petals of her youth, pulling them off the stem one by one, just like Nanny had taught her to do in the park one Sunday afternoon when Batya was five. "He loves me, he loves me not. He loves me, he loves me not. He loves me," Batya murmurs into the night. No question, Grisha is fierce. The unforgettable sight of him at the table lingers in her mind for a long time, and the scent of him in her bed persists throughout the night, while "*Violino Tzigano*" whirls through her dream.

* * * * *

She awakens to the shrill ring of the telephone.

"My aunt wants to see you," Grisha announces. "I told her that I want to be with you for at least as long as you are in Rome."

He has already set a limit on our romance, she thinks, getting dressed. Soon she is on the way to Madame Berent's, hoping that this kind lady, who is now corresponding with her mother and re-establishing their old friendship, is not learning things that may turn her good thoughts about Batya into the old criticisms she has been trying to escape.

"My aunt is not feeling well today. Come on," Grisha says to her at the door. She follows him into the bedroom, where Madame is lying in a large bed. An armoire of blond wood stands opposite the bed, its glass window draped in curtains of blue and white polka dots, much like Mother's dresser in their Warsaw home before the war.

"Sit down, child," says Madame, pointing to a chair. A variety of pills lie scattered on her bedside table, along with a half-filled glass of water that looks as if it has been there for a while. Madame's hands are bony and twisted with rheumatism. The skin on her face is crinkled like dried fruit; her body appears childlike and frail in the folds of the pink bed jacket. She is coughing.

"Just an attack of asthma," she says, seeing Batya's concern. "Don't worry," she adds, overcome once again by a spasmodic cough. Grisha gets a fresh glass of water and hands her several pills. She swallows them obediently and lies back against the pillows, pale and spent.

"These are the lasting gifts of war, my dears," she says, admitting to more than mere asthma, "and my time in the camp. In the freezing weather we had no proper clothing. The fear destroys your insides too. Every time the kapo walked into the barrack to make an announcement, I'd start coughing and choking from sheer anxiety. He was not one of the bad ones. He even brought me medicine. And these," she says, trying to stretch out her fingers, "these rheumatic fingers I acquired while carting heavy pots of soup to German quarters at the camp in below-zero weather. My fingers would freeze to the handles and the Nazi guard there would tear them away so hard it hurt. My hands haven't stopped hurting since. And this," she points to a scar on her left shoulder, "was when I ripped my skin climbing over the barbed wire during the revolt at Treblinka, when everyone started running. But I was too far away from the opened gates and too near the barbed-wire fence. Even though an inmate put a blanket on the wire so we could climb over more easily, some of the prongs were exposed and ripped our skin."

She stops for a moment, too weak to continue. "Only I, a few men, and maybe one other woman survived. We ran into a forest and, after that, nothing is clear. I was saved by a Polish peasant woman. Bless her good heart." She dozes off and a minute later wakes up with a start.

"Thank God for Grisha," she whispers. "He helps when Anushka is not around. After the war," she continues her story, "I ended up in a French DP camp, where I applied for a visa to America, but they sent us to Italy to wait and I never left."

"What about the kapo—was he a Jew?" Batya asks, thinking of her father. Had he been there as a kapo, surely he would have been less cruel than the Germans.

"Yes, the kapo was a Jew, who could be both good and bad, depending on who was monitoring him. But that is a story for another time, my dear," replies Madame and sinks back into sleep.

Shaken by Madame's tale, Grisha and Batya stay by her side glued to their seats, watching her toss in her sleep as if she were dreaming of something from her troubled past. After a while, she wakes up and starts talking again.

"Batya, your mother wrote to me. She feels that you should have stayed at home a few more years till your children were older. But, of course, your children are already teenagers. I didn't have any more children after my daughter died, but I suspect if I had, I couldn't have left them no matter what. But I am not judging you." She stops as a violent cough shakes her body. When the cough subsides, she looks shrewdly at Grisha and Batya.

"I know what you want to tell me. I was young once." She lies back and breathes with difficulty. "Go in peace, the two of you. Anushka will come here full time. Your lives have to be lived today, not tomorrow or in a month's time. I know, I know. Love does not wait and love isn't eternal either. People are fickle. Who knows about love, anyway?" She motions for them to leave and closes her eyes. Batya doesn't want to leave, but Grisha insists.

"Don't take it on so. She is old and sick. Let's go for a walk," he says. Batya feels caught in the web of Madame Berent's camp story, her illness and her mother's gossip. She feels guilty for taking Grisha away from the ailing woman even for a minute.

"Guess what, Batiusha?" he says on the street. "Later today I am getting these two gold teeth replaced. Want to come with me?" He explains that in Soviet Russia the wealthier people had gold teeth put in to replace a missing tooth and the poor ones had the silver. Implants or porcelain crowns were unheard of.

"Sure. Now you'll have all the ladies chasing you," she teases.

"I don't need ladies. I am just a poor immigrant. And one lady at a time is enough for me."

One at a time? But she brushes that aside. Instead she revels in that magical air about him. But she must be realistic: it is much too early to think of this relationship as anything lasting.

She waits at the dentist's for hours. When he comes out, Grisha's teeth are all white and he looks even more handsome than before. He stops at every shop window along Via del Corso, looking at himself in the glass, exposing his teeth like a werewolf. "These are only temporaries. But already I look better. Don't I?"

"But of course," she replies, unable to contain her admiration for him.

"We are not far from the Jewish ghetto. Let's go there for a bite to eat."

They pass between the Theatre of Marcellus and the arch of the Portico di Ottavia into the Jewish ghetto, where the walls of dilapidated buildings regulate the light on the narrow streets. Some are dark because the tall tenements hide them from the sun, but in the open piazzas, sunlight illumines the streets and the yellow stucco walls. They come upon a square bustling with cafés. Farther down, high among the trees, nestles the white dome of the Great Synagogue.

Seated in the Café Judaica, she is fascinated by the fact that this quarter was once a ghetto. Searching for something familiar, some thread that ties her to this place, she overhears a conversation of a man at a table nearby talking to a group of tourists: "The Germans surrounded this ghetto on October 16, 1943, on Shabbat, and raided the quarter by going door to door in the early morning, waking up the sleeping Jews. They gave them a few minutes to pack. About one thousand Jews—men, women and children—were taken to the Military College of Rome. They were all deported to Auschwitz and only fifteen people survived."

"This ghetto sounds similar to the one in Warsaw but for the great difference in the number of deportees to Treblinka," Batya tells Grisha.

"I heard of it," he replies. "My parents were both murdered in Treblinka. They were gassed on arrival by carbon monoxide from diesel or petrol. Nazis also took away my friend Zoran, who saved my life.

"After the war," he continues, taking a gulp of wine, "a mutual friend found my aunt and told her that I was living in a Russian village under an assumed name."

"What happened to you before that?" Batya asks carefully. His sudden openness takes her by surprise.

"I was ten years old during the war in White Russia. My father brought me to Zoran, who took me in. I told him my name was Grigori, but he chose to call me Grisha. Eventually, I came to think of Zoran as my father. There was something wild about him, though loving. He played the balalaika and the harmonica, and could he dance!" Grisha's face lights up as he speaks.

"We travelled in a horse and buggy from village to village, then by train, till we found a half-burned, deserted shack that belonged to one of his relatives in a village near Warsaw. We lived there quietly while Zoran fixed things for the folks around, who were none too friendly and paid him a pittance. But we always had enough to eat. I helped him gather and chop wood and feed the few chickens we had.

"One day, I went to the forest to pick mushrooms and came home to find Zoran gone. The peasant next door told me that German soldiers had taken Zoran away and in all likelihood they would send him to a concentration camp for sheltering a Jew. I didn't know I was a Jew then. I was in shock and abandoned for the second time in my life, but I continued to live in our shack and fend for myself by doing chores for the peasant next door. I waited for my mother and father to come for me. But they never did.

"After the war, the peasant next door dug up a painted chest from under a tree next to our shack. It was Zoran's and it contained his documents. That's when I saw my name—Grigori Alexander Rubin—written on my birth certificate, and I found out I was a Jew. Soon after, a man came from a Jewish agency and took me away.

"He connected me with my aunt, Madame Berent, who had been married to my father's brother. At that time, she was in a displaced persons camp. Some years later, after her husband died, I was able to get out of Belarus and she invited me to come and live with her."

"What happened to Zoran?" asks Batya.

"Not that long ago, a friend wrote to me telling me he had found out that Zoran had died in Treblinka. Until then, I wasn't sure what had happened to him. I loved him…" Grisha's voice breaks off.

"I am so sorry," Batya says, wiping her eyes.

"I have lived all this time trying to forget. But sometimes, like being here in the Jewish quarter, things come back. And you make me remember," he adds, almost accusingly.

"I should go to Poland just once to honour Zoran and my parents," he says, his voice thick with emotion. "To see the killing ground where they were murdered. Maybe that will put an end to my bad memories."

"I have always wanted to go back there," says Batya. "Right now I am much closer to Poland than I was in Canada."

"I never wanted to go back there," he says. "On the other hand, if you go, can I come with you?"

"Come with me?" She hadn't even thought of going herself. How could she? She barely had enough money to come on this trip. And what about her flight back to Toronto? A wild thought: maybe she could move it ahead for a small charge.

Grisha must have sensed her hesitation. "If it's on account of money, I can borrow some from my aunt, enough for both of us. You can pay your part of it back. But I don't mind. If you don't pay her back, I will."

His wanting to go with her surprises her so much she is speechless. What started out as a spark between them seems to be turning into a full-fledged affair. *An affair and a trip to Poland seem unlike twins.* She thinks with a twinge of mistrust.

She remembers all her aunts, uncles and cousins who perished in Treblinka, leaving a huge vacuum in their family, which only grew larger when Tereska vanished. It may be right to visit those places and pay respect to her family. And perhaps learn the truth about her father. The last thought brings her back to her ultimate purpose of this visit, even though Poland was not on her list.

"When could we go?" Grisha presses her, his eyes flashing with mischief. *This is like an adventure to him*, she supposes. *Not so for me.*

"We will need visas." He is already thinking ahead, and there is excitement in his face, which a moment ago was taut with grief.

"You know that I am going to Venice the day after tomorrow and will return in a week's time. Maybe then we can go to Poland," she says, her voice uncertain. She wants to be with him, but in Poland things will be different for her than in Rome. Poland is a hurt place in her heart, while in Rome being with Grisha might prove to be an act of healing.

"I didn't know you were leaving so soon." He turns away from her. "I'll try to book hotels but we need our passports," he says, looking out into the street. "Then we will get the visas when you come back. Remember, I am waiting for you." They leave the restaurant and he kisses her goodbye at the bus stop.

I'll miss him, she thinks, walking down the street, and this magnetic pull she feels towards him turns to doubt. Can she really trust him? It takes a lot of courage to trust a stranger, and she is too much of a coward to place her faith in a stranger.

Nor has it escaped her notice that he turns his head at all the pretty women passing by. She feels that prick of jealousy and the uncertainty of his true feelings for her. Will he really be waiting for her when she gets back? She thought it strange when she met him, that such a handsome man would not have some loving woman in his life.

It is almost evening and the sun is low on the horizon. It will soon be dark, but she is not ready to go back to the hotel. She wants to return to the site of *Bocca della Verità* to try to find what she might have missed on her first visit. She takes a taxi.

The square and the church are empty now. She enters the portico and walks up to Mouth of Truth, its face partially lit in the pale glow of the setting sun. She no longer sees it as a puzzle in her father's life but as a missing piece in her own. The face, the silence, the grey facade of the old church, the fresh memory of the ghetto all evoke in Batya something akin to a prayer for freedom, a release from bondage, anger and blame. A feeling of liberation she had not felt even at the end of the war.

Mouth of Truth stares at her, challenging. She yearns to touch it now, to feel the marble smoothness of its skin. She moves slowly towards it and stretches out her hand to trace its features like a blind person who wants to discover the face of a loved one, to sense their meaning beyond the face itself. With her eyes closed, she fingers the scar, the crack, the eyes' hollows, and the outline of the lipless mouth into which her hand has suddenly slipped.

She has for so long wondered about this sculpture and its replica in her purse, their connection to her father and to herself. She has been for so long conflicted about her Jewishness. There were many times even in Canada when she longed to walk into a church like the one here. Perhaps this was still a remnant of the Christian Beata side of her. And yet she is no longer the frozen Batya she was then, during the war when she had to lie about being a Jew and long afterwards when she felt hidden inside herself. There were times in Canada when visiting Christian friends, she would not reveal her identity, fearing their dislike of Jews. Now standing motionless, her hand trapped inside the Mouth of Truth, somehow unable to withdraw it, she feels ashamed.

It is now fully dark and only a pale street lamp glow softens the harsh expression of the sculpture's face and its burning eyes.

"I am a Jew," she says loudly to the *Bocca*. "This is the truth I am proud of and not ashamed. I am a free Jew now. I am Batya--no longer Beata."

Warmth envelops her body, travelling down her arm and into the fingers frozen inside the mouth. Something has taken hold of her hand, gentle but firm and reassuring, like the clasp of her father's hand that held hers in just such manner when they walked on the terror-filled streets of Warsaw, past the SS officers beating two old Jews and laughing at them. How well she remembers her father's face and its look of compassion for the two old men. Her father, who always told her to speak the truth, but who failed during the war. Her beloved father, this was the man she worshipped and not the other man, the policeman.

Feeling strangely liberated, Batya gently pulls her hand out of the mouth. The *Bocca* stands silent and stony in the evening dusk. But Batya no longer feels silent, inert or hidden. She stretches her arms towards the darkening blue sky and stands tall. She feels like dancing. Another chapter of her journey is about to begin. She is standing at a juncture of her life, loving this moment, feeling as if she were a part of everything around her: the ruins, the river and even the strangers that pass by. She longs to be able to love wholly, to be loved, and not keep her feelings hidden by the past, like the half - -moon above, its face partly in shadow.

Chapter 18

Venice

A few steps away from the Santa Lucia station, Batya finds a city so different from any other she has ever imagined or seen. The Grand Canal sprawls like a superhighway, its banks glistening with the domes of churches and ancient buildings. But she has no time to admire the riches in front of her. She must find her hotel. A vendor at a fruit stand gives her directions.

"Lista di Spagna there," he says, pointing to a street that extends to the left of where she is standing. Pulling her bag into the narrow passageway, she sees the neon sign for Hotel Lorenzo.

The lobby is small, crowded and fogged in by cigarette smoke. Her room on the main floor is little more than a damp cave. A narrow bed with an iron headboard and a wooden cross above it stands in a corner. The only other piece of furniture is a table holding a candle stuck carelessly into a glass ashtray, next to a lamp missing a light bulb. A door opens onto a washroom closet where the showerhead hangs directly over the toilet seat.

The dinginess reminds her of her hiding place in that Polish village. There was also a cross hanging on the wall over the bed and a cold floor where Lena made her kneel each evening to pray. She made Batya cross herself and recite the Lord's Prayer and finger the rosary, which Batya had thought at the time was a beautiful necklace of beads. Beata would move her lips to the Lord's Prayer while Batya would pray for the safety of her parents and Tereska, and hope that Bolek would not return home from one of his Saturday-night drunken orgies.

The oblong window of her Venice hotel, partially covered by a heavy shutter, looks out onto a narrow street with many shops side by side. It is almost dark but there is still a trickle of light coming through. Batya puts her things away on a shelf and goes into the street in search of food.

The air is warm. Tourists and locals mingle, walking in and out of stores laughing and chattering mostly in Italian, though other languages fall into her ears, among them English, Russian and even Polish. She chooses a trattoria right on the canal not far from the hotel.

Sitting at a table for two surrounded by people laughing and talking, she feels very much alone. She thinks of Grisha, his intense eyes meeting hers across the table. She imagines sharing a meal with him and the secret feelings of passion that only the two of them know. Does he love her or has he already found another diversion while she is gone? She thinks of Joseph and a feeling of guilt makes the image of Grisha vanish instantly.

Batya takes out her notebook and shares her thoughts with its pages. She looks up, mesmerized by the strip of pink-grey sky, as the last of the setting sun reflects in the ripples of the dark water. After a meal of pizza, she pays the bill. Walking along the canal she hears a confluence of disparate sounds: her heels clicking along the pavement; the water gurgling and swishing as the *vaporetti* plow through the canal; the music flowing from the gondolas—a soprano singing an aria from *Tosca*; the meowing of cats mating in some corner of the Lista d'Espagna. She shivers in the warmth of the evening. But there is nothing for her to fear here, she tells herself, in this unusual place where everything seems to flow in concert with the water's current.

Back at the hotel, she telephones Signor Moller.

"Ah, Mademoiselle Lichtenberg. In Venice at last. How good it is to hear from you," he says, sounding pleasant and glad.

"Why don't you meet me tomorrow at the Campo del Ghetto Nuovo?"

"That will be fine, signor. I am just not sure how to get there," Batya answers, eager to meet this gentleman at last.

Moller gives her directions and promises to wait for her.

* * * * *

The entrance to the Jewish quarter is an inauspicious archway through one of the many buildings that line the mouth of the canal like crowded teeth. A narrow passage leads to a wider gateway, which narrows and then widens again as Batya passes through several piazzas towards the main square. Gondolas bob below the bridges, moored next to the ramparts. As in Rome, light plays a game with shadows depending on the size of the passages and the height of the buildings looming above. She has been told that these buildings once housed Jewish people, who had to build upwards because of the insufficient space allotted them in the ghetto. She looks up at the windows discreetly veiled in white lace, and wonders about the human stories behind them.

The faces of the people passing by in the opposite direction seem pensive, as if preoccupied. She had read in one of her guidebooks that this was the first Jewish ghetto, where in the sixteenth century the Jews of Venice were forced to live. She conjures up images of oppressed Jews walking through here. Jews like herself, descendants of Abraham and Isaac, slaves of the pharaohs, merchants of Venice—Hitler's persecuted Jews, ghosts passing through the centuries in and out of this place, driven to the trains, going to their deaths not knowing their fate. Up till now only a handful of historians and a few survivor-writers have told the world of how they were persecuted, of their inhuman suffering and the struggle and courage it took to survive.

On reaching the large ghetto square, she sees an elderly, white-haired man, tall and very thin, standing in the shade of a tree next to a café. He is wearing a light beige suit, a burgundy tie and a straw hat with a black ribbon. He is leaning on a cane. She stops and looks at him intently.

"Are you Signor Moller?" Batya asks.

The man nods and, removing his hat, bows. "So you must be Madame Lichtenberg-Mintz," he says in accented English and smiles. She notes how his small nose juts out of a well-groomed moustache and the light of kindness in his grey-blue eyes.

"At last we meet," the man says, taking her hand and grasping it tightly. He leads her to a table at the outdoor café. "Let us have an excellent coffee," he gestures. "Right here."

"I knew your father in the Warsaw Ghetto," he says simply. This is just what she had hoped for. What she is hungering for. He orders cappuccinos and almond cakes. She takes the velvet pouch out of her purse and pulls out the silver disk. The sun, peeking through the branches of a tree above the café, infuses the cavernous eyes with light.

"The story of this piece is not simple," says Moller, staring into the silver face, then covering it with his hand as if shielding her and himself from its eyes. They sit in silence for a moment until the waiter returns with coffee and cakes.

Moller, pensive, his hand still covering the disk, stirs his cappuccino, while Batya surveys the spacious, simple square enclosed by tall, narrow buildings and a brick wall. The few trees appear to be growing straight out of the tiles that pave the ghetto ground. Next to one of the trees is an old well, and several shops have Hebrew letters painted on their windows. On the far side, children are kicking a soccer ball against the brick wall, mindless of the seven bronze plaques affixed to it. The bricks are pink-red, just like those of the Warsaw ghetto wall. Every brick wall she has ever looked at reminds her of that one, laid by Jews, who were forced to build their own prison wall brick by brick.

"Recently," Signor Moller says, breaking the silence, "it has come to my attention that a man in Poland was awarded the status of a righteous Gentile for saving Jewish lives. I won't go into how I know this. But suffice it to say that my wife's sister, Lilya, still has contacts in Warsaw.

"I know that this honour was not earned. The man, who once was your father's friend, later became his enemy. He was a greedy man who extorted money from Jews for hiding them during the war and then, when they had no more money left to give him, he informed on them. Your father was forced to sign away his property to this man in order to save all your lives. Otherwise, the man threatened to inform on you, to tell the Nazis of your hiding places."

How does he know all this? she wonders, but dares not interrupt. Of course, he is speaking of Rogacki. He seems to have the same information as Karp and Madame Berent, and maybe more. Thank God Moller has not mentioned the gossip about Papa being a Nazi collaborator.

"Yes," Batya replies. "He was the one who hid my sister,...her voice falters. My little sister who was later taken away from his house by the Gestapo," she says, choking on the words.

Moller puts his hand over hers. "I learned," he continues, "that your father initiated a lawsuit against this blaggard after the war. He accused Rogacki of blackmail and extortion of property. Rogacki asked for the money to pay off the Gestapo in order to get your sister out of headquarters, where they held her. Or so he said."

Batya does not know all these details about Rogacki, and she can no longer withhold her questions. "How do you know so much about my father and this man?"

"After the war, I met a lawyer, a mutual friend, who told me these things. Then the lawyer died and I lost track of your family."

"How did you meet my father? Do you know anything about him while he was in the Warsaw Ghetto?"

"Let me tell you the story from the beginning. I am an Italian Jew who met my Polish wife here in Italy while our families were vacationing on Capri. It was love at first sight. You remind me a little of her. She was petite and blonde, with big blue eyes and high cheekbones. I called her Cara." His eyes look far into the distance and grow misty. "She died while we were hiding in a village and my life was shattered." He speaks so quietly she has to lean forward to hear him.

"Is it her name inscribed on the back of the silver disk?"

Moller nods, wiping his eyes with a handkerchief. "I made this piece here in Venice in the spring of 1939 for my wife's birthday, just before she went back to Poland. My Cara staunchly upheld the concept of truth as opposed to lies. When she saw the *Bocca della Verità* in Rome, she loved what it symbolized. The idea of truth appealed to her high sense of morality.

"Just before the war erupted, Cara took the children to Poland to see if she could get her mother and father come back here with her. She took the silver disk, insisting that it was a part of me going with her.

"On arrival, my wife discovered that her mother was too ill to travel. She decided to stay for a while to help her father cope. Then the Blitzkrieg happened and it was too late to leave. She wrote to tell me she had to stay for good. I knew that she would not be able to live with herself if she left her parents, so I immediately set out for Poland. I did manage to get there through devious routes, handing out bribes as I went. Before embarking on my journey, I had hidden diamonds in toothpaste tubes, inside the lining of my jacket and inside my shoes. When I was crossing the Polish border, I remembered I had a diamond in my change purse that I had forgotten to hide. When I saw how they were checking everything, I swallowed it. You can imagine how I had to find and retrieve it at the other end."

Moller attempts a grin and with trembling hands, lights a cigarette. "It was while we lived with my wife's parents that I met your father. His law office was in the same building where I opened a small shop and made jewellery I tried to sell, along with the pieces I had brought with me. But soon after that, our businesses were banned, our trades and professions forbidden. Polish borders were sealed, and in the year that followed we were herded into the ghetto.

"We moved from Leszno to Nowolipki Street just before the ghetto wall was sealed. I went to the Judenrat, the Jewish council, begging for a job. They told me to go to a place where Czerniaków, the chief of the Judenrat, was building a place for homeless children. They gave me a hammer and took me in. The home took almost a year to finish. One day, while I was still working there, putting in the finishing touches though the place was already functional, a Jewish policeman appeared with six dirty, starving children. The face under the cap looked familiar and I recognized your father from Leszno Street, where he had his law office. He greeted me with a smile. 'Look,' he said,

'I am now the father of six more children.'

"He had a large package under his arm, and when I asked him what he was carrying, he opened it and showed me a huge bolt of blue cloth. 'A woman down the street has a sewing machine,' he told me, 'and I will ask her to make some loose clothing for the children.'

"He asked the attendants to wash the children and shave off their hair. He told me that the building he was living in was quarantined for typhus. 'Lice are spreading the disease,' he said, 'and the street children are covered with them.' The six children were washed and dressed and given soup and bread.

"I continued to work there for some time. Each day your father would bring in more street children and have them tended to. Some were so emaciated that I wondered how they were going to make it until the next day. But, after a little food in their stomachs and care from the women who worked in the place, they improved. I thought then that your father was the greatest human being I had ever met. If you could have seen how he treated those poor orphans. He would read his own poems to them and tell them funny stories with each visit. And they'd look at him as if he were a magician. Even Korczak* himself would have approved.

"After we finished working on that children's shelter, I was sent to another, where I would fix things and be given a bowl of soup and a piece of bread to eat. I would eat the soup and share my piece of bread with my family.

"The next time I ran into your father, he came in limping and his face was the colour of seaweed. We had a glass of tea together, and he told me a Nazi officer had beaten him when he refused to carry out his order to make a Jewish man kneel in front of this officer.

"He said that these were terrible times and that he regretted ever becoming a policeman. He told me that at first he was supposed to be keeping the peace in the streets to prevent smuggling and looting. It was May of 1942 and your father did not yet know the fate of the entire Jewish population of the ghetto. And even then, most did not believe the truth of what went on there. The truth was inconceivable.

"In the meantime," Moller continues, "deportations grew worse and, finally, the expected and feared raid on our building came. Nazi soldiers stood with their rifles poised to shoot anyone who disobeyed, while the Jewish police hustled the inhabitants out of the building. Your father was one of the policemen on the job. When our turn came, I offered several of the policemen pearls. They couldn't take them, they said, because if it was noticed, they would be shot. So we were pushed into the street with our bundles and, to-gether with the rest of the line, walked to the Umschlagplatz where cattle cars waited to deport us." Moller pauses, his breathing shallow and hoarse. His hand nervously fingers the silver disk. He looks at it directly for the first time since Batya handed it to him and examines it, touching it with reverence, as one might a religious object. Then he clasps it with both hands to his chest, his eyes brimming with tears.

"My wife," he continues in a choked-up voice, "and her sister, Lilya, were sobbing. My two frightened children were clutching at their mother's skirt. I was terrified of being separated from my family and wanted us all to stay to-gether. I didn't believe that it would be better to get the children out first.

"I was wrong," Signor Moller goes on, his breath coming out in rasps. "How I wish now that I had sent my children to the Aryan side earlier, just as your father did. They could have survived."

Moller pauses and cannot speak, his eyes full of tears again. After a while he resumes. "We had barely reached the Umschlagplatz deportation depot when my wife fainted, catching the attention of a Nazi officer. Suddenly, your father appeared out of nowhere and intervened. 'I'll take care of this, Herr Commandant,' he said to the officer who stood there with a dog. Just then, someone's ear-splitting scream diverted the Nazi's attention. Your father, with Lilya's help, picked up my wife and told us to follow him. I grabbed my two children, one under each arm, and your father took us to a truck near the en-trance to the ghetto that had just been emptied of people brought into the depot.

"We climbed into the truck and he lowered the tarpaulin cover over the back. 'I have to leave you now,' he told us. He was fearful that someone might have seen what he was doing. Then he left but soon returned with water for my wife. We stayed hidden there for a while and then, after the deportees had been herded into the trains, he came back and told us to get off the truck and run back into the ghetto. Before we could, something happened and we had to hide a while longer where we were.

"A Nazi soldier saw Shimon helping us. He dragged him away, and turned his gun on him, but Reykin, the head of your father's unit, intervened. So in-stead, the Nazi beat your father so hard he lost consciousness. The Nazi then went somewhere else, and we got out of truck and ran back into the ghetto.

"When we were back inside the ghetto, I saw your father swaying on his feet and groping the walls of a building like a drunken man. I tried to give him a diamond wrapped in a tiny piece of black cloth as a gift for what he had done, but he waved it away. Then I remembered the *Bocca della verità*. I told him that I had made it myself in happier times, and I wanted him to have it. He refused to take it as well, so I just threw it at him. 'Take it!' I told him. 'It's not a bribe! Let it stand for the good you hold sacred!' Your father looked at me in bewilderment and, clutching the disk in his hand, fell to the ground. Another policeman came by and took him away. I heard that he was disabled for quite some time."

Batya lowers her head, as tears gather and fall onto the table. Moved to the root of her being, she prays for this to be the truth. At last she has found out how her father got the silver disk.

"It was at this point that I started believing in God," says Moller.

"And yet there were more of those deportations at Umschlagplatz and people going to the trains," she says, still looking for answers.

"As I see it, your father had to harden his heart to withstand what was happening in front of him. Sometimes, a person is forced to divorce themselves from all their senses just to keep going and to fight for survival, not only their own but their family's. But your father's heart, had the ability to soften when it came to the ghetto children and to us."

"What happened to you when you returned to the ghetto?"

"I immediately began using some of the jewellery I still had to get us out of there. I did not see your father after that. We managed to get out of the ghetto on a truck packed with labourers. For a gold bracelet, the driver agreed to hide my children under a blanket and, somehow, we made it through the checkpoint. It was night by the time we got out of the truck, and we walked through the countryside until we came to a little village. We knocked at the door of a house and when the farmer opened the door, he looked at us with fear in his eyes. His wife crossed herself a hundred times but when I showed them my two diamonds, he let us in. He hid us in a stable until almost the end of the war."

Moller stops talking, his face ghostly white, his hand clutching his chest.

Batya is frightened. "Can I help you? Can I get you something?"

He shakes his head and takes a pillbox out of his pocket, swallowing a tiny pill.

"Perhaps we should stop for today," Batya says, even though she is eager to know the end of his story.

"I must continue, dear girl. I must tell you the rest of the story. I need to tell it to you," Moller says. His colour somewhat improved..

"The farmer was very good to us," he goes on, "but, just before the end of the war, someone in the village told the authorities that the man was hiding Jews. We left immediately when we heard this and hid in the forest. One night, German soldiers came and found us, ordered us into a clearing and told us to line up next to a row of trees. They shot at us and when they thought we were all dead, they left. Wounded in the arm, I crawled over the bodies that lay on the ground towards my wife and children. They were dead. I felt that my life was over. In a daze, I kept on crawling, not knowing or caring where, but ended up back in the farmer's barn. His wife bandaged my bleeding arm and I fainted.

"The next day, I heard cannons booming in the distance. Someone said that the Russians were advancing and the Germans were running away from the village. That night, I buried my family in one grave in the forest." Moller stops, his eyes now closed, as if he were back there where it all happened to his loved ones.

"The farmer let me stay until the Russians liberated the area. After the war there was chaos, but I got my papers and, as soon as I could, I left for Italy." Moller wipes his forehead with the back of his hand. He is growing paler by the minute, his eyes darting back and forth like those of a snared animal. "I will always wonder why my wife and children died and I lived."

Batya strokes his arm.

"When I came back to Venice, I discovered that all my other relatives had been taken to Auschwitz. Life seemed to have lost meaning. Man becomes feeble in the face of such disasters. On the one hand, he feels he is a super being and can make miracles happen. But in the face of such tragedy, he discovers he is limited—a lonely traveller with no power to change the outcome of things."

"What did you do when you came back to Italy?"

"I started up another jewellery shop. It was my trade. The shop was very popular with tourists. After years of working, I decided to go back and visit the camps in Poland. I went back to the village where we had been hidden and, quite by chance, found my sister-in-law Lilya still alive and living there. Finding her was like seeing a ghost. She told me how she crept away on all fours from the shooting in the forest, even though she was wounded, and how she survived in a farmhouse where a peasant took her in. After a while, she married him and they had a son. But the peasant died soon after the baby's birth.

"Lilya is as good and kind as was my wife, bless her soul. I thought of marrying her but was afraid that a marriage like that would not survive. Too many ghosts would come between us. In any case, I brought her and her child back to Venice, where she lives in an apartment next to mine. We are very close, although she won't talk about the past."

A flicker of light in this tragic tale. Moller is not alone and Batya feels glad. "Please go and rest now," she begs him.

There is so much to take in. Moller's story is compelling, and he speaks as if he were unable to stop the force of the testimony that has been driving him since the war. Maybe he has had no one to talk to about this, just as she hasn't.

Moller goes on. "Some of the Jewish policemen became vicious men without morals. One can blame the Nazis for this, but a man has a choice— although a choice made at the end of a gun is no choice at all. Those who generalize and put all the Jewish police into one bad lot also blemish the good ones and set themselves up as judges.

"As it is, your father picked up the children off the streets and found shelters for them. In the end, even he couldn't save them. All the children in those orphanages were sent to Treblinka, but Nazis were the ones who sent them there, not your father."

"Do you really believe that?" she asks.

"I do. The Jewish police worked like animals about to be shot for the slightest disobedience. The Umschlagplatz became a treacherous arena of deadly games. Jewish police didn't carry guns. They didn't kill. Besides, Nazis had their own henchmen, their police, their gendarme guards, and collaborators from other countries to do the job, and these were far more cruel."

Moller pauses. He has obviously had enough.

"How can I ever thank you for sharing your story with me? For showing me my father?" Batya asks. "Hearing you speak is like hearing my father speak to me."

Moller is from the same mould as her father, a man of honour, a survivor, an intelligent man who believes in telling the truth. "It was my duty to tell you what I knew about your father, and it is I who thank you for listening. So few want to listen, and there is such a huge need to tell the truth.

"Now, if you would let me have the silver disk till tomorrow, I promise to return it to you at the same time, in the same place."

"Of course," Batya says.

"My dear," he says in a barely audible voice, "I am not a well man and need to rest now."

"Will you be all right?" Batya asks. He stands up with difficulty and leans on his cane. She offers him her hand but he refuses help and soon disappears into one of the buildings on the square.

As Moller leaves, the sun drops behind a cloud and the square darkens. Overwhelmed by what she has just heard and reluctant to leave the ghetto, Batya walks mechanically over to the wall to examine the seven bas reliefs and finds that they depict scenes from the Holocaust. In one, soldiers point rifles at the victims, just as they did when she and her family were in the line-up of people heading for the trains. Among the children in the line she envisages herself and Tereska, and among the policemen, she imagines her father. Wanting to learn more about the plaques, the artist and his work, she wanders into one of the shops in the square, where a young man wearing a yarmulke is busily sorting Italian beads into boxes. The shelves are lined with books and counters cluttered with glass boxes full of beaded jewellery.

"Do you speak English?" she asks.

"Yes, I do," the young man replies.

"Do you have any literature on the artist who created those bronze plaques?"

"I can tell you that they are the work of Arbit Blatas, a Lithuanian artist. Those plaques out there were recently dedicated by the mayor of Venice in honour of Jews who died in the Holocaust. We have a book about the work, but we only have one English copy left."

"I'll take it," she says without hesitation.

"Have you been to the old synagogues in the square?" he asks. "They give tours," he adds, "but not at this hour."

The shopkeeper puts the book inside a brown paper bag and hands it to her. She feels as if she has just been given a gift. She goes back to where the bas reliefs are and sits down on a bench opposite the wall. She opens the book to examine each of the seven scenes, reading their respective captions.

Kristallnacht
The Quarry
Punishment
Execution in the Ghetto
The Deportation
The Revolt of the Warsaw Ghetto
The Final Solution

A sprawling memorial on another wall depicts the trains. Children's banging a ball against the walls of the ghetto, disrupts her meditation.

She stays there for a moment longer before returning to the hotel.

* * * * *

The next morning Batya awakes to the sun blazing through the dirt-speckled window. She finds something healing in this light which brings clarity to the hidden places in her mind. Her appointment with Moller is in the afternoon. Meanwhile, she takes a morning walk to Piazza San Marco. On the way, Batya stops at a *maskareri* shop and peruses hundreds of masks. So many to choose from!

She tries many masks but none feels right. Nothing works. The masks she has worn in her life were not merely faces; they were identities—dramatic roles that felt uncomfortable and false. *What would the masks of Beata and Batya look like?* she wonders. Finally, she picks out a harlequin mask whose velvet hat has triangular points tipped with golden bells. More than any other, this one suits her mood. The eyes are empty of expression, like those of the silver disk when there is no light in them. She puts on the mask and sees in the mirror that the harlequin's eyes are no longer hollow. She has filled them with her own. When she laughs, the eyes brighten; when she is serious, the eyes sadden and darken. There is her answer. She buys the mask and leaves the shop. *One's whole life, she reasons, is like the harlequin mask with eyes empty of expression. It all depends on what you put into the sockets of those eyes to give them life.*

The bells on the harlequin's velvet hat jingle inside the paper bag as she crosses many bridges and piazzas, following the arrows that lead to Piazza San Marco. The great piazza is filled with people and pigeons all shuffling through it against the backdrop of the Doge's Palace. The light is bright but not blinding. Shop windows sparkle with gold and silver, and she stops to purchase gold earrings for Miriam. She buys a silk shirt for Sam and a silk cravat for Moller, to show him her gratitude. Then she boards a crowded *vaporetto* back to the Guglie station in Cannaregio. Once again, it is time to meet with Moller.

The ghetto square seems different today. Yesterday, the children's soccer ball banging against the walls disturbed her. Today, she feels the children's presence as a sign of redemption. A new generation is playing in the same square where Jews were once gathered for death. Now there is life and laughter and even hope. Moller is waiting for her at the café; only this time, he is not alone.

As Batya approaches, she is taken by his companion's fine silver hair coiled at the nape of her neck. A classic beauty dwells behind the web of wrinkles on her face. Moller appears even more frail than yesterday, but the elegant lady steadies him as he stands up in greeting.

"This is my sister-in-law, Lilya," he says.

Batya shakes Lilya's hand. "I am so happy to meet you. Signor Moller has spoken of you."

"I told you yesterday," says Moller, "that we were the only ones who survived from our entire family. And, as you know, your father also saved Lilya from deportation."

"I have heard much about you and your family from Carlo," Lilya says. Her English is very good and her voice has a sonorous lilt to it. "You are also from Poland, aren't you?" Lilya doesn't wait for Batya's answer. "Italian Jews were protected until the end," she says. "Carlo always reminds me of this. But in 1943, when the Nazis came in, Jews were rounded up in this very square and taken away. There are not many of us left, but for those who live here now, life is good."

Moller nods in agreement. He squeezes Lilya's arm and Batya senses the affection between them.

"I have something for you, my dear," he says and hands the familiar pouch to Batya. "Here is your silver disk. Please, look at it."

Batya takes out the medallion and finds a silver chain attached to it.

"Signor Moller..." she begins, but he interrupts her.

"Read the inscription on the back."

In honour of Shimon Lichtenberg,
Who came to our rescue.
With gratitude and affection,
Carlo Moller and Lilya Panicz
July 31, 1942

Something inside her heaves, as if a stone is moving in an effort to come loose from where it has been solidly wedged. "I don't have the words," Batya manages. Lilya hugs her and Batya feels the older woman's wet cheek.

Moller's eyes have tears in them too. "When survivors cry, they don't cry for nothing. They cry in memory of their lost loved ones," he says.

Batya looks at her two new friends and knows that this moment the three of them share will live in their memory for a long time to come.

"Have a look at the synagogue here in the ghetto," Lilya says, showing Batya the pictures she has brought.

"What a treasure!" Batya exclaims, admiring the synagogue's velvet interior. "I wish I could have gone inside, but I'm afraid there is no time now."

"Then you will come back," the lady tells her.

"Yes, I must come back," Batya promises. She takes a small package with the tie in it out of her purse and offers it to Moller, then hugs Lilya.

"I should be going now," Batya says. "Thank you. Thank you for everything."

"Please write to us," entreats Moller. "Let us not lose contact."

The two walk away, their arms linked. Seeing them together she can't help but wonder how a world full of treachery such as the black Holocaust planet could spawn such a new and tender love.

Chapter 19

The plane circles Warsaw. When the clouds unveil the city of her birth, Batya feels as if she were an alien landing on some ravaged planet. To her surprise the city she sees from above is not what she had thought she'd find. Certainly not like the city she had left after the war.

"Look, Grisha," she shouts, grabbing his arm and pointing downward. "No ruins now. Warsaw stands intact again, see? The Polish spirit must have brought it back to life."

She remembers the vanquished city only too well: its buildings demolished, main roads and streets obscured by mountains of debris and twisted staircases; rooms and partial walls dangling in mid-air from burned buildings. But despite the new structures in place of the rubble and the dust, the remnants of that old world—her father's world—are alive in her mind. Maybe, somewhere here, Tereska is strolling along some street, having forgotten her family. Maybe by sheer chance Batya will find out what happened to her sister.

"My father's old world is here," she tells Grisha, as if to validate her mind's wanderings.

Grisha looks at her sceptically, but is silent. She is preoccupied, reconstructing the past, fragment by fragment, to make Warsaw once again her own city—once good, once treacherous. Duality always seems to pop up its Janus head. Even Papa was two people. She must find a way to help herself come to terms with the father she doesn't know.

The plane touches down. Is it possible that she is back in Warsaw?

"Don't torture yourself so," Grisha says, "The world doesn't give a damn; only you do."

What is he saying? she thinks. He was the one who wanted to come with her. Maybe he is sorry now. She is afraid to ask.

Grisha picks up their bags and heads for the exit. In the terminal, the customs officer carefully inspects their passports and visas. He looks at Batya pointedly and asks how long she has lived in Canada. After a few more questions, he lets them through to the baggage claim.

Soon they are on their way to the hotel. The red streetcar still travels along its tracks, she observes. The parks are resplendent in their greenery, just as she remembers them. Tall linden trees line the wide streets, as they did long ago when she would look up at the sky through their green lace, while munching on little dried bagels on a string. Her nanny had bought them at a kiosk still standing right there, near the Tomb of the Unknown Soldier.

"How," she says to Grisha, "can I connect emotionally with this Warsaw to the one I remember as it lay in ruins after the war. Or the one even before the ruins?"

"You can't. I am often confused between what I remember and what is," says Grisha. "Everything changes and your memory is just a trick of the mind. Not the real thing."

"Oh? I don't agree with you at all," says Batya, disappointed in the things Grisha is saying. *His voice has anger in it,* she thinks. Soon her attention turns to what is in front of her and lost in the memory of what came before. She iremembers so well the pre-war wide boulevards, bright, happy streets where she and other children played. But too soon they started losing their innocence.

There is nothing left of the past, Batya thinks, *except what I came here to find: the remains of a long-gone family, my home.* Is it foolish to think that she can redeem the honour of the lives and deaths of her relatives by remembering them this way? *No,* she thinks. *But it is perhaps the only way, I can recover a tiny part of myself and the childhood I lost, my relatives and, most of all, my sister.*

The taxi driver stops half a block away from the Bristol Hotel, his finger on his lips.

"Will you change your dollars for some of my *zlotys?*" he asks. "Here," he explains, "we can buy more for a dollar than for a *zloty*, and I will give you more zlotys for a dollar than the bank will."

Batya and Grisha exchange looks. "This is the black market, so typical of a Communist regime," he whispers to her, but complies and pulls several bills out of his wallet along with a few photographs that fall to the floor of the car.

Batya bends to pick them up, but Grisha's hand stops her.

"Don't," he says in an agitated tone of voice, but it is too late.

One photo shows Grisha and a dark-haired girl standing in front of an

Italian bistro. She is smiling. She is beautiful. The second one reveals Grisha and the same girl sitting in the café with their arms around one another. The date stamp indicates the time Batya was in Venice, ten days ago, when she sat by the canal thinking of him.

"It's not what you think," he says. "She is a girl I knew in Russia, and when she came to Rome I had to show her around."

"I don't believe you. You've changed towards me. I noticed it when I returned to Rome."

"It's your own fault for going away," says Grisha.

That hurt. She thought she got free of being blamed and being made to feel guilty when she left Vancouver.

"Do you love this girl?" she asks, forming the words with difficulty.

"I loved her once, but we parted and went our separate ways," he replies. "She is from my village, and she became an orphan when her parents were murdered. She is Roma, a Gypsy."

Her image of herself with Grisha in love, is collapsing. She had a gut feeling something was wrong, and she doesn't believe that his relationship with this woman is over. *Be strong,* she tells herself. *You are here with him only for a short time.* Yet the snake of jealousy coils around her heart.

They stop in front of the hotel and enter the lobby, the driver trailing behind with the suitcases. While waiting for their room, Grisha squeezes her hand but Batya withdraws it from his clasp. The empty space between them creates a feeling of nothingness and dulls her excitement of being here.

The hotel is old, still in its nineteenth-century decor. It smells of home-cooked food and strong perfume wafting from the female clerk at the counter. Most noticeable are the crimson velvet drapes framing the windows.

Batya forgets her pain, fixated on the décor, fascinated by the languages she hears spoken: French, German, Russian and Arabic. Most of all she loves hearing her native tongue, Polish. So familiar is this language she loved as a child. It was here in Poland that she formed her first impressions of nature's bounty and of human nature's good and evil. Here she found true beauty of this land while roaming among acacia trees, smelling the flowers and tasting luscious berries right off the bush. Here she first observed the life of insects and felt their sting, heard the birds sing and watched squirrels collecting their nuts. Here she experienced the sour taste of hunger, the bleakness of the ghetto streets and the sound of bombs falling on the city. Here she wrote her first poems.

Grisha is restlessly walking up and down the lobby in front of her. "Warsaw is not where I was born, but I can appreciate its charm. Except that we are waiting far too long for our room. In fact, we are being totally ignored," he says impatiently.

The taxi driver, who has been standing behind them with their suitcases, murmurs that there is something else they must do to get a room despite having made a reservation. Grisha listens carefully and does as the taxi driver bids. He places a U.S. ten-dollar bill in each of their passports and approaches the female clerk behind the desk. He smiles at the perfumed clerk, who examines the passports, nods knowingly, then hands him their keys. They go up to their room followed by the taxi driver with the luggage.

"I picked this old hotel," Grisha says after the well-tipped driver leaves, "because my aunt told me that it was one of the few buildings spared during the bombing."

"See," Batya says, looking through a dirty window, "there is the governor's mansion guarded by four lions and the statue of Józef Poniatowski, and over there is Krakowskie Przedmiescie Street, leading to the Old Town. I remember walking here with my father and stopping in a *cukiernia* for a pastry. I can still smell the sweet vanilla of the little cakes filled with custard that my father used to order. Maybe we can find them after we eat dinner?"

It must be the euphoria of being here that helps her put aside Grisha's obvious indiscretion, even though he will not own up to it. *But maybe he was betraying the other woman? Not her? Maybe this is her punishment for betraying Joseph?*

Batya makes a conscious decision to go through with her visit to Poland and deal with her memories and feelings somehow, though deep in her gut she is full of misgivings about Grisha. How could she have been so stupid? All the signs were there when Grisha stared at every girl that passed by.

"I guess I am not pretty enough for you," she says bitterly, immediately regretting the self-effacing words.

"You're being silly and childish. Besides, I never promised you anything," Grisha says angrily. "Nothing has changed. I still care about you."

She doesn't believe him, except that he is right. He never did promise her anything. What was she expecting in a short-term relationship with a stranger?

The act of pretence begins. Batya is conscious of how completely she has abandoned her Beata double, her master pretender. It is she alone, Batya, who must deal with the world in all its complexity and survive in it, today, now.

At the hotel restaurant smelling of cabbage and beer, they dine on delicious beet borscht and meat-filled perogies, accompanied by an excellent Polish vodka. Later they take a stroll down a street that runs parallel to the Vistula River.

"Not far from here," says Batya, "on Bracka Street, before the bombing, there was a department store where they sold toys and had a puppet theatre. Mother used to leave me at the theatre and go shopping. I was fascinated by the small stage and the puppets in colourful costumes."

She gathers from his silence that Grisha is not interested in her childhood remembrances. But she was filled with such wonder then. The puppets danced across the stage, their body movements guided from above by barely visible strings. She wanted them so much to be real but at the end of the show, when she walked up to the little stage, she saw they were only wooden puppets.

Mother returned from shopping with a doll as a gift for her. The doll resembled one of the puppets on the stage but did not have a string attached to it. Batya could do with it as she pleased. The doll was supposed to be a baby like her new born sister, Tereska, her mother had said. After touching the baby doll's porcelain face and straw like wisps of hair, Batya threw the doll to the floor in anger and stamped her feet in front of her mother. She didn't want a puppet baby. She wanted a real baby like Tereska, whom Mama and Papa doted on.

Grisha walks beside her in silence. Has she been raving, going on too much about herself? Here he is moving forward in the present, and next to him she is retreating into the past.

They enter the *Stare Miasto*, an old town square surrounded by tall, narrow buildings with red roofs standing shoulder to shoulder, each no more than four or five storeys high and each a shade of beige, cream or grey. In the centre of the cobblestone square rises a lofty statue of King Zygmunt, ruler of Poland in the sixteenth century, carrying a cross. There are a few eateries around the square where the horse-drawn carriages known as *doroshkas* stand, waiting for customers, just as she remembers them from before the war.

Walking way past the Old Town, they reach a flat, grassy park with benches in the shade of trees and bushes where people sit and chat next to a large stone memorial. She has seen pictures of it in a book. A sign on a post confirms this is the Warsaw Ghetto Memorial, raised to the ghetto fighters. *My God,* she thinks, *I am standing on the ground of the Warsaw Ghetto.*

"Look at this. Dogs run around barking and people pass by, unaware they are walking on what once was the killing field," she says to Grisha.

"The city, like a person, has to move forward, you know," he replies, "despite its history."

The several bronze figures on the memorial seem so real: a father holding his frightened child by the hand, the mother with a baby next to him. Their faces express terror and outrage; their bodies are bowed in humility, as if praying for salvation.

People bustle by on the sidewalks and cars speed in and around the streets that once were the ghetto. And underneath the squat black marble memorials along Zamenhof and other nearby streets, rages the tragedy of the Jewish people.

At Mila Street, Grisha recounts the story of Mordecai Anielewicz, the leader of the ghetto fighters, and his bunker at number 18. "After all that, here is your memory. Nothing but a black granite stone inscribed with the names of the heroes," he says sardonically.

"It's still an honouring, so they wouldn't be forgotten," she says. "They saved the honor of all Jews by refusing to be sent to the gas."

'And they all died in the process."

On Zamenhof, she reminds him of the thousands of Jews who walked along this very street in a long dismal line to the trains on Stawki Street. And suddenly there it is: the Umschlagplatz, where the line halted.

She envisions her father in the distance, in his policeman's uniform. He worked here on those few fateful days in July of 1942. Now all that remains is a grey monument inscribed with words that no one is reading.

She sees him again, now standing on the grassy field outside the memorial. Never fully believing he is buried in a distant Toronto cemetery, she senses him as an ever-present ghost in her life.

Batya and Grisha sit a long time on the benches within the walls of the Umschlagplatz monument reading the inscriptions in different languages about the Jews who left here for Treblinka on tracks that no longer exist. How difficult it is to connect herself to that fear and the hunger. How impossible to convey to Grisha what she is feeling.

There is her father again at the red-brick remnant of the ghetto wall still standing, just as he was standing then, when she was leaving the ghetto. She touches the wall as if touching her soul and becomes mute like Grisha.

They backtrack through a park and find themselves on the wide boulevard of Aleje Jerozolimskie, Jerusalem Avenue.

"This is where I lived before the war," she says. "It is such a wide street that only through an underpass can one get safely from one side to the other. Here we are at the building. Number 47, that was our home. It seems to be almost like it was in 1940, when my family and I were forced out to live inside the ghetto."

She takes Grisha's hand and guides him into the courtyard, where a group of boys are playing. One small boy in a tattered jacket runs over and, looking up at them with a roguish expression on his face, says, "Go away, you don't belong here!" He senses that they are foreigners. She sees in him that little boy in rags stretching out a soiled hand begging for money in 1939, when she walked with her father hand in hand along the same street in front of this building. Papa went into a shop and bought the boy bread, chocolate and apples. Papa believed that little children should not handle money, but should have enough to eat.

The little boy is right. She no longer belongs to this old dilapidated dwelling where she was happy once, for such a short time. Here, before the war, her family gathered together and laughed and played. How she used to love her walks with Papa. It was her very own hour with him, and Papa treated her as if she were his only little girl. He spent so much time with her, even after Tereska was born, when she felt Mama no longer loved her—walking along Aleje Jerozolimskie, a grand street with many shops. The trees here, which once were tall, must have been replanted and grown up again, but not as tall as they once were.

Grisha points to a man in a leather jacket standing on the corner smoking and watching the passers-by. "That guy is the Polish KGB," he says in a low voice. "I see them everywhere."

"Strange," Batya says. "I am so wrapped up in the past I don't see the present."

"That is precisely your problem, Batiusha. You are in a space I cannot reach. Not so with me. I am fully in the present."

"Maybe you should try to reach me where I am," she says." And maybe you're right, but I am not the only one here with a past," she reminds him. "What about yours?"

He shrugs his shoulders, takes her hand to his lips, and for a moment she feels comforted and attracted to him again. Yet it is obvious the connection between them is not as passionate as it was before they came to Warsaw.

She now makes a conscious effort to enter the present, to be in sync with Grisha. She notes that there are very few cars on the road compared with North America, and she has not as yet seen any women drivers. There are line-ups in front of small cave-like shops where they sell bread and milk. This Warsaw is much different from her pre-war Warsaw, where food was plentiful. Looming over them on Aleje Jerozolimskie is the city's tallest structure, a rather traditional building called the Palace of Culture and Science. Stalin's gift to the Poles.

They return to the hotel, painfully aware that a cloud of silence has enveloped them.

The next day, they eat breakfast still steeped in that silent fog. *Maybe the omnipresent past simply makes words irrelevant*, she thinks. When both she and Grisha were children, they could hardly use words to describe their emotions. Now, they have become again the children who were once made speechless by the fear of war. At least she knows it is so for her.

"Why is this happening to us?" she asks, trying to overcome the chill between them.

"It's the heat," Grisha says.

She nods but she knows better—*it's not the heat; it's the memories*.

They leave for Marszalkowska Street, where Batya was born, stopping at Café Ziemianski for her favourite pastries. This is where her mother used to take her to eat slices of *dobosh* torte, cream-filled *babas*, and *pączki*, the jam-filled doughnuts whose sweet vanilla scent takes her back to better times. As they wait in the line-up at the bakery café, things seem more normal. The aromas of baking connect her to the pre-past, as she often refers to the pre-war period of which she has few memories, the sweet, buttery vanilla scents evoking the sweetness of her short childhood before the Blitzkrieg.

They load up on their favourite cakes and walk to a vaguely familiar park where they sit on a bench in front of a pond with swans. So engrossing is the aroma and the taste of the pastries that she almost forgets Grisha sitting next to her. When she offers him a pastry, he refuses. She is transported back to the cake shop, remembering how in the first days of occupation they were not allowed to have cakes and tea there because they were Jews. The same restrictions applied to the park where they were now sitting, and in schools and libraries as well as the theatre where she had seen her first Shirley Temple movie and Walt Disney's enchanting *Snow White*. Her beautiful world suddenly stopped that day on September 1, 1939, and the word "Hitler" became a synonym for terror in her child's mind.

"Where are you again?" Grisha asks, giving her a mild poke. There is annoyance in his face.

"Don't you know?"

"You must know by now that I am not as affected by this city as you are, Batiusha. Don't forget I was born in the Ukraine."

She looks at him as if he is a stranger. How remote and stern he has become.

"Besides, I do not intend to spend my whole life navel-gazing," he adds angrily. "I came here to pay my last respects to Zoran and then I am going to forget everything."

"You did tell me what happened to you. You cried when you remembered."

"It was just a sentimental moment. I was telling you about Zoran and my parents and I guess I got carried away. I am sorry now. I thought we would come here and have some fun too."

Her half-eaten pastry crumbles to the ground as she studies his face, looking for the man she thought he was.

"Anyway, I hate digging up past tragedies. It's all in the distant past. There is nothing for me here." Grisha's words fall harshly on her ears.

She had thought that sharing this experience would bring them even closer together. But there is no point now. She will not change the focus of her trip, which is to honour her family and the memory of them that still lives in these streets.

The discord between them creates tension. She feels tired after their long walk and the sadness she experienced in the ghetto streets. Back in the Old Town they stop for another meal in a restaurant, where Grisha orders a bowl of *bigos*.

"I must admit this reminds me of Zoran," he says. "He often cooked such a stew for our midday meal: sauerkraut, onion, wine and sausage, or another type of meat if you could get it. This is so good." He smacks his lips and his face brightens.

"You see, you do cherish those past memories," she says.

"Do you still love me?" he asks out of the blue.

She looks at him, amazed by this sudden outburst. Love was never really mentioned before. "I don't know," she replies honestly. The word "love" seems an anomaly here in Warsaw, especially now.

He smiles and raises his glass. "To your beauty."

Who can resist such a toast? she thinks, emptying her glass, pouring herself another and smiling at him. The wine helps ease her anxiety. Back in the hotel room, a semblance of love returns at night, but she is locked inside its darkness, filled more with desperation than with passion.

Chapter 20

In the morning, after breakfast, Grisha wants to take a stroll in the nearby park. "I'll wait for you in the hotel lobby or in the room," he says.

Batya agrees to meet him later. She is off to the Jewish Historical Society to search the archives and find more information about her father. If not there, where?

The cab driver says he can't stop in front of the building because the street is barricaded. She gets out of the cab and a young boy runs up to her. "You come, I take you to building," he says in broken English.

"How do you know where I want to go?" she asks.

"I know. Many people come here," he says with a funny little know-it-all smile.

After he leads her to the door, she gives him several *zlotys* and watches him run away. He reminds her of a beggar boy who shouted at her when she came away from the ghetto wall in 1942 after leaving her father. "You little Jewess, I saw you," he yelled. "You don't belong on our side of the ghetto wall. Get back to where you came from." But this boy was not mean. *Who knows?* she thinks. Poland is full of mysteries. Maybe the spirit of that little boy is trying to redeem himself in another boy, by helping her. Maybe such coincidences are possible.

She walks into the building that once was the Great Synagogue of Warsaw until it was bombed. The man who looks like a guard regards her with suspicion, but when she speaks in Polish and asks for information on the Jewish police, he nods knowingly and takes her into the archives section of the library and tells another man to get her the information. After some moments, he returns with a file that has her father's name on it and hands her a thin book. "This is a master's thesis on the Jewish police, written by a student."

Strange, she thinks, taking the book back to her reading table. So far, all the information she has received from Moller and Berent has soothed her, but there is still so much she doesn't know for sure.

The title of the thin Polish volume translates to *The Jewish Police of the Warsaw Ghetto*. She is wary of what she may find in its pages, considering what she had read elsewhere. She can't fathom why a Polish student would pick such a topic for her master's thesis, unless her aim was to show Jews in a bad light.

First it describes how the Judenrat formed the Jewish police core on the orders of a Nazi commander. The following chapters repeat much of what Batya has read in the library at home. Next, the author writes about the Polish court's prosecution of Nazi collaborators among the Jewish Ghetto Police. Here Batya comes across the names of six accused policemen. In each case, the individuals in question appeared in court to testify on their own behalf. Their testimonies all speak of how they tried to survive under unbearably difficult circumstances. Each of the policemen who gave his testimony was acquitted due to insufficient evidence and discharged—all but one, a policeman who was not present in court, her father, Shimon Lichtenberg.

She rises from her chair wanting desperately to escape the nightmare of this discovery. The man who seems to be in charge of the files, blocks her path on the way to the exit. He scrutinizes her every move. She remembers that she is in communist Poland. "You left your purse," he says in a loud voice. She looks back at the table she was at. There it is on the chair. She turns around.

I must stop running away and face what is in those papers. She thinks frantically, returning to the table. She has never felt more alone.

Trying to compose herself, she examines each word of the thesis trying to grasp what is written here. She feels dampness on her face, her neck. Drops of sweat drip onto the page. She sits on the edge of the chair, her body tensing into a coil of nerves, as she reads on.

> *During the occupation, in the Warsaw ghetto, working in the capacity of a Jewish police officer, Shimon Lichtenberg acted against the Jewish population of the ghetto when, during resettlement, he behaved with extreme cruelty against his people. He took bribes from the victims in the form of money and jewels and treated them badly. Everything pointed to the eventual prosecution of this policeman, but the Court was informed on September 20, 1949, that Shimon Lichtenberg had died that year in Toronto. Consequently, his case was dismissed.*

If only she could disappear, vanish forever into non -being where she has been most of her life. Feverish thoughts creep into her mind. *Why did this woman have to write this, years after Father's death, and where did she get her information?*

Now the archivist is watching her. Her throat feels constricted, as if a noose around her neck were pulling tighter and tighter. Another cut into the wound from the past. Where is the father in whom she had unshakable faith throughout the years, the faith and the love that helped her cope somehow? Like that day when Papa, standing on the bank of a river, was teaching her to swim while she, submerged in the water up to her neck, hung on for dear life with only her toe touching the bottom. "Let go," Papa insisted. "Let go and you'll float." But she couldn't let go for a long time. Papa, who had just had surgery and couldn't wade into the water with her, stood there and waited patiently until her trust in what he was saying triumphed over fear. After a long struggle with herself, she had let go and miraculously floated.

Here it is in black and white, a scathing indictment against her father, bringing an even greater burden to her already guilt-ridden conscience. She should not have survived to have to witness this. She has no right to live.

It is too late for self-- reproach. Instead she must face the truth. She must think, pull herself together. Papa always insisted on objectivity. Was it not unfair and unethical to accuse a dead man who could not defend himself? Was this student's research thorough? Batya has her suspicions about how this information might have reached the Polish court. She had read that they shot all the Jewish collaborators in the Ghetto, and yet after the war Papa was invited into the provisional Polish government to head the legal department.

Moller had spoken about Rogacki and how he had won his case against Shimon L. by lying in court. She reads in a newspaper clipping she finds in the file that there were witnesses in Rogacki's favour. The court recognized the testimony of a woman by the name of Maria Orlicka, whereas Papa's only witness was rejected by the judge as biased because this witness was a distant cousin. *What a farce,* she thinks. Long ago she heard her father tell Mama about how, despite the fact that he was married, Rogacki kept a mistress by the name of Maria Orlicka, and after the war when his wife died of cancer, he married her. Therefore, her testimonial account was by no means unbiased.

Batya cannot clear her father's name without access to the legal files and the sources of this woman's thesis. It will be difficult, if not impossible, to obtain the files under the Communist regime. Authorities tended to regard a snooping foreigner from the West with suspicion.

In what little her mother ever said about the war, Batya knew that she hated Rogacki. She remembers her father speaking of the time when they were running from the Nazis, how Rogacki chose that very moment to blackmail him. She hadn't understood the circumstances then, and her father had not enlightened her further, but it all seems true now. Madame Berent's belief that Rogacki lied to get revenge for her father's accusations against him and even paid off witnesses to lie was further evidence. Even outsiders like Moller supported this version of the truth, but his word won't help her now.

She asks the file keeper to photocopy the part of the thesis that accuses her father. The man now seems sympathetic and agrees to get her the required material. He even offers her coffee but tells her that he is not allowed to give out information. When he returns with the designated pages, he suggests that she read the source of Mrs. Larski's thesis where that terrible paragraph about her father appears. Mrs. Larski, says the biographical note, is now an instructor at a Warsaw University.

He looks up the source of the paragraph and, sure enough, it is as she thought. The Larski source is precisely the court statements given by Rogacki and Orlicka, copied verbatim into the thesis.

"The source she used is a lie," Batya cries out. "This swindler lied to get back at my father!"

"But can you prove it?" says the archivist, half-smiling. "Look, I found something for you while searching through your father's file. Here is a photocopy," he says, handing her a piece of paper. The writing appears to be part of an article or an essay. "Read it," he instructs. "I am doing you a special favour."

> I knew Shimon Lichtenberg in Warsaw before and during the Holocaust. Before the war he was a most respected lawyer well on his way to be appointed a judge. In the ghetto he cared for the homeless and hungry children. Not only did he find homes for them, clothing and food, but he protected them from being deported for as long as he could. I praise him deeply for that.
> —by Jerzy Konarski

To have found this bit of redemption felt like the loosening of a noose around her neck. The noble Mrs Larski had discounted this affirmation of his character. If only Batya could tell her that. After thanking the archivist, she rushes back to the hotel to phone the university in hope of finding Mrs. Larski.

"I am sorry," says a man's voice, "Mrs. Larski no longer teaches here."

"Can you give me her address?"

"We do not give out such information to strangers" is the curt answer.

What can she do now? It is dangerous to snoop around in an Eastern Bloc country with spies on each street corner. She will contact this writer on her return to Canada, where she can find a lawyer to help her. But even then, will she have enough proof to clear her father's name? How difficult it is to chase history and how impossible to correct its errors. But at least she knows now that Larski's statement about her father is mostly a dirty lie. Not all of it though—not about Father at the Umschlagplatz, where he was seen on the day of deportations. Will she ever know the whole truth about his role there and what he felt about putting Jews on the train to Treblinka? The thought that he could have done this sickens her to the core.

Chapter 21

On their way to Treblinka death camp, Batya experiences a sense of dread, she had on hearing Madame Berent's story of the death camp, coupled with the knowledge that Papa may have helped to send Jewish people there. She looks defiantly out the window at the Polish scenery, trying to calm her thoughts.

It is now late summer and the morning is balmy. They leave the city in a hired car with driver and travel along a road surrounded by serene fields and forests, the leaves on the trees a brilliant green. The sun shines through a white membrane of mist. She can smell the wheat, tall enough to hide a small child.

The driver stops and asks them to wait in the car. He disappears into the forest then returns shortly with a handful of luscious wild strawberries such as can only be found in these forests. They feast on the fruit's red sweetness, but Grisha looks even more unhappy and distracted than the day before, behaving as if he has been forced to come here. Batya doesn't tell him about her findings in the archives. Why complicate this difficult journey with more sadness?

They arrive at the town of Malkinia, where the railroad track that has followed them along the road splits. One section runs towards Treblinka and ends mid-track, as if someone had pulled out the rails.

"These," explains the driver, "were the rails that took the transports into the camp. They were partially destroyed. Trains and lives ended here."

This ground conjures up more than a killing field and the burning and rotting of flesh. This ground has been sanctified by Jewish blood. Batya thinks listening to the driver.

They walk towards a sign that reads *TREBLINKA*. A few metres past it, they come to a wooden shack. On the outside wall hangs a large poster of Dr. Janusz Korczak's face. His eyes express the tragedy that befell his people and his children. There is nobody else in sight.

They walk along a wide forest road, calm and pastoral at first, surrounded by a grassy field. This is the road along which her people walked when they came here, the ones who weren't already dead by the time the rail car doors opened. To one side a tall hunchbacked stone hugs the road, then another and another. They resemble humans turned to stone like Lot's wife. The deeper they venture into the camp site, the more stones line both sides of their path—stones that look like grave markers, each inscribed with the name of a lost Jewish community. Farther still, they come upon a field of stones of various sizes and shades of grey, hundreds of them representing the lost *shtetls*.

While all the stones commemorate the names of the lost communities, only one stone has the name of a person written on it. Batya reads the inscription: *Janusz Korczak i dzieci*—Janusz Korczak and the children, all murdered. Another memorial stone is marked with the words "Never Again" in many languages, including German.

The stony desert has a tall, awkward memorial at its centre. Made of smaller rocks, it is clunky and has the shape of a giant mushroom. An eerie hum vibrates around it, louder than she has ever heard before in any countryside, louder now until her eardrums feel as if they might burst. *This emptiness, these stones, this buzzing sound is all that is left of our family and of others,* Batya thinks, trying to put names to the faces of those she remembers.

Aunt Lola with her dark, brooding face, who was childless.

Her husband, Zygmunt, a tall, pale man who was funny.

Aunt Maryla, brown-haired, with delicate skin, who had a lovely singing voice.

Batya's cousins, happy-faced Zula and Jurek, whose face was always sad.

Auntie Fela, a dark-eyed, dark-haired widow who had three grown children, Halina, Irena and Adam.

They all died here in Treblinka.

And Uncle Mietek with his big questioning eyes, a young doctor with a future, who taught Batya to dance the foxtrot. Father told her that Mietek was taken to Mauthausen and never heard from again.

She recalls a room in the ghetto where the family often gathered. *Even there when they were all together, there was laughter and animated conversation. A glimpse of happiness at just being with each other and sharing the little food the family could scrape up for their supper. Two of the older cousins, Halina and Irena, were standing in front of a cracked mirror, combing their hair. Aunts and uncles were talking about going to America after the war; the girl cousins wanted to take ballet and piano lessons; Adam planned to go away to a school in France. Grandmother looked on at her family with love.*

In the evening, everyone said goodbye and returned to their ghetto hovels before the curfew fell and before Nazi police came out to torment the few Jews still wandering in the streets. Her aunts, uncles and cousins promised each other to meet again the next day.

Except on the next day, no one came. Grandmother had died from a heart attack during a police raid on her room that night. Their own room, which only the day before had been filled with familiar faces and voices, now stood silent and empty. Someone said they had seen the family on the train to Treblinka. Why didn't Papa get them out?

It is impossible to believe what has transpired in this place. In what world could you imagine trains arriving with people packed like sardines, without food or water, some stifled to death on the way? The immediate disrobing and being made to line up for the showers. The subsequent gassing of humans whose dead bodies were discarded into mass graves, the Jews themselves forced to carry out this horrid task. And to think that some survived. Dear God! Poor Madame Berent!

Grisha is nowhere to be seen. She calls out his name but hears no response. *Why has he left her in this vast field of buried corpses?* She wanders, stumbling over the stones. She is lost and alone, just as when she was parted from her father at the ghetto wall.

Anxiety turns to panic. *Where is the way out of here?* She walks on and finally sees Grisha sitting on the ground by the broken train track, chewing on a weed.

"Why did you leave me there?"

"I wanted to check on the driver. I wanted to see if he was still waiting for us." His voice is cold. She knows he is lying and that he has simply forgotten about her.

"I don't believe you," she cries. She turns away. Despair grips her as she falls onto the grass. The grass feels cool on her face but the earth exudes an unnatural smell. She sits up. She must be on someone's unmarked grave. Or a mass grave. She examines the spot for bones protruding from the earth. "We can't sit here," she cries. "It's disrespectful."

Grisha doesn't move. He regards her with an ironic smile. "You've become irrational. Like a drunk. Compose yourself. Isn't acting this way in front of the dead also disrespectful?"

There is contempt in his eyes. He is right. She is shaky and her mind is racing. Maybe she is going mad. Maybe they both are. *Encountering a monstrous truth can kill you,* she thinks.

He has chosen to run away from memory, probably afraid to share his grief, if he even feels it. Just like her mother who chose to forget. Trembling, she walks down the road and gets into the car, her mind still wandering among the stones. It is impossible to leave this place behind. The words she heard about Papa are with her as well. *No, Papa is not that man,* she thinks, anger with the writer charring her insides. She cannot go back to Warsaw. Not yet. She must make two more stops before they return to the city.

She tells the driver to take them to the village where she had once lived in hiding. They ask someone and soon find the village and the street. She remembers a little white house hidden by trees. There it is now, nestling among the green branches like a white dove. It looks the same as it did then. She rings the bell at the gate.

At first no one comes, then a petite woman appears from around the corner where the house and the garden meet. She eyes Batya suspiciously. "What do you want?"

"I used to live here during the war when I was a little girl," Batya replies. "Can you let us in, just to look?" A man comes out to the gate. They remind her of the couple with whom she lived then, so many years ago, though they are different folk. They whisper to one another in Polish. The woman nods and the man opens the gate to let them in. Grisha opts to stay outside. Batya follows the couple into the house and her heart almost stops. Nothing has changed inside.

The woman says that the couple who lived here throughout the war years and afterwards died, and that it was the man's relative who sold them the house.

Through a partly opened door she sees only one evidence of change: a small washroom added onto one side of the hall. Even the staircase is still the same. The same stairs to the loft, which old Bolek had climbed to hide her books and then bargained with her to get them back in exchange for sex. He also used bread as a bargaining tool. Nausea rises to her throat at the thought of Bolek.

She stands transfixed at the entrance to the room where the old man abused her. This room off the kitchen, where he sat by a stove with his pipe when she was nine years old, is as vivid now as it was that day. His pants undone, his member out, he slowly gets up and walks towards her, holding out a piece of bread. She recoils against the wall, a cornered animal. She had never seen a man's genitals before. When he sees that the bread won't work, he tries to bribe her with a book she loved to read over and over again. He approaches again and asks her to remove her panties. He examines her private parts, and

she cringes. He goes back to the chair dragging her by the arm and starts playing with himself, urging her to touch him. His member feels like rubber to
the touch and she tries to pull her hand away when, grunting and gasping
like a bull, he flops back into the chair.

This is the very first time she has remembered the scene in its entirety.
She knows now it was not a dream but a fact of her childhood, the repressed
memory an obstacle between her and Joseph during their lovemaking.

She enters the little room to the left of the hall and waits there until she
feels calmer. This was her room, dark except for a small window. She can still
smell the mould growing on the damp wall next to her bed, as it was in 1942.
The wood-framed window looks out onto the garden and partly onto the
road. How often she stood there, a prisoner looking out, hoping against all
odds to see her parents come up to the gate. In the winter she would trace
her fingers around the edges of the icy flowers that formed on the window
pane, watching the rivulets of melting ice drop to the sill. The snow outside
lay packed partway up the window. In the spring she watched the snow melt,
uncovering the black earth, and she marvelled at the awakening of the trees
and shrubs. In the summer the garden was rich with bushes and green fruit
trees, the blossoming jasmine, acacia and sweet raspberries, colours that burst
from the flower beds and from the wildflowers that grew around the fence. It
was through this window that she first saw her parents finally returning along
the dirt road and felt joy like no other she has ever felt. But the joy would
soon be marred by the news of her sister's disappearance.

In the kitchen she notices the same yellow tile stove with a pipe that led
to the ceiling, the only source of heat, and the old wood-burning stove with
its iron doors where Lena cooked. The same dark wooden credenza that held
Lena's treasures, looms tall in the dining part of the kitchen.

"Oh," she exclaims, looking out the window, "here is the tree where my
father, when he came to visit me hung a cage he had built for a squirrel he
caught so I could have a pet. I dreamed of having a furry pet I could take to
bed with me and snuggle up to. But the squirrel was wild and bit me. He lived
in the cage for a while and when the cage was left open, he ran away."

The woman, who has been following her around, listens and points to a
brown squirrel climbing the same tree. "Maybe it's his grandchild," she says,
smiling. The elderly gentleman, smoking a pipe, sits in a chair—the same
brown chair where half a century before, Bolek sat. The kind couple offer her
a cup of tea, but she refuses, thanking them profusely before going outside.

She roams the familiar garden and sits in a canvas chair under one of the elm trees. For the first time since it all happened she feels grateful to the people who made it possible for her to live and to survive. Papa, who arranged her escape from the ghetto; the woman who brought her here; the old couple who took her in; and the village folk who never informed the Gestapo that she was a Jew. Full of gratitude, she touches the gentle jasmine flower and breathes in its scent. The garden, even in those days, was her refuge and a place for imagining that life could be a fairy tale, if she pushed away the ugly and embraced the beautiful.

When the couple come into the garden, she knows she has outstayed her welcome. She asks them if they know a man by the name of Jan Rogacki and tells them a little about her sister.

"He lived in Otwock," she tells them, "a town not far from here."

"We don't know these people," says the woman, shading her eyes from the sun with her hand. "Do you have a photo of your sister? You might send it in to the Otwock paper. Maybe someone in the town will recognize her."

Yes, Batya thinks, *I might just do that.* She thanks the couple and walks out onto the dirt road where Grisha is moping by the fence. She tells him of her immediate plans.

The driver takes them to Otwock. He happens to know where the newspaper office is. She has Tereska's picture in her wallet. She had thought it might come in handy because she still had hope of finding traces of her little sister.

A man standing in the doorway of the building approaches them. Batya discovers that he is the editor of the town paper. He seems sympathetic and invites them into his office, where he picks up a pad to write down the facts about Tereska.

"I will print your story in the next edition of the paper," he says, taking down her telephone number and address in Canada. Then he makes a copy of Tereska's photograph. She thanks the man, offering him one hundred *zlotys*. He hesitates.

"Please, take it," she says, "as a token of my gratitude." She leaves the newspaper office, satisfied that at last she has done something about Tereska, who, in her mind, has been missing all these years without anyone really knowing or trying to find out what happened to her.

Next they stop on Szkolna Street. The editor has given her directions to the Rogacki villa. Batya gets out of the car while Grisha stays inside with the driver. Two dogs inside the high fence start barking and rush to the gate. Her father once told her that Rogacki always had vicious police dogs guarding his house. A young man comes to the gate.

"Who are you?" he inquires through the iron slats. The look on his face is harsh.

"Who are you?" Batya counters, feeling bold. "Where is Jan Rogacki?"

"Why do you want to know?"

"I am looking for my sister, Tereska Lichtenberg, who stayed with him during the war."

The man grimaces. "Aha, you're the Jews my uncle tried to save. He is dead. I am his nephew. What will you give me if I tell you?" He sounds pompous and arrogant.

What load of crap is he handing me? she wonders, her heart pounding. "Do you want money?"

"And why not?" he replies.

"First, tell me what you know," Batya demands.

At this point an elderly woman leaning on a cane joins them at the gate. "I am Maria Orlicka, the owner of this house. What can I help you with?"

So this is Rogacki's lover, Batya thinks.

"What happened to Jan's wife? The Rogackis were friends of my parents, the Lichtenbergs." Batya presses on, aware that she is being rude but she doesn't care.

"Oh, I know who you mean," says the woman. She and the young man exchange conspiratorial glances.

"I am Jan Rogacki's wife. His former wife died of cancer," she says.

"Do you know what happened to my sister, Tereska?"

The woman frowns and turns her face away from Batya. "You forget about her. Do you hear?" she says sharply. The dogs are still barking like mad. "Wait here," she adds and goes into the house.

They wait. The young man stands by the iron fence like a mute guard while Bata leans against the locked gate wondering why the woman said what she did. After a while, Orlicka returns.

"Here," she says and hastily shoves a yellowed envelope through the slats of the gate into Batya's hand. "These belonged to Jan's former wife. I don't want them. Now leave or I'll call the police," the woman threatens. "I am not going to tell you anything." She turns and walks back into the house, the young man trails behind her not bothering to hide his wicked grin.

If only Batya could have challenged this woman about her testimony against Father. But what is the use when the damage has been done? It would take an enormous amount of work on the part of many people to repair the harm, if that were even possible.

Grisha is still in the car, waiting. She opens the envelope Orlicka has given her and finds photos she has never seen of Tereska. A beautiful little girl looks up at a tree. In another she is tied to a doorknob by a rope. How cruel! Her parents said that Rogacki did not treat her sister well, that he tied her up in case she decided to go out of the house. Just like a dog. Poor little girl. How terribly she must have suffered, and she was only five years old.

Batya leans against the car window, her strength spent. *So much sadness to take in,* she thinks. She observes Grisha's dispassionate face. Grisha, the fiery Gypsy, who has changed so drastically on this trip. Maybe her own feelings for him have cooled as well? Maybe they both became who they really were in the first place, cold people afraid of love—she an idealist, longing for emotional fulfilment; he the realist, fulfilled by the gratification of his body.

"What has happened to us?" she asks.

"Life," he responds. "There is nothing romantic about reality."

"I don't agree."

Grisha looks at her, saying nothing. She is too full of today's events to think of anything at all. But she does admit to herself that her dreams of love and romance are just grains of sand in the desert of life--her life.

They return to Warsaw, each retreating into their own worlds. The following day they pack and leave for Rome in that same frozen state. Treblinka has writ itself into their hearts and minds, at least into hers.

Before they part at Leonardo da Vinci airport, Grisha makes a feeble attempt to be gracious. He kisses her on the cheek, just as he did that first time in the elevator. She puts her hand up to her cheek just as she had done then and the sensation is just as sweet, though much less intense. She wants to tell him that he was the first man with whom she had experienced physical abandonment, the first time she felt completely liberated from taboos and from the past. That he had validated her sexuality and thus transformed her. But she is silent.

"I am sorry, Batiusha. I never meant to hurt you. But we are different, you and I. To be as honest with you as you were with me, I admit that the girl I once loved came back into my life while you were in Venice, making everything terribly complicated."

Batya cringes but no longer feels jealous. During this emotional trip she had accepted that a parting of ways would be inevitable. They had given each other as much as they could, but theirs was not to become a relationship that would sustain their deeper needs for understanding and commitment.

*Love is the only way to grasp another human being
in the innermost core of his personality.*

— Viktor E. Frankl, *Man's Search for Meaning*

Chapter 22

Toronto, Autumn 1982

On the flight back to Toronto, Batya makes notes of all that has happened since she left home. True love for a significant other is not after all what she had imagined it to be. Madame Berent described it one way as "fickle," Marta in another way as "Men are pigs." *Neither is real. Those are poor extremes. The love I feel for my children is real and solid, like Papa's love felt.* She closes her eyes and leans back in her seat imagining her father's warm hand guiding her safely through the dangerous streets of occupied Warsaw. Then, Grisha beside her on a flight to Poland, too quiet, almost indifferent; in the car with Joseph, arguing about the new dress she was wearing to a party; Julian's angry eyes at the table in the café, and her mother's rejecting words.

Is it because those people couldn't love or can't show love as she has not been able to do for many years, or is she at fault for choosing the wrong people, the wrong men? Her mother? No choice there. Or maybe it is she who cannot love them completely? Emptiness crouches at the pit of her stomach, wearing the harlequin mask from Venice whose hollow sockets lack soul until someone's eyes fill them. Or like the eyes of the Mouth of Truth, empty until light brings them to life.

After what seemed an endless burrow through the clouds, she is back in her Toronto apartment where she finds a letter waiting, in a thick envelope like the one she had received earlier from her mother. She tears it open, her heart drumming up a storm. A stack of pages falls out with a letter.

> Dearest Batya,
> I have been worried about you. Mrs. Berent telephoned me and spoke highly of you. But then she said that she felt you were under a great strain and were roaming the country searching for the truth about your father. Perhaps you have found it already.

I wanted to keep the truth from you for as long as possible to spare you the horrible details of our life in the ghetto. By shielding you, I may have done more harm than good. No matter what you might think of your father, he was a good man.

Let it not be on my conscience any longer that I have been lying to you. It never occurred to me before that I owe you the truth. Maybe I have kept secrets from you for too long.

I am sending you the remaining pages written by your father near the end of his life. I am begging you to return to Vancouver. Your children need you. I miss you. Please forgive me if I have done you wrong all these years.

Your loving Mama

P.S. Max sends regards.

Is this for real? Batya wonders, startled by her mother's letter, her apology and her plea for forgiveness. *Everyone is begging forgiveness these days, including me, but can sins committed against one's children ever be forgiven by them? Can anyone ever forgive themselves for having done wrong to others?*

It is late evening but Batya is wide awake, reading her father's memoir, hearing his voice again telling his story.

Chapter 23

Testimony of Shimon Lichtenberg

Toronto, 1948

If it is true that good dwells in truth, then I pity all you, truth seekers, at least on the Jewish side of the universe where the sun is eclipsed.

In the Warsaw ghetto, we lived amidst lies and surreal scenarios. I saw a man steal a coat from his neighbour when he wasn't looking. I myself visited darkly lit rooms hidden behind armoires where people painstakingly falsified papers for those who had money to live on the other side as Christians and lie about who they were. This was a huge business in the ghetto.

I saw a man greedily choking down a piece of bread as hungry people around him begged to know where he got it; but he wouldn't tell. Nothing was a matter of conscience any more. Stealing and illegal smuggling took place in the most unlikely corners of the quarter because those activities could save you from dying of starvation. I was witness to much smuggling through holes in the ghetto wall. Bribing was rampant, particularly for the Jewish and the Polish police, and even the German soldiers on guard at checkpoints. People said that most Polish police would take bribes to let the smugglers do their job if they could have a part of the take. Sometimes even the checkpoint guards got in on the act.

What people wouldn't sell for money, food or safety! They would sell their soul for a winter coat or a loaf of bread. They would steal food and let another go hungry. The new rules my people lived by were born of necessity and deprivation. Moral behaviour gave way to every man for himself. I began to despise the ghetto community and despised myself even more for having become a hunted animal as well as a predator who would go after what he needed to stay alive.

Most things we did there were merely diversions along the path to imminent death. Can you believe this truth? I myself can barely believe that the torturers devised a scheme by which they used their prey to carry out the torture of their own people.

First, they forced us to build the wall and pay for this partition that cut our population off from the world. Next, they used us to keep the streets free of vandalism, usury and smuggling—or so they said. They used Jews to enforce their curfew and to taunt their own people. Together with—and against—our fellow prisoners, we daily performed the perilous art of surviving.

I wandered through streets full of crazed humans looking for food and work, and looking for an exit from this ungodly place. I even prayed for salvation. Those poor Jewish souls praying by the windows, their frail, yellowed arms barely able to put on the *tefillin*—the leather ties with black boxes holding the Torah, fastened onto their shrivelled arms and bodies davening in the window. And yet, in their half-closed eyes I saw a world of another kind—a godly world of light where faith ruled supreme.

We were all helpless in the ghetto, but I thought that those who were religious had at least the power of their faith. I wanted to believe as I watched them dying. Secretly, I hoped that a greater power existed somewhere in the universe, but if there was a God, then I was angry with him for having abandoned me. When my prayers were not answered, I sought another kind of power, an escape from being a victim.

In 1941 we heard of how Terezin (Theresienstadt)in Czechoslovakia had become a ghetto and a concentration camp at the same time. That is how I saw the Warsaw ghetto, where almost five hundred thousand Jews were methodically annihilated in body and spirit. We had factories where the predators employed slave labour. Starvation, killing, disease and death paraded in the streets dressed in the uniform of the SS. We lived at the point of a gun, surrounded by enemies. People in the street became suspicious of one another. Even former friends and neighbours were suspected of theft, bribery and treason. One good man, whom I knew personally, proved capable of all these transgressions when his life was being threatened daily.

Many broke curfew, cloaked in darkness, to see if they could find a deal for a sack of potatoes or a warm coat, or to hide in some old, half-burned building to avoid getting caught for deportation in a raid on their part of the ghetto.

I managed to find a room for my old father and his brother, my uncle. When I visited them, I'd find them lying listless in bed, next to one another.

The room stank of disease, urine and rotting gums. I tried to bring them soup, but they were weakened beyond eating. I would take Batya to visit my father, whom she loved because he had taught her to read and write. But she became frightened when she saw two sick old men lying side by side, their yellow teeth swimming in a cup of dirty water.

One day the soldiers ordered my uncle and my father out of bed and forced them onto the street. An SS officer told them to bow before him, but my father could not do this fast enough because of his badly shaking legs and arms, as he was suffering from Parkinson's disease. Then the inevitable happened. The uniformed monster shouted, "These old men are useless!" He shot and killed my father and my uncle. I found them lying crumpled on the pavement. I was both terrified and relieved that they no longer had to suffer—as my wife had felt when, not long before, her mother had died of a heart attack. The family had deemed her death a blessing.

Our situation was becoming more desperate by the hour. Money was running out, food rations were lean and it was winter. With no heat or proper clothing, we were always cold, the children especially. I watched horrified as my two girls and my wife were wasting away. Tereska would chew on her hand, creating saliva that she would then swallow, smacking her lips. Batya lay in bed lethargic and staring into space. Marta would stand in line for hours to collect our family's meagre rations, then hope to get back home without someone even more desperate snatching the food out of her hands along the way.

There was no employment available at the Schultz or Tobbens factories where I had hoped to get a job as a guard. Many men were joining the police force. There was no pay for police work, but the police and their families were exempted from being sent to a labour camp. Because I wanted to live and to save Marta and my children, I decided to try to get in. Even if it meant I had to become someone other than the kind of person I was, our situation had made me ripe for this kind of work. Of course, my metamorphosis into another, harsher person had been taking place ever since we were imprisoned in the ghetto.

I went to see an old friend, Reykin, who worked in the office of the Judenrat. I applied and went through the process of interrogation. My credentials were good as I had an honest record of a sizeable legal practice and, to the best of my knowledge, the respect of my clients. I passed. I was given a cap with the insignia *Jüdischer Ordnungsdienst,* an armband with the blue Star of David and over it written, *Jüdische Ghetto Polizei.* With it came a yellow badge as well as a rubber stick. My first job was to patrol the streets after curfew.

For a while we were safe from deportation, but I soon found out that to feed his family, a ghetto policeman had to partake of the black market.

Many of my colleagues, including myself, most of us educated, cultured men, believed that working for the Judenrat in the ghetto was the only path out of harm's way. Although it was not a path that led away from sin—only from the immediate inevitability of death. The Judenrat, that small governing body of Jews in the ghetto, was already despised by the Jewish populace. What the people didn't realize was that the chairman of the Judenrat, Adam Czerniaków, had no real power over his people's living conditions and was completely answerable to the authority of the Nazis.

Adam Czerniaków was ordered to report regularly to the office of the Gestapo, where Commissar Heinz Auerswald hung over him like a vulture over a wasted body, demanding goods and services from the Jews. This was in April 1941, before Auerswald started ordering large quotas of Jewish heads to be deported, at a time when the ghetto was experiencing a relative calm before the tempest.

We consoled ourselves by reasoning that the Judenrat and the Jewish Police were at least better than a governing body composed solely of Nazis and their police. At least Czerniaków, who had to play a double agent, negotiated as best he could for food and shelter for his people.

Jewish policemen were admired at first. They were supposed to keep order in the ghetto—to check the petty thieves and marketeers. We were also ordered to control the children who tried to sneak out to the other side and scavenge for food to feed their families. If caught by the Polish police, they might get away by giving them all of the food. If caught by Jewish police, they were reprimanded then ignored, or maybe asked to give up some of the food. If captured by Nazi guards, they could be shot and killed.

As the situation in the ghetto worsened, the people grew to dislike the Jewish Police, who appeared to wield more power than the average person in the ghetto. They saw Jewish policemen who were neither hungry nor dressed in rags nor begging for bread, so they took out their hate and misery on us, the so-called keepers of order.

In my new position, I patrolled the dark streets watching the smuggling shadows drift here and there, obligated to stop them but not doing so. Some nights I would hear a "Halt!" then shots as the shadows fell to the ground. I learned to hide in the doorways and hallways of deserted buildings.

Every so often a group of German soldiers or policemen would pass by and kill or beat anyone who broke even the smallest of rules. If something happened on my watch, I was called in and reprimanded for not being on the scene. Any Jewish policeman suspected of helping his own people, against German orders, would be severely punished.

One day, on duty as a guard, I found another way of putting food on the table.

Children, being smaller and less noticeable, did much of the smuggling. Men, who took chances with their own lives, devised a system whereby goods were smuggled across in boxes or pots and delivered at night to the Jewish cemetery. We were hired to stop them, but some of us eventually figured, why not overlook their crime if we could get some small reward of food in return for letting them go?

The goods came by devious routes like the Okopowa Street cemetery and were heaped onto wooden carts meant to be carrying dead bodies. Some of the ghetto people were getting rich, but I stuck to smaller pickings.

One evening, a thin boy suddenly appeared inside the ghetto. It looked as if he had slid underneath the wall where bricks had been pulled out. He stood in front of me small and awkward. His pockets and jacket, which he held together with his hands, were bulging unnaturally.

"Please, sir," he wailed. His gaunt cheeks and pale skin gleamed in the moonlight. "My father is starving."

He started to run away but, knowing that I may have been watched, I stopped him, as was my job.

His arms rose up in defence, even though I had no gun. His jacket sprung open and out fell several rolls and potatoes. We looked at each other and I knew that I couldn't take these things away from him, though I was supposed to.

I reprimanded him and he begged me to let him keep the food for his brothers and sisters. He scrambled to pick up the rolls and stretched out his skinny arm, offering them to me. I envisioned Tereska and Batya eating them. Not so long ago, I had fed beggar boys on my street and now maybe, I thought, that act of generosity had turned around. I took one roll and thought, I'll cut it and give each of the girls a half.

How low I fell that evening. I felt like a thief. But when I got home and saw how my little girls greedily filled their mouths, each with her half of the bun, practically swallowing it in one gulp, while Marta, herself starved, looked on, I felt justified. The next time I patrolled the wall, I would take two or three rolls.

I saw a Jewish woman snatching another woman's basket and running away with it. The victim cried for her lost bread as if she had lost a loved one. Another time a man, seeing another man carrying a bowl of soup jumped on him like an animal and, spilling half of it, grabbed it out of the other's hands. The one who had been robbed fell to the ground licking the spilled-over soup. Whenever I could, I tried to look the other way. How could I punish these poor people?

Still, I felt the ghetto people's hate. I saw disdain in their eyes, their manner of speaking to me and the expression on their faces. They were seeing the enemy. And yet, when they flouted the laws, many Jewish policemen covered up for them. Once, several men attacked me in an alley, tearing off my badge, then pulling off my jacket and boots. I had to hit them with my stick, the only weapon we policemen carried, to get them off me, and eventually they ran away.

After many such incidents, I hardened, but not enough. I still had that gnawing in my gut when I saw death prowling the ghetto streets.

The people's hatred for us grew. I felt despised and useless and soon fell into a state of indifference, perhaps as a form of defence. I searched for a way to quit what I was doing and still go on living. But that kind of noble thought belonged to better times. I had abandoned my principles. They didn't matter here. All that mattered now was to get by from day to day. To escape death— to live.

I confess to you that I felt like a character in a Kafkaesque world, where reality was mutilated and distorted. More and more each day I was moving through the hours, doing things automatically, as I was ordered to do them. I was a lawyer metamorphosed into a policeman. I tried to find meaning, even in this distortion of a life. Yet I found myself playing a role in a gruesome plot alongside other once-decent souls driven to immoral acts by our predators.

It was the beginning of the year 1942. I walked through the days and the nights on aluminium legs, patrolling the wall until I'd drop onto a mattress for a few hours of tortured sleep. Even in my sleep I saw the grotesque images of the day's work.

Nevertheless, I continued to perform my policeman's duties under the watchful eye of the police chief of my precinct. One night, I heard a feeble cry at the doorway of a building. A brown heap lay on the pavement. I lifted the filthy rag and saw the face of a child, thin and white against the darkness.

Its eyes were huge medallions filled with tears of pain and loss. For the first time in months, I felt something move in my heart.

In this abandoned child's face, I saw the faces of my own children and what could happen to them, were I or my wife no longer able to care for them. I picked up the withered little body and carried it to the orphanage on Sienna Street. A woman opened the door. From the look on her face I knew that they were overloaded with orphaned and sick children. But she gathered the child into her arms. I told her that I would bring food. The door closed and I, back in the cold, felt warmer knowing that that poor creature would be safe, for a while at least.

I continued to patrol the streets at night to make sure that no one wandered around after curfew. We were finally getting paid, though the amount was meagre, but at least I was able to secure a little food for my family and a degree of safety.

One morning at the Judenrat office, Czerniaków announced that SS-Sturmbannführer Hermann Höfle had commanded us to fill a huge daily quota of Jews to be taken to the Umschlagplatz. Czerniaków said that if these quotas were not filled, many more men, women and children would have to be dragged from their homes and deported to the camps. How to respond? Never had I, nor any of my colleagues, anticipated facing such an inhuman dilemma when we joined the police force.

The deportations began and with them, a reign of terror in the ghetto streets. As parts of the ghetto were raided and Jews taken to the Umschlagplatz, I saw how some of my colleagues had already adjusted to this cruel task. I watched as one of my friends from pre-war Warsaw dragged a Jewish man and woman out of their home, the stony look on his policeman's face revealing none of the compassion I believed he felt in his heart.

Another policeman in an apartment belonging to people about to be evacuated was filling his pockets with money and jewellery as a favour for letting them go. He moved on to the next apartment. My job was to make sure that all the inhabitants were taken to the courtyards for an identity card check and to ensure that the policemen did their jobs. When I went after one man, he tried to slip some money into my pocket. At this point I didn't know whether I was being loyal to this old acquaintance, his eyes filled with fear, or loyal to the Jews who were left behind, or thankful for the money, of which we had so little. I chose to ignore that particular apartment so as not to attract attention, but had to move on to the next. I, too, was being watched by others higher in command.

There were many similar incidents, but I didn't realize until the day we were ordered to raid a certain district in the large ghetto that I had found my dark side.

I admit now I continued this work not only because I was afraid for my family's lives but because I was also afraid for my own. I wanted to live. Oh, how I wanted to live, even when I was filled with disgust and horror at what I was doing. When a group of us raided a building, it was not peaceful and orderly.

I burst into a dingy room. I ordered a woman with a child to come outside. She threw herself at me, her thin arms tugging at my coat. She pulled a wad of bills from somewhere and waved it in front of my face. The greed in me took possession and I was reaching for the money when a German guard's voice at the door hollered "Schneller!" again and again. He pointed his rifle at us, and I quickly hurried the woman and child out of their room into the courtyard. A German officer there checked the woman's identity card and pointed her and the child to the street. There they joined the endless throng of Jews evicted from their homes on their way to Umschlagplatz, where the cattle cars waited to take them to Treblinka. I walked away, my body stiff like a puppet's, while helpless rage burned inside me.

Later that spring, we found out by word of mouth from someone who managed to escape by jumping off the train just before arrival at Treblinka and walking back into the ghetto, that the rumours were true. Treblinka was not just a labour camp but an extermination camp. Many of my colleagues didn't want to believe the truth. Some naively thought the Jews were being sent to work in the East. Now we knew for sure that Treblinka was a death camp, where most people were gassed on arrival. The victims would be told to strip and go into a shower room to be cleansed. But no water awaited them there, only gas. What kind of a vile mind could have devised such a system of rail track and wooden boxcars snaking human beings towards the end of life? Our tragedy too was Warsaw's proximity to this lager.

The machine fed on itself. The ghetto was simply a prelude to the death camp. The Jews did all the dirty work in the ghettos and in the camps. As if by a curse cast upon us, we Jews were forced to lead ourselves to our own deaths.

Perhaps, to survive among beasts, one is forced by the law of nature to become one. It occurred to me that I was living in apocalyptic times that marked the beginning of the end for civilized human beings.

In July 1942 the mass deportations began taking place daily. "Where have you been?" barked Reykin, my supervisor, when I reported for work that first day. "We need help with getting these Jews to Umschlagplatz." He spoke as if he himself were not a Jew. How he had changed from the kind, compassionate man I knew and admired before the war. I wanted to shout back at him, to resist, but could not. I became a coward. Hating myself, I led a group of Jews out of their homes towards the cattle cars.

I will never forget that day. The long line of deportees shuffling into the Umschlagplatz, the smelly cattle wagons standing silent, their open jaws waiting, as Germans, Ukrainians and Latvians in SS uniforms, with rifles and vicious dogs, waited for us Jews to commit their crimes for them and with them.

I wanted to close my eyes so I would not see the mass of Jews walking to the deportation depot, the men, women and children being led to hell and annihilation. Their wailing was so pathetic that, for a moment, I felt relieved not to be one of them. Yet I was a victim in another way: my gut was sour with guilt. I was a tormented man, my conscience a raw wound, yet I couldn't stop. There was no redemption here, only cold-blooded evil. I felt myself going mad. The people tore at my coat and they pleaded but I went on with my task like a robot, unable to stop.

Chapter 24

Batya can read no further. Her eyes are blurred, her soul tearing apart as she chokes down the sobs. *Can I come even close to feeling the agony that Papa must have felt?*

She looks around the apartment and sees another world. Bright and clean, it is now a much more welcoming place than it was when she first arrived from Vancouver. The only thing that needs tidying is the half-empty mug of coffee on the worn table in front of her. *But is that the only thing that needs tidying in my life?*

She has resisted buying more vodka since she returned to Toronto. She should feel stronger for knowing the truth, shouldn't she? She has heard from people who were there, who knew him, that her father was a good and honest man. But now, reading his own testimony, she understands that Shimon Lichtenberg suffered terribly, recognized his weaknesses and, when tested, gave in to his own darkness.

How can she accept this new version of Papa? Can she forgive him for what he has done? For leaving her a legacy of wrongdoing? But who is she to forgive after what she has done—breaking up her home and family?

There are still more pages to read, but she cannot continue. She has been reading for hours, until it got dark and the apartment turned cold. She will put the pages away until she is ready. There is much to do and think about. She has her children to consider. And Joseph to face.

And her mother. Is she closer now to knowing why her mother has shut herself off from the past for all these years? Was it to protect her daughter? To keep her family together, to forget the dark things they did to keep themselves alive? *I must call her,* she thinks. *I must tell her that I better understand why she has kept these secrets to herself, but that it was the wrong thing to do. You don't lie to your children.*

Batya picks up the phone to call, starts to dial, then thinks, no, even though she has reached out to her, Marta will not really have changed. If I call, she will deny what Papa has written. She will only lecture me about how I should be home with my children.

She is not sure she is ready to forgive her mother, but then again, she thinks about her own sins. Has she the right to forgive? Can she ever forgive herself?

She longs to speak with Sam and Miriam. She has missed her children so much. She dials the number of her family home, holding her breath. She imagines the pleasure and puzzlement in Sam's voice when he hears hers. If Joseph answers she will hang up. Several rings later, the voicemail clicks in and she hears Joseph's recorded voice—he even sounds angry in the recording—and she hangs up. What could she say? That she might be coming back… sometime? She has become a coward who doesn't feel ready to face her family. She must finish what she set out to do. She bundles the papers together, empties and rinses out her mug in the sink, then turns out the light and heads to the bedroom. Drained and tired, she tosses and turns, praying sleep will come soon and that it will be dreamless. She will continue reading her father's testimony tomorrow and then decide what to do next.

Chapter 25

Testimony of Shimon Lichtenberg

Toronto, 1948

I know what you are thinking in the comfort of your living room. I ushered the Jews to the trains. Yes, I didn't help them and I didn't push them but I stood there as they were boarding the cars, prodding them on with my stick. I tried to avoid their eyes, but when I did gaze at one and two and then the whole lot of them, I saw in each my own despicable fate. Like them, I was in a humiliating and wretched state of existence.

In another world, when I studied Aristotelian thought, I had thought about the problem of free will. My own people! How could I have dragged them out of their homes? I was utterly unwilling and yet I did it. Something kept me from doing the right thing. In this cesspool of evil, my own once strong will was broken, my soul paralyzed, and only two choices left—to survive or to die.

As the trains were being loaded with human cargo, Nazis ran around with their barking dogs, bellowing orders and pointing guns at us, the police, in case we didn't complete our work to their satisfaction. Once the wagon doors were slammed shut, the train would be moving on.

If he is lucky, a man will have a moment of realization when he knows he must recover some decency in himself while there is still time. That day, I felt it. I knew what I must do when the opportunity arose. I turned to move away from my gruesome task. I remember a German soldier with a dog on a leash making his way towards me shouting, "Machenzi schnell," and then he hit me across the legs with his rifle.

As I fell, the Nazi became distracted by someone's shrill scream. I got up with difficulty and limped out of sight, somehow escaping his attention. I hid at the edge of the crowd, crouching till the pain in my leg subsided. A family was passing in front of me, and I saw the woman swaying on her feet. I forced myself to stand up so I could help her. After that I remembered nothing.

When I came to, in our room in the ghetto, I had an excruciating pain in my back and my head. My hand was clutching a curious round object carved in silver. The face etched on it wore a petrified look, as if in response to a horror it beheld.

Several policemen informed me that I had disappeared from my post at the train loading, thus disobeying Reykin and a German guard. When I finally returned to my post, I was beaten and taken to a local prison. No one seemed to know what had happened between the time I disappeared and the time I returned. I only remember a lot of shouting, then pain and nothingness. Nobody saw me during my absence. Those in power assumed that I had deserted my post and I was suspended from my policeman's duties for five days then taken to the Gestapo headquarters at Aleje Szucha for interrogation.

I was brought into an office. An SS officer pulled out a little black book and shook it at me. I recognized my address book. It must have fallen out of my pocket or they had found it on me while I was unconscious. "What does this mean?" he shouted in German. Then he got up from behind his desk and stood over me, his eyes menacing, his hand pushing the book into my face. I knew what they did to people here.

"You are a spy and for this you will be shot," screeched the SS man. "Unless," he added, suddenly smiling, "you co-operate with us."

There was a loud knock on the door. A German soldier walked in with a click of his boots and a Heil Hitler and said, "Herr Obersturmführer, there are some Jews to see you."

The SS man nodded and walked back to his desk. "Let them in," he barked.

The door opened and in walked the chief of the Jewish Police and Reykin, my supervising officer. I nearly fainted. They were there either to crucify me or to save me. They spoke in German. The chief of police said that I was very useful not only to the Jewish police force but to the German police. I did not understand. Beyond a few incidents of speaking with the German police in good German when trying to pacify them, I had had no dealings with them.

"Get him out," barked the SS man again, pointing at me and smiling at the chief of police.

The soldier took me downstairs to a crowded, cage of a cell where the stench of diarrhea made me gag. Inhuman shrieks came from the end of the hallway where the torture chamber was. My fate was sealed, I thought.

Three days later the soldier who had brought me down returned, followed by Reykin. I was released from the squalid cell and Reykin took me outside, where a rickshaw returned us to the ghetto. I was speechless at this miraculous outcome. Hardly anybody came out alive from Gestapo headquarters on Aleje Szucha.

Reykin confirmed my thoughts. "You're lucky," he said. "Marta came to me at night with your two little girls to plead your case. In the morning I took her to see our chief, who took one look at her and liked what he saw. She begged him to save your life and he gave in, providing she would have dinner with him that night. Marta apparently acquiesced. I cannot tell you what transpired next except that here you are."

Although I recognized the taste of sour phlegm in my mouth, this information took time penetrate my skull. When it did, my thought was, what do we all have to become to survive this inferno?

"But so what?" Marta said when I got home.

"It's disgusting that you had to fling yourself at the chief of police."

"I had to get you released, didn't I?" she cried.

"How did you do it? Did you sleep with him?"

"Look, we had a few drinks, I got very drunk and he offered me and the children a meal. Then they went to sleep in the room next door, while we listened to some music and I remember him kissing me and that is all I remember. I was afraid to refuse him for fear he wouldn't get you out."

Under normal circumstances I would have hit her, but I knew that this would never have happened under normal circumstances—or would it? The drinking was turning her into a slut, I thought. But was I being fair? Relationships in the ghetto were desperate, tenuous and as uncertain as life itself. There were desperate young women who would snuggle up to a policeman for a favour or two. I had given in to temptation myself more than once with one or two women. And after all, she had done it for me. I still loved my wife, so I composed myself and swallowed the rot. I was getting used to its taste.

The chief of the Jewish Police was a convert. He considered himself Aryan and was good friends with the Polish police, since he had once been a colonel in the Polish police force. They threw parties and drank together, sometimes joined by the German policemen. The chief was well liked and had clout among the Nazis. Because Reykin's wife was a sister to the chief's wife, the chief respected Reykin, and Reykin could not have proved his friendship to me in a more persuasive manner. I was definitely beholden to him, and that scared me. I owed him.

Like the chief, Reykin also admired Marta for her beauty. It made her the toast of our division and made it easier to obtain favours from admirers who knew how she loved bimber—a very strong ethyl-alcoholic brew made from potatoes. I found it gut-wrenching but she drank it in large quantities. I knew that she drank to kill the fear. It was the drug that helped her live through these terrible times.

Life continued in the same state of anxiety and terror, particularly now with deportations in full swing, and then what I was afraid of came to pass. Reykin finally reminded me of my debt to him. Each policeman was forced to supply a quota of Jews to the Umschlagplatz, but Reykin wanted me to help him not only with mine but with his quota as well, since he claimed I knew more people than he did.

People were saying that a few policemen had quit their jobs and run away, but I was not ready to throw away my cap and my badge. I felt that I had no choice, I tell you. I was lucky to be alive. Still, the Gestapo had not returned my address book and so I had lost my contacts with the outside world: the addresses of my pre-war clients; information about Jewish friends living abroad and on the other side of the wall, anyone I might turn to in case of need.

It was not in my power to save others, but I had to use whatever power I had to save my family. I didn't realize how desperate I had become until that day I let my children go, when fear for their lives became my master.

A Gentile lawyer I knew occasionally came into the courthouse in the ghetto. I met him there and he offered to take a message to Jan Rogacki. A week later a message came back that Rogacki was willing to take one of my girls. The Rogackis were childless, so it made sense that they could adopt our little girl. Batya was older than her little sister but still only nine. I wanted her to go out first, because her size meant it would be much more difficult to get her through a hole in the wall.

But this wasn't in the cards. Batya fell ill on the day she was supposed to leave and I had to send Tereska, my three -year-old, instead. I put her inside a black duffel bag and took her out in the middle of the night to where there was a hole in the ghetto wall, far from any checkpoint. A friend of Rogacki's was to come to the other side of the wall after I sent word. Several drunken Polish policemen passed by and glared at the bag, but since I had my police-man's uniform on they didn't stop me. They pointed to the bag and cackled, "Black market, eh?" before stumbling away.

My child, huddling beneath the blanket, was quiet as a mouse. After they passed by, I looked inside the bag where she lay trembling. Her big eyes were filled with terror such I had seen before in other children's eyes, and when she saw me, she started whimpering. I took her out and cuddled her till she quietened down. I kissed her face, her hair and her little cold hands. Suddenly I heard a whistle, a sign to let me know that someone was on the other side to take Tereska away. Quickly I placed her back in the bag.

A wave of foreboding washed over me. I held the duffel bag in mid-air, reluctant to pass it through the wall to the man on the other side. Another sense told me it was too late. I quickly completed the act of separation from my child. No words passed between the man and myself. I heard a sob, "Papa, Papa…," from inside the bag, her cries piercing my soul until it bled. Soon her voice and the footsteps faded away and Tereska was gone. Shrouded by darkness I went home numb, unable to cry, as if I had lost my ability to feel.

When Batya got better, it was her turn to leave. I did not know how Batya would survive being severed from her parents, but reason dictated that I must save her from the ghetto. I slurped some of Marta's alcohol to blunt my senses, and then got Batya up very early in the morning, before curfew was over. We walked down a cold dark street. I, terrified that a nasty colleague or a German policeman would spot us, Batya, her trembling hand in mine, eyes petrified in a pale face.

We went to a part of the wall made of wood but laced with barbed wire. Another policeman, whom I had asked to meet me there, helped cut out a plank, making an opening through which Batya could crawl to the other side. Throughout the procedure, she remained pale and mute.

Again I hesitated. I knew that only ten percent of children had so far survived the ghetto, and that the chance of survival on the other side was much greater. My child clung to me, her little body wracked with silent sobs, but when I tried to soothe her and tell her it was dangerous to cry, she understood. She stopped and fell back into her frozen state.

Once she was through the wall and I was still holding her hand, I gave Batya her false identity paper and told her that I would see her soon, knowing well in my heart that this might never be. Someone I had arranged for came to take her away, and I watched my second child disappear around the corner of the Aryan street, clasping a strange woman's hand. I banged my fist against the wall and the barbed-wire prong tore the skin off my hand.

When you sever a tree from its root, it dies. My poor little Batya and Tereska. Would I ever see my children again?

The ghetto Jews kept on complaining, hurling insults at us policemen. They called us a mean lot of thugs. One man called me an "advocate of the devil." and said if it weren't for the Police and the treacherous Judenrat, all his family and friends wouldn't have been deported.

His accusation hurt. But I could understand. Hate flourished here like a poisonous weed. Crazily, I tried to defend myself. "Chairman Czerniaków is saving thousands from deportations by handing over a small quota to be deported. He has to appease the Nazis or they will seek revenge and everyone will go."

I approached the poor beggar and tried to give him a few *zlotys* to appease his misery. His eyes were blazing with anger or maybe it was hunger or simply madness. I wasn't convinced myself that I was telling him the truth. The relationship between Czerniaków and the Nazis was based on the blackmail of cruelty, and in my opinion it rendered the chairman of the Judenrat helpless.

Later I found out that Jacob Reykin, by that time head of the Jewish Police, had been shot and killed by the Jewish underground. Although I owed him my life for getting me out of the Gestapo headquarters, I couldn't help noticing how he seemed to have transformed into a monster, behaving as if he also hated the Jews. "In this hellhole, it's every man for himself, Shimon," he once remarked.

While Reykin was alive, I had tried to distance myself from him. But it was too late. I had become involved with the machinations of the police force and was made Reykin's confidant and right hand. I began to experience the corruption that beset the force as day by day he and other policemen, myself included, got tougher, less compassionate and more compelled to cling to our jobs.

While our children were facing their new lives outside the ghetto, and Reykin was rotting in his grave, the raids on the ghetto homes continued. One day, first thing in the morning, we heard that a section of the ghetto would be evacuated and that the men at our precinct would be commanded to do the job. We filed out onto the street and our new superior described what was about to happen.

"Your group will run en masse, not walk," he ordered, "into the buildings in the designated area. You will enter the apartments and command their inhabitants to get out. You know the rest. They will be sent to Umschlagplatz."

I looked at the men standing in rows around me. Their faces were strange masks both grim and indifferent. The eyes were filled with fear, lips set in a tight line. The cheeks, taut as if set in stone. I might have been projecting my own feelings onto their faces.

"Now go to it," our commander barked. "If not, we will have to answer to the Gestapo." Men treated as beasts became beasts was my motto these days. The hate I had developed for those who gave the orders was eating at my insides. Yet, as I have said before, I couldn't stop. I became a machine without controls, without a turn-off switch. After a raid, I'd hide in some corner like a beaten animal, guilt sawing at my entrails. I suffered pains in my gut, uncontrollable vomiting and diarrhea.

Having recognized a certain similarity in our fates, I became like Reykin. I did help to get people to the deportation depot under orders of my commander and the Nazis. I never killed anyone, although I might have hit someone who was out of control. Still, those who saw what I did despised me. I was undoubtedly a target on the Jewish underground's list.

By now I was desperate to get out of my situation. I thought I might work as a guard at the Schultz factory, where Germans employed slave labour. The Jewish workers sewed German uniforms and fur collars onto jackets. If you were lucky, you got a slice of very old bread and soup made of potato peels. The job was hard to get and the first time I applied I was turned away.

The next time I applied I got it. The Jews working there observed me suspiciously as I, still in my policeman's uniform, stood watch over them, in anticipation of Nazis storming in unexpectedly to check out the place. I thought I could protect these Jewish laborers by warning them of Nazis' raid on the place ahead of time.

I had to get Marta out of the ghetto while I still had the protection of my police badge. I knew of a man who falsified documents. I got what little money I had to give him and knocked on his door at night. He peeked through the curtain and on seeing a policeman, ducked. I forced the flimsy door open and, pointing my rubber stick at his face, made him do as I asked. He worked feverishly to produce two false documents, mine and Marta's.

There were rumours around the precinct that certain functionaries and their families were either being shipped off to Treblinka or murdered, if not by Nazis, by the underground Jews who took revenge on the ghetto policemen of higher ranks. Although I was only a guard now, I had enough of a reputation at the factory to be hated by the Jews who worked there.

The day I sent a message to one of my former clients on the Aryan side for help with Marta, I was again called to duty at Umschlagplatz. The high police command told me that the German police, to whom I was already known for smuggling my daughters out of the ghetto, had threatened that if

I didn't obey this order, they would deport both me and Marta.

I left my post at Schultz and went to the dreaded Umschlagplatz where, once again, I performed my policeman's duty. Again and again the victims begged and pulled at me until I could barely hold myself intact. Yet I went on with my task.

After the cattle cars were shut and ready to depart, I caught a glimpse inside one of the wagons. Huddling together were Marta's sisters and their children. May God, if He exists, forgive me.

Later that day, I received a message from my former client, a kind doctor with a wife and two small children. The message said that if I could get Marta out of the ghetto in the next day or so, he would come to help her only if she feigned illness. I sent a message back via one of the policemen, who had a pass to the other side of the wall, saying that I would try to get Marta out to a German factory in Aryan Warsaw the day after next. At least I could save her. I never told Marta about her sisters. The words were strangled by the guilt I felt for not having been able to rescue them.

Marta was then working at Schultz too, and I got her an identity card to that effect. On the designated day, she had been drinking. By some miracle she sobered up enough to get into the truck of Jewish labourers who were going out of the ghetto through the checkpoint to work in a German factory for the day. We parted without passion, both frozen with fear of what might happen. We could not allow ourselves to feel deeply. Marta seemed almost unaware of the goings-on around her. Yet when she left, I knew that I would feel empty and lonely until I saw her again.

The group was to return in the evening, but without Marta. I had hoped the doctor would have done as he had promised – to come and take her away from the factory on the Aryan side as a woman who had suddenly fallen very ill. She would then be taken to his house and set to work as a governess to his two children, to avoid any suspicion on the part of neighbours who might think that the family were helping a Jew.

Marta was fair-haired and green-eyed and that facilitated the operation, just as this "colouring" helped with our own two daughters. Non-Jews were quick to point fingers at the dark-haired and dark-eyed men, women and children, with darker complexions and large noses. These were the stereotyped Jews, who had to hide in the attics and cellars so as not to be seen, while the fair-coloured Jews could live on the surface, though tread carefully with their fake documents to prove they were Christians. I myself was one of the fair-haired.

According to her false document, Marta was a baptized Christian woman by the name of Eva Rupicki. If the scheme worked, I was to meet her at the doctor's home after I escaped the ghetto. Two days later word came through a friend that the scheme had worked, and Marta was safe.

The following morning, as the ghetto police hastened to the Umschlag-platz for another harrowing day of loading up the cattle cars with human cargo, I threw away my cap and badge and lowered myself into a sewer. I had to tie an old handkerchief around my mouth to stop gagging from the indescribable stench that came from the water around my feet. I was submerged in darkness and mud several feet deep, thick with excrement. The walls themselves seemed to be moaning with the suffering that took place there. Someone's flashlight revealed the white face of a woman bending over an inert child, propped up against the wall by a blanket. Wasted bodies of what once were human beings flitted by like phantoms in the mist rising from the cesspool we were in. I thought of them as fogmen floating through the vapours of the sewer.

They were dishevelled, wide-eyed, with hair that appeared to have risen off their skulls, rags covering their bodies and faces. The singular instinct of a simple animal fighting for survival kept them alive. They pressed on, every so often climbing steps upwards to what were the unattainable stars above these lower depths, but each time they lifted the sewer cover they saw soldiers standing about, and they lowered themselves back into the inferno. Germans knew that Jews were escaping the ghetto through the sewers.

I became one of them now. Horrible nausea kept rising to my throat. My clothes became tattered and smelly, my body drained of strength. I felt as if I had fallen into a bog so deep I could never lift myself out. So many times I wanted to quit. To let myself rest against some wall and die.

I stopped for a while to get my breath and sat there huddling against a wall. How could I get out of this crypt of putrefying bodies and souls? When I was a boy I ran from the outside into myself whenever things got bad. I closed my eyes, trying to obliterate reality so I could go on. Images came to me, expressions of what I was feeling, and instead of seeing rats and victims moving through the cesspool of steam and mud, I saw human creatures as the eternal seekers of truth.

The fogmen blow from the lungs of the past—death-oven ashes and bombs' foul dust. They float beneath the bruised stars of Bethlehem and David in the graveyard hour of the nowhere land. The mother of darkness clasps these human nebulae to her charcoal-nippled breasts filled with tar. And the fogmen grope the grime of the earth, for that crushed seed of truth that once was theirs.

That I could still find words to transcend the evil I was facing, gave me the courage to press on. I was driven in this dark hour by a desperation born of a glimmer of hope—to see the light again and to see my two little girls and Marta. I even prayed to God as I shuffled through the muck.

I don't know how long I lasted. Eventually, through some inexplicable surge of energy, I pulled myself up and took a chance on a manhole cover I could barely lift, thinking, let come what may. I climbed out onto a street bathed in a bluish light. At last I could look up and see the moon and the starlit sky. Thankful to be alive, filling my lungs with air, I flitted, a fogman myself, through the empty streets of Warsaw to the doctor's house. When I saw Marta standing at the door in her grey maid's uniform, I felt as if I were beholding a queen dressed in all her finery.

The doctor helped Marta get the rags off me. They threw them away and gave me clean clothes. I sank into a heavenly bath. After one blissful night of rest, we rose at dawn and, not wanting to endanger the family, we ran into the countryside. Marta, dressed in a peasant skirt with a kerchief tied around her head, I, in a rough pair of breeches, a heavy cotton shirt and a lorry-man's cap. False documents were our only weapons.

Chapter 26

Batya stops reading. There is only so much she can absorb at once. There is too much to process, too much to bear. She aches for her father, mother, her lost sister, and for her lost self.

Her return to Vancouver is imminent. She must gather all her strength to face the family and friends she had left behind so suddenly. She must survive the accusations against her. If she learned anything this year, it is how to fight the feelings of victimization she had been conditioned to feel for so long. She must not withdraw into depression or alcohol for survival. Unless she stands on her own two feet, she will never heal from the wounds of her past. Like her father she must gather her last vestiges of strength and courage to pull herself out of the gutter.

At least it will be easier financially. A letter from Mother's lawyer, Gerald Saltman, has informed her that the written statement from Madame Berent has made it possible for her German claim to be processed. A bulk sum of the claim should arrive soon at her Canadian bank. Besides that, she plans to apply for a job teaching English as a Second Language to immigrants.

She has also received a curious note from Julian Karp. He would like to talk. Would she call him as soon as she returns?

There is nothing from the children. When she phones home again no one answers. She should call her mother and thank her for Papa's notes but decides to do it in Vancouver, thinking that any conversation at this stage would best be conducted in person.

She spends the next few days putting her things and thoughts in order, for her return to Vancouver. When the jetlag wears off, she telephones Karp. Despite her newly found strength and resolve to sound self-confident, she is tongue-tied when he answers the phone.

"Julian, it's Batya. I am back."

"Where were you? I wanted to see you."

"I had to go away. To Italy. What is this about?"

"Italy?" He sounds mystified.

Batya is not about to offer an explanation.

"Never mind then. I don't want to discuss what I'm thinking about on the phone. What are you doing now? May I come to see you?" he asks.

Now it's her turn to be curious. *Why not,* she decides swiftly, and gives him her address. Thirty minutes later, he is at the door handing her a bouquet of yellow roses. He appears more handsome than she had thought him to be the last time they met and certainly more pleasant. He kisses her hand as Polish men do when greeting a woman.

"Thanks for the flowers," she says, surprised but pleased. "Sit down. I'll be with you in a minute. I must find a vase."

She is almost relieved to be in the kitchen by herself for a moment. The roses have a lovely scent but ouch, a thorn snags her finger, which starts to bleed. She quickly runs it under the tap and puts a bandage on the wound, then returns to the living room with the roses hastily arranged in a glass vase.

Karp is seated in a comfortable chair reading from a volume of Milosz's poetry he had found on the coffee table.

"My favourite Polish poet," he says, thumbing through the pages.

"'Campo dei Fiori' is my favourite poem," she says.

"I know it well."

"Then you must know that Milosz, who was not a survivor," Batya continues, "or a Jew, for that matter, chose to speak of the Warsaw ghetto and the carousel in this poem. I find it so inspiring, especially since survivors themselves are still mostly silent about what happened."

"Ah, but you are wrong," says Karp. "Survivors are no longer silent. They are writing, publishing memoirs and speaking. They are giving their testimonies on videotape for posterity. As a matter of fact, I will be looking at those testimonies as part of my work here. If you are interested, I could show you some of them."

"Survivor testimonies on video?" she exclaims. "Yes, I would very much like to see them. Have you videotaped or written your own story yet?"

"No, I have not. But I've thought about it. I always felt that my horrible childhood has influenced the way I cope with things. The problem is that no one, not even our parents, understood what we children went through. And so we grew up silent, carrying in us a whole other world, separate from the reality of the present."

"I find that I have always lived in two worlds. The past one and the present one. Haven't you?" She says, thinking of her Beata and Batya dichotomy..

"Up to a point, I suppose. I have yet to find out what makes me tick," he replies cheerfully. "There is hope for us yet. Although there are still many things I don't yet understand about the past."

"A drink?" she offers, not quite knowing what else to say, and reaches for a bottle of vodka.

"Please. I take mine straight."

"Let's toast to a long and healthy life," she says, raising her glass, remembering Grisha, the gypsy.

They click glasses. He looks around. "Are you going away?" he says, pointing at the open suitcases she has not finished packing and her clothes littering the furniture.

"In several weeks I go back to Vancouver for good. I have children there."

"How old are they?"

He listens with interest as she tells him about Sam and Miriam.

"Do you get along well with them?"

His question startles her. Up till now she has only dealt with those issues herself. Or confided in Antonia.

"Moderately well," she answers, tight-lipped.

"It's not easy, is it?"

"No, it isn't. Do you have children?"

"No, I don't," he replies curtly.

He sounds unhappy. Batya can't imagine Julian Karp being anything but confident, so sure of himself, knowledgeable and mature. Although he is probably not all he seems to be. Maybe he too has his own split personality and like her, can't always cope.

"My children think I am a victim," she blurts out, remembering Miriam's scalding words. Instantly she is angry with herself for talking about her children.

"Yes. Maybe they need to understand better where you are coming from. Problems arise between child survivors and their children," he says. "If you didn't have a real childhood yourself, it's hard to understand your children's feelings and needs and, in turn, help them. But adult survivors often don't want to look at the truth," he continues. "Denial is a mechanism, a cover-up. Think of the carousel in front of the ghetto, its cheerful music drowning out the desperate voices." He looks at her with a wry smile. "Sorry for the lecture."

"So you are saying we are all walking around in denial?" she asks, intrigued and ignoring his apology.

"I think some survivors are in denial and others are simply unaware of how the Holocaust has affected them. In any case, most pass their pent-up feelings and unresolved issues on to their children. Despite their successes in the outside world, they often fail to look into the dark places in themselves and deal with what they find there."

"As I've been trying to do," she says, thinking that Karp has just described both her mother and herself.

"I am sure you've been struggling with this," he goes on. "It's been a painful struggle for me too."

"It is a hell of a struggle, facing the past," she says.

He looks at her intently. "Maybe talking about it would help? As it happens, I will be in Vancouver to discuss the survivors' testimonial project. In the U.S. they have already started taping survivor experiences."

She shakes her head. "The prospect of talking about my childhood frightens me."

"Perhaps your children would understand you better if they knew the whole story."

"I don't think they want to hear it," Batya said.

"But your childhood experience has affected them, whether they realize it or not. Many have to live most of their lives with parent survivors who are silent about their experiences. They do have questions. They want to know why you are the way you are. The group I'm working with on this project calls this the intergenerational dialogue. When they asked me to help them, I took a course on how to interview survivors of trauma."

"It's great that you are helping with this project," she replies, suddenly feeling very tired. She knows her words sound hollow.

He looks at his watch. She dislikes that characteristic in the people she is speaking with. It reminds her of her cold and super-efficient stepfather.

He gets up to leave and she is glad to see him go because the subject matter has exhausted her. She walks with him down the hallway. "I have filled your head with difficult issues," he says apologetically. "Let me give you a hug." He puts his arm around her.

She feels a surprising warmth in his touch. A silent spell of tenderness bonds them to each other for the moment, and she feels better disposed towards him.

"Please let me know if you want me to interview you in Vancouver," he says quietly.

She pulls away, surprised. He might as well have been asking her if he could see her again. People never say directly what they mean. And this is Julian Karp, of all people, the man who hated her guts just a few months ago.

He hands her his business card. "Here, on the back, are the phone numbers where I can be reached in Vancouver. Look, I am sorry about our first meeting. I should not have said the things I did. Perhaps we can continue our discussion sometime next week?"

He is a curious mixture, she thinks. *An intellectual, a cynic and a kind human being. But now he is all business.*

She takes his card by the door and he leaves without any further ado. She thinks of Grisha and his first kiss. But this was different. She and Grisha were at odds about the very things that forge a common bond between her and Julian. She could not be with someone who wanted to forget.

* * * * *

A few days later Julian invites her to hear a survivor speaker. She never heard the term "survivor speaker" before. She can't imagine who would want to hear anyone speak about the Holocaust.

He picks her up on the evening of the talk and they drive to a community centre auditorium where a sizeable audience is already seated and waiting. The master of ceremonies introduces the speaker as a well-known figure in the Jewish community, a philanthropist and a businesswoman.

A combo consisting of a violinist and a pianist are seated on the stage. The lights dim and a woman steps up onto the podium. She speaks of a program for homeless children and says that this occasion is a fundraiser.
Batya looks at Julian. "It's okay. I paid for both of us," he says, taking her hand, but she immediately withdraws it feeling awkward.

A petite, middle-aged woman walks onto the stage and is introduced as Doris Goldstein, a survivor of the Lódz ghetto. There is loud applause, after which the house grows silent and she begins to speak.

Her voice comes loud and clear through the microphone, but it takes a while before Batya actually begins to hear what the woman is saying and before her mind begins to grasp the content of the presentation. It is as if she is resisting the event in some way. Batya has kept her own memories mostly to herself but for a few mutterings to Sammy and Antonia, and a little to Julian. When she tried to speak to Grisha, when he saw how much these memories boiled in her blood, he rejected her. And then there were those here in North

America to whom the Jewish genocide was a matter of "Well, it concerned only the European Jews."

The speaker's passionate tone of voice overtakes Batya's self-absorbed meditation. Doris Goldstein speaks of hunger, imprisonment and the terror of the ghetto dwellers, and she speaks of deportations and the losses Jewish people suffered when forced to leave their homes and all their possessions, then led to their deaths..

"The memories of these terrifying experiences have never left me. They give birth over and over again to feelings that defy language. Yet I and other survivors are compelled to speak of it, regardless.

"People who lived through those times lost their belief in the existence of inborn human dignity and goodness. I, for one, have had problems with trust and faith, although I have not lost hope that goodness still exists."

Mrs. Goldstein's words make sense. Batya thinks of the good and bad in the people she knows: her father, Joseph, Grisha and Bolek, and even herself and her mother. As she listens to this woman's harrowing war experience, she remembers the voices of Madame Berent and Signor Moller telling her their stories. *In a way, this survivor,* she thinks, *is telling the story of others as well, of those who survived and those who died.*

Doris Goldstein is describing the conditions of the Lódz ghetto. "The facts are," she says, "that Chaim Rumkowski, known as the ruler of that ghetto, was given more power by German authorities than his counterpart, Adam Czerniaków, chairman of the Judenrat in Warsaw, although like Czerniaków, he was completely answerable to the Nazis. But because of his efforts in industrializing the ghetto population and its huge productivity, the ghetto lasted longer than Warsaw's. The Lódz ghetto existed until August 1944, when the remainder of its population was transported to the death camps of Auschwitz and Chelmno. It was the last ghetto in Poland to be liquidated. Some 18,000 people in the ghetto are believed to have died during a famine in 1942, and altogether, about 43,500 people died from starvation and disease.

"On one occasion, Rumkowski pleaded with parents to give up their children for deportation so the rest of the population might survive. But I, still a child, survived this purge by helping a man in a paper factory. He later hid me in a wooden crate and covered me with cardboard while the children, hundreds of them, marched to the trains destined for Chelmno, where carbon monoxide in gas vans killed them. I ask you then, how can one not feel guilty for having survived?

"Eventually, we were deported to Auschwitz," she says with difficulty, "and from there onto a death march in freezing-cold January of 1945. Survival was almost nil. We were sent on this march to die. A few of us survived…and here, words fail me.

Thank you for listening."

Her voice breaks down and she takes a glass of water and speaks no more until the question period. The auditorium is as silent as a solitary cell. Batya feels humbled by the words of this survivor and by her suffering, so much so that her own story seems unimportant. She is grateful to Julian for bringing her here.

After the talk, they line up to say a few words to Mrs. Goldstein. When it is finally their turn, Batya hardly knows what to say.

"Thank you so much for sharing your experiences with us," Batya tells Mrs. Goldstein. And suddenly tears come. "I was so very moved by your words," she manages. The petite woman touches her shoulder and nods, looking at her knowingly.

There is a line-up of people behind her, but Batya stops to ask a question that has been bothering her. "Do you think the child survivors, the ones who were not in camps but survived as hidden or ghetto children, have worthwhile lessons to teach?"

Doris Goldstein looks Batya straight in the eye. "My dear girl, but of course they do, and so they should teach."

Batya and Julian leave the hall arm in arm. They part on a friendly note and promise to see each other in Vancouver.

On the plane Batya takes out the last batch of her father's notes.

Chapter 27

Testimony of Shimon Lichtenberg

Toronto, 1948

Night fell and we were deep inside the forest. Once I loved the thick fern, the mushrooms, the berries and the tall trees surrounded by moss. Now the forest threatened us with prowling Nazi guards and their dogs, hooting owls and, above all, the terrible darkness. We dug ourselves deeper under a tree where there was already a hollow in the ground. We covered ourselves with our thin coats and fell asleep, hoping no one would find us.

As soon as light filtered through the branches, we rose and went farther, towards a neighbouring village. We ran aimlessly from hamlet to hamlet. Marta's shoes were so worn her toes were sticking out of them. We had to fill them with leaves.

We came across a band of underground fighters who at first turned their guns on us, then mercifully let us pass without questions as we really looked like two village peasants. Even when we lay down to sleep on those cold and terrifying forest nights, and even though I was too numbed to reflect upon it fully, in the far reaches of my mind those few bloody days at Umschlagplatz were inscribing a permanent stain on my conscience and into my dreams.

We became fugitives. It was spring and still very cold and unwelcoming to those fleeing the enemy without a roof over their heads. We ran into other Jewish nomads like ourselves wandering the forests and the fields. They told us that the last group of Jews to be deported from the Warsaw ghetto had resisted the Nazis and fought for the honour of all Jews, holding up the final front before Hitler completed the destruction of the ghetto.

"You should have seen them," said one young Jew, who had fled with his mother because she wouldn't leave the ghetto by herself. He told us of how the Jews got ammunition by trading with Poles. They built bunkers where they hid from the enemy but at daylight scattered themselves in places from where they could shoot. They stunned the Nazis with their meagre weapons and a small group of fighters held them off for a few weeks, and the Nazis fled. "But the bastards returned," he said, "with an even stronger army machine. They burned the fighters out of their dark bunkers into the light of day, only to be shot and killed. To the end they were a triumphant army, our ghetto Jews."

Hearing him speak I felt ashamed of having escaped and wished that I had been one of those brave young people.

We could trust no one. One night at a farm where a peasant had let us hide out for a few nights in exchange for a gold bracelet, we saw the vermilion sky over Warsaw and we heard this peasant laugh and shout, "Hey! Can you see? The Jewsies are frying!" The ghetto was being levelled.

On the run again, we moved from barn to barn, sometimes sleeping beneath the forest trees wrapped only in our coats. We crept like hunted animals towards the town of Otwock, where Rogacki, who had taken in our daughter Tereska, lived. When we knocked at his villa gate after dark, he came to the door, opened it a crack and, having seen me, said, "Go away. Your presence here can only bring us trouble. Everyone around here knows you and Marta, and someone will only end up reporting you and us to the Gestapo."
"I just want to see Tereska," I begged.

Rogacki told us that was impossible. He said the he was hiding her elsewhere because someone had already told neighbours that she was a Jewish child.

"Then lead us to her. Give her back to us," I implored.

The open crack in the door narrowed as Rogacki added, "That is a bad idea. Go away quickly before you are found out." The door slammed shut.

I could hardly believe that my good friend would deceive us. But I suspected that something was very wrong and that he was keeping the truth from us. Troubled by our child's uncertain fate, we crept away from the Rogacki villa towards a nearby town, midway between Otwock and the hamlet where Batya was staying with the couple Mrozek.

After miles of walking through an endless field of harvested wheat, we reached the town but avoided the main road for fear of being discovered. With what strength we had left, we pushed on until we came upon a lonely farmhouse at the edge of town next to a forest. A large hound almost jumped over the fence as we approached, barking ferociously and exposing a set of large, sharp teeth. Just as the dog was about to launch another attack, a man rushed out of the house and called him back. The dog sat quietly next to his master, but continued to growl.

The man opened the gate. The dog followed him from behind. With no small amount of trepidation I approached him. He was tall, middle-aged and dressed in a brown jacket, beige pants and high leather boots. Next to him, I felt like a beggar in my mud-stained breeches and a torn coat. Marta's clothes were also soiled, her face tired and smeared with the earth on which we slept and crawled.

The man looked at us quizzically.

"What are you folks seeking here?" he asked politely.

"We are from Warsaw, where we lost everything in the bombing. We are looking for a place to live and work," I said, having no idea what work I was fit for there.

"May I see your papers?" the man asked.

I groped in my pocket for our false identity cards.

He examined them carefully and then scanned us up and down.

"Hmmm. Felix and Eva Rupicki, baptized Catholics," he read slowly. "Many folks lost a great deal in this war," he said. My hunch told me that the man was kind and maybe even compassionate.

"I have a room you can have, but I live alone with my young daughter and need a housekeeper. In exchange for lodgings, some food and a little pay, would your wife be willing to take this on?" he asked now, examining Marta, who had managed to wipe the dirt off her face.

"Also," he continued, "I need a forester for cutting trees. Can you do that?" he asked me. I eagerly agreed both for myself and Marta, knowing nothing about cutting trees.

"Good then. Your room is in that little house near the barn. You will find all you need there."

My instinct proved to be right. The man was humane, and I had the feeling that he knew we were Jews. I thought then that if it hadn't been for decent Poles, many Jews would not survive. And so we started to live quietly in this seemingly uninhabited part of town. Marta, who never knew how to cook, did a fair job of cooking simple meals consisting of soups, stews, potatoes and vegetables. Fortunately she didn't have to go to market, because the farmer had a cold cellar where he kept potatoes, turnips, carrots, onions and apples as well as sides of bacon and fat sausages hanging on a string. When he'd go into town he would ask Marta if she needed things like bread and butter. In fact, he and Marta got on famously. More than once, I'd catch them laughing and sipping tea mixed with spirits. I didn't interfere, so long as it didn't go further.

It was the end of 1943 and I found myself at loose ends. I didn't want to endanger Batya by visiting her at this time. The hell I had left behind was still churning inside me, and I spent all my angst on axing trees. In that task I had the help of one peasant who was always drunk and unsuspecting. Or so I thought.

One day, the tree he cut fell on me after he yelled that it was going the other way. He came up, looked at me with crazed eyes and slurred though the large spaces between his teeth. "You folks don't belong here," he cackled. "What is a guy like you doing felling trees?" Then he stomped off. I picked myself up and felt a sharp pain in my left side from the tree, but more than that I felt danger lurking.

Thankfully, he vanished after the tree incident. I had to be in bed for some time to heal my injury. The blow exacerbated the beating I had received from a Nazi officer in the same area of my body. My lower back and left kidney never stopped hurting even after I got better.

One Saturday morning at dawn, on our day off, Marta and I decided it was time we walked over to Mrozeks' place. It was cold and dark outside. The endless fields were covered with snow. We hung on to each other and trekked through the blowing snow like members of a lost tribe, wandering through an icy desert. We heard noises made by animals and people, and after a while it was hard to distinguish one from the other. By late afternoon we reached the hamlet. I knew the house and street from a previous visit, before the war, where this couple, grandparents of our friends, lived. They were very poor but had offered to take in Batya for a small sum of money.

The shabby house stood darkly against a clouded sky. There was movement behind the white lace curtains, and candles shone through here and there. Though we were out of the ghetto cauldron, we felt that danger still lurked. Marta shivered next to me while I clutched tightly against my chest the only gift I had to give to Batya.

As we approached the hut, I thought I saw my daughter's little face in the window. The feeling of seeing her again was hard to contain. So filled was I with gratitude and gladness for this moment that I ran like a crazy man up the stairs and pounded on the door. The old woman opened it and there was my girl hiding behind her as if she were afraid of us. Had we changed so much? Her face was very pale, with huge blue circles underlining her eyes. When I took her in my arms, she felt as fragile as a flower that had been plucked and left to wilt by the wayside.

She put her thin arms around my neck and I felt her tears on my skin. I handed her my gift. She sat on my knee with a frozen expression on her face and a body that was as tense as an arched bow. She stretched out her hand and gingerly took the pouch. The silver disk fell out onto her lap.

"What is it, Papa?" Batya asked timidly.

"It's something of a mystery," I replied. "Think of it as a secret we must one day unearth." The strange little silver disk with a face on it was the object I had apparently brought home one day from Umschlagplatz, but I could not remember how it came to be in my possession.

The old woman, Lena, was nervous. I saw it in the way she fidgeted and looked first at us, then out the window. "I am waiting for Bolek," she said, twisting her bony hands. I knew she wanted us to leave. We were a dangerous burden.

We stayed only an hour and as we were leaving, Bolek staggered into the hut very drunk and mumbling incoherently. The two men who brought him in eyed Marta and me with interest and suspicion, or so I thought. I took Lena aside and told her where we were staying in case she could bring Batya to us. After the ghetto, I didn't trust anyone. I had learned to take chances that had helped to save us all so far. All except Tereska, and I could not get her off my mind.

Saying goodbye to Batya was painful both for us and for her. Her little hand would not let go of mine. She clung to me like a leaf to a branch shaken by wind. I could hardly let go of her. I was bruised by goodbyes. And besides, I was worried about the drunken Bolek. What if he told those men that Batya was a Jew?

The next weekend, I left Marta at home and set out for the Rogacki villa. It was deserted save for the toothless caretaker, who knew me from before the war when I would visit the Rogackis. He said that the owners had all left and he didn't know for where. He was lying, I felt it. I interrogated him, trying to intimidate him, but he gave me no information. I had no recourse but to return home to Marta, who was in despair as well. We imagined the worst but not nearly what was yet to come.

I went back several times but each time was told that the Rogackis had left for an unknown destination. When he spoke, the caretaker averted his eyes, never once looking me straight in the face. "I would stay away if I were you. You will be recognized," he warned me. I knew him to have been a decent man once, so I took his advice and left. Only the crazed dog barked at me, foam dripping from his jaws. After that, I stayed away from the Rogacki villa.

We went back to our unheated cottage, where we stayed throughout the winter of 1944, huddling beneath a pile of blankets Marta found in the owner's home. Somehow we survived, occasionally going into the big house to warm up in the kitchen. We decided to wait till spring before we made another move to try to get Tereska back. By then, I thought, the snow would no longer be up to our knees when we walked for miles without proper shoes or coats.

But by that time, the farmer was keen to get rid of us as the Nazis were everywhere, taking food from the local farms. He decided to move to another town. Marta and I were becoming more and more desperate to know what had happened to our child. Our family was scattered around these unfriendly villages. By now it was December 1944, and we thought maybe the end of the war was in sight when we heard the sound of cannons booming from the East. The Russians were advancing, but no one knew for sure if they would defeat the Nazis.

We had to leave our room and on Christmas Eve, Marta and I stole into the first barn we came upon in a small village not far from where Rogacki lived. We crept inside undetected and huddled in the hay, where at least we could sleep. The next morning the farmer-owner of the barn stomped in drunk, holding a bottle of brew, and found us. He was not like the others, scared of strangers, but in exchange for a few nights' sleep accepted Marta's woollen sweater and a cameo pin she had managed to salvage from the ghetto.

"It would do for the wife's Christmas present," murmured the man, who introduced himself as Antek Kozukh, between swigs of bimber. He even shared the rot gut with us and so it warmed up our empty stomachs.

Feeling restless, I started rummaging around the barn and found a piece of wrinkled cardboard and a child's mostly used-up box of paints tossed into a corner. I needed to express the love and the longing I felt and the frustration of not being able to hug my children and tell them that this too would end someday. Dipping the worn paintbrush in a bit of snow outside, then in the leftover paint, I was able to paint flowers as a symbol of the two girls I so loved. What came out were lilies of the valley, next to which I wrote a poem that I kept till this day.

> Lilies of the valley, fragrant bells
> Infant faces on lithe stems

Sisterly souls, golden sunbeams
You strain your arms towards your absent parents

Flutter white bells, ring out wistful and tender
While the wind bends your heads and clouds hide the sun
But wait! When the wind dies and the sun awakens
I will gather you into a bouquet once again
And fold you close to my heart.

Papa
Written on Christmas Day, 1944
Hiding from the Nazis in a Polish village

I was hoping to give the poem to Batya when I saw her next. It gave me some comfort to think of our reunion.

Soon, however, the worst of all things happened. I suddenly saw Rogacki though the partly open barn doors. Then, when he pushed them wide open, he loomed big in the doorway, and my heart was bursting through my chest. He walked over to where Marta and I were huddling in the hay on the barn floor and hovered over us. I stood up while Marta lay almost frozen on the ground. He was always taller than I, but in the days of our youth it never mattered. It did that day.

"Where is Tereska?" I managed.

"Where is Tereska?" he mimicked. "If anything happens to her, you have yourself to blame," he said. "I told you not to hang around the villa, where you are known from before the war. You aroused suspicion among the folk. Someone informed on her."

"Where is Tereska?" I repeated. So he is blaming me, I thought, for something he is guilty of.

"Your daughter is in the hands of the Gestapo. I promised them a bribe to get her out."

His words were like a hot poker into my belly.

"I want you to sign your apartment building in Warsaw over to me if I am expected to get her out."

What a bastard he was. How could I have ever trusted him? I couldn't think straight. What to do? The father in me wanted to do everything possible to save his daughter's life, in case Rogacki spoke the truth. The lawyer in me strongly felt that what he said was a hoax and blackmail.

He had betrayed our friendship. He was well dressed, well fed, bearing the posture of someone with power like a Gestapo man and not a second-class citizen as most Poles were during the war, other than those who had joined the underground. That is how I saw him—so much so that even big Antek, the peasant, looked scared. I was fairly certain it was Antek who had given me away to him.

Rogacki pulled out a pen, a piece of paper and a gun, then called Antek to witness the signatures.

I hesitated.

"If you don't sign right now, I will expose Batya's place of hiding and she will be taken by the Gestapo and then who knows?" he said in a commanding tone of voice.

I signed without another thought.

I gave away my building in Warsaw to him. It was all I had left to return to if I ever lived through the war. I was nothing now. A nobody. Then I heard Marta whimper from the hay and realized that she still needed me, as did Batya.

Although it was now dangerous to stay in Antek's barn, we had nowhere else to go. I could not bring myself to look at Antek; I so wanted to kill him. Still, Marta and I agreed to stay there that night.

After the other men left the barn, I left Marta alone for a few hours and went back to Rogacki's village, asking anyone I met on the road if they knew of my daughter and what had happened to her. Folks in these villages knew everything that went on, but as before no one wanted to tell me anything, until an old peasant smoking a pipe said he recognized me from before the war as Rogacki's friend. He told me to follow him if I gave him some tobacco. I happened to have a few cigarettes, the last of my supplies.

The man took me to the edge of the village forest. He picked up a naked tree branch and started digging the frozen ground under a tree. He poked and he poked. "Here," he said. "Look for yourself."

I wished my eyes were burned out. I wished I were blind. I saw a ditch poorly covered with earth, which partly exposed a pair of little legs clad in socks and worn little shoes that resembled the ones Tereska had been wearing.

I stood there dumbfounded. I was denying the nightmare that was really happening. My body was rejecting this with every nerve and muscle. Of all I had been through, nothing matched this. I was certain I had lost my senses forever.

"She was murdered three days ago," he said matter-of-factly.

So Rogacki already knew my daughter's fate when he had come to blackmail me.

I left the peasant and crept away like a wounded animal. One thing I knew for certain. I would not tell either Marta or Batya about this. Let them think that our daughter was lost to us. Crazy thoughts buzzed in my head. How did I know for sure that those were her legs? On the way home I pulled my hair out of my skull in exasperation. To think I had been stupid enough to send my daughter to a traitor.

On return I found Antek waiting for me. "Don't you know," he said, drunkenly slurring his words. "The mister that came to see you was a Gestapo man. You know what I mean. I couldn't help what happened."

I hit him in the face I don't how many times, until he lay lifeless on the ground. His wife ran out of the house screaming. I grabbed Marta's hand and pulled her away from there. We ran until she could run no more. We rested somewhere. In my foggy mind, nothing mattered.

After another long trek through a huge field in deep snow, Marta and I found a place where the owner allowed us to stay in his barn in exchange for housekeeping chores. The sound of the booming cannons came closer and closer; the Russians were nearing our village.

The next day I took Batya away from Lena and Bolek. My child was in tears, saying that Bolek was not being nice to her and was doing dirty things. I believed her, even though Marta thought Batya was making up stories.

"How important is what he did to Batya, when he saved her life, Shimon?" Marta said. I didn't agree with her, but there was no time or way to go back and deal with the man. I believed my daughter because I knew that she always told the truth. The day I took Batya away from the Mrozeks, the child was frightened to the point that when I touched her shoulder, she jumped like a wild thing. I contemplated once more the dual nature of man and how good and evil could coexist like conjoined twins.

I had to tell the man who took us in that Batya was our niece, because the names in our papers were different. Batya would have to call us uncle and aunt. From the day I brought her to us, she became mute and wouldn't say one word. We lived in that room, the three of us as best we could under the circumstances, with Germans still crawling about but never suspecting who we were. The Russians were coming closer and closer. When I found out that they had liberated Warsaw, I decided to set out on foot to find living space for what was left of my family.

In Warsaw, I found some old friends who were good to me, among them the doctor who had rescued Marta on the Aryan side and taken her in until I got out through the sewers. I found an apartment in one of the few buildings still standing on Lwowska Street; I was also offered a job in the provisional government of Poland in the legal department.

I went back to the village to get Marta and Batya, but they were gone. The man where we lived said that they had packed up and left after I did. So I travelled back to Warsaw and wandered the city streets for days looking at every face of woman and child I passed by. I went to every corner of the city that was familiar to both Marta and me.

Finally, I ended up on the street where we used to live, from where we had been driven to the ghetto. Clutching at the last straw of hope, I found our building still intact. I walked into the courtyard and there beside a dried-out fountain were two human beings sitting dejectedly on their suitcases—Marta and Batya.

We hugged and cried for what seemed like hours. They told me that after I left they had managed to follow me on a train with Russian soldiers. I told them I had a place for them to live on Lwowska Street and I had a job. As the three of us walked down the debris littered street past the drunken soldiers and general chaos, I felt that despite everything that had happened, the three of us were together. Somebody from above was being benevolent and forgiving, I thought.

Our happiness was but a short sojourn from misery. I now had to counter the threats and the gossip spread by my former friend Rogacki, who had become an avid enemy. Since I had given him the rights to my property under pressure, I accessed all my known contacts and managed to secure my property as still belonging to me. I felt that justice would be done once the courts knew that I had been blackmailed.

Marta and Batya, with whom I had not shared Tereska's fate, kept asking questions about her. I could not bring myself to reveal what I still found hard to believe. I couldn't speak of it as it was too terrible, so I deluded myself into thinking that maybe by some miraculous intervention Tereska was still alive and what I saw were another child's legs.

After many months of searching, I contacted Rogacki again, only to have him chase me away with a gun in his hand. Then he had the nerve to call me a Nazi collaborator and a traitor to Poland. I returned home a bitter man, never divulging any of this to either my wife or my daughter.

On Marta's insistence, we spent weeks after the war visiting convents, schools and orphanages in Warsaw and the vicinity. Maybe by some miracle we would find Tereska alive. We were given free access to these places, to various classrooms where students would stand up as we entered and we, in turn, would search each girl's face, hoping to find our lost child, only to leave bitterly disappointed.

"She must be dead," said Marta after days and days of fruitless searching. Rogacki had disappeared as suddenly as he had surfaced and was nowhere to be reached, nor was his wife or his mistress. It was the most difficult thing we had to face—the loss of our daughter.

In the meantime my brother-in-law from Canada eventually found us through the United Nations Relief and Rehabilitation Administration and asked that we go there as soon as possible. I wasn't keen on leaving but my wife was adamant.

"We have lost everything," Marta said. "Tomek is my only family. I want to see him. I must! I hate living among the ruins around us and inside us. I want a new life," she cried.

Neither she nor I wanted to live under the Soviet occupation of Poland and the possibility I would be forced to become a member of the Communist Party, were I to survive my present government post.

Personally I did not think that a complete renewal in our lives was possible, even though I wanted it to be—if not for me, for my family. I had no recourse but for the love of my wife and child to comply with Marta's wishes and leave Poland for a better life in North America, without knowing the fate of our beloved daughter Tereska.

Finally, tired in body and spirit, we arrived in Toronto, Canada. Soon after our arrival, I felt pain in my body where I had been injured. After many trips to the doctor and several surgeries, I found out I had cancer.

The various roles I have had to play in my lifetime have left me with just one—a Jew with a terminal illness, imprisoned in bed by my ailing body. During the time of my illness, I even tried to launch a suit against Rogacki, leaving the case in the hands of a very good lawyer in Poland. But my foe came to court with the same terrible accusations against me and the case was thrown out. I had lost. With Rogacki, the score remains unsettled.

For the loss of Tereska, I blame only myself. I should not have placed her with Rogacki.

If I had to live my life over again, I would do some things differently. Although I didn't manage to save my younger daughter, I would still have given my life and the lives of others to save my family from death.

The other day, Marta was out working and I lay as usual in bed and in pain in a dark room, trying to scribble the last words of my testimony. On the other side of our bedroom, divided by a partition we built, to give Batya some privacy, I saw a light and supposed that my daughter was still up, listening to the radio. Unable to stand the loneliness and the pain I was feeling, I called out to her.

She quickly came to my side and asked me, "What is the matter, Papa?" But I didn't have the breath to respond. I knew my end was near. I wanted her to promise not to forget what happened to us and the Jewish people.

Mostly I wanted to ask her to forgive me. I knew she wouldn't understand, but I felt that one day she would. She looked frightened. Perhaps this was too much to ask of such a young girl. I squeezed her hand and felt her answering response. I tried to sit up, but the pain was getting stronger, so much so that I must have fainted.

The next thing I knew, an ambulance came and took me away. I was glad to be away from the place where I had created such unhappiness. I saw Batya looking out of the window when they were lifting me into the ambulance. As the ambulance screamed down the street, regrets raged in my head. A man wants to settle scores and make amends before dying.

I thought of my parents. I no longer felt the bad blood between me and my father. I no longer agonized about my relationship with him. But I will always wonder whether he loved me.

My mother, who loved me more than life, died in an obscure village where she stayed after the war. It was only two weeks ago a letter arrived to tell me that, and I grieved. She died alone, as we had left Poland without her. I secured some money for her from the sale of a small property she owned with her siblings. But money does not assuage loneliness. Only Batya cried when we were saying goodbye to her. Marta never did get along with my mother, and I was always busy. I had it in my mind to bring her over once we settled down, but now it is too late for everything. Mama, please forgive me.

I beg forgiveness from G-d , my family and my fellow Jews, and leave myself to their judgment.......

Chapter 28

Vancouver, Autumn 1982

The writing breaks off. Papa was obviously in a great deal of pain even as he wrote these final words. *The word forgiveness again,* Batya thinks out loud. *The impossible and difficult word that is supposed to cleanse us from all our sins, erase our heartbreaks and deaden our memory. Dearest Papa, for so long I have longed to hear from you, about you. I have lived on the memory of your love for me, and that alone helped me survive. Thank you for this and for your difficult but honest words.*

The flight attendant stops at her seat. "Are you all right, ma'am?" she asks.

Batya nods yes. But is she all right? Could this woman and all those sitting around her watching her cry even remotely comprehend what she has just read? The flight attendant stoops to pick up some of the pages that have slipped onto the floor of the plane. She thanks the woman, slips the pages into her bag, and straps on her seatbelt, readying herself for landing.

There is no one to meet her at the Vancouver airport and she is glad. With Papa's words echoing in her head, how could she possibly smile in greeting? Besides, she hasn't even phoned the children to let them know she is coming. *This is all wrong*, she thinks. *This constant distancing of mine must stop, this being a "remote control" mother.*

Antonia has offered Batya her home while she and her family are away. Batya declined. She wanted to return quietly, on her own terms. In fact, she has made a reservation at the old Sylvia Hotel till she gets her bearings, till she finds a home to go to. Vancouver makes her nervous; it now feels much less friendly to her than Toronto, which she would never have left had it not been for the children. She came back for only one reason: to make them believe that she never really left them, and that none of what happened between her and Joseph was their fault.

She drives her rental car through the quiet Vancouver streets. The hotel at English Bay is near Stanley Park, an oasis of lush greenery almost in the city centre. Autumn is beginning to paint its colours on the deciduous trees, and the evergreens, firs and cedars, gleam in the sun like dark emeralds against the vast stretch of water and mountains.

At the hotel, she telephones Sam and Miriam. Sam's nineteenth birthday is coming up in a few days, and the family always celebrates by throwing a party at home.

"Hi, Mom," Sam says. "Why didn't you let us know you were coming? Are you back for good?"

"I have much to tell you, sweetie, but not now."

"Mom," says Sam, his voice strained.

"What's wrong, Sammy?"

"Miriam is upset."

"Why?"

"The housekeeper quit. You know how Dad relies on Miri. Even with the housekeeper there, she still has to do everything."

Of course Miri is upset, Batya thinks. *The poor girl is carrying a load that should have been mine, her mother's.*

"On top of that," continues Sam, "Dad's girlfriend wants to move in."

Batya shouldn't be shocked. She wasn't exactly alone in Rome; why should Joseph wait for someone who isn't there? It is childish of her to have expected him to. Antonia had intimated in one of her letters that a number of single women were already standing in line for him. Yet she has never thought of Joseph with another woman. She has always felt him to be there, if not exactly a safe harbour, at least a mooring place. But now he is no longer there, not for her.

"Tell Miriam not to worry," Batya says, hiding her dismay. "I will speak to your father and be there soon, so together we'll get the house ready for your birthday," she says, feigning good humour.

At night she lies awake, thinking about how things at home are changing. Joseph is planning a life without her and she will have to plan a life of her own. Unable to sleep, she looks in the newspaper's classified section and underlines several possible places for rent. She can't possibly stay at Antonia's, with the cats and the occasional domestic quarrels and she can hardly afford to stay in a hotel.

In the morning she reluctantly phones Joseph at his office to ask whether she can come to the house and help with the birthday party. "I can't talk to you now," Joseph replies, "but yes, do go to the house to help the kids with the party," he says curtly and hangs up.

Batya immediately starts looking for an apartment. After a day of hunting, she finds one that is furnished and ready to move into a week from today.

In the next phone call she makes, her mother invites her to lunch. The conversation on the phone is as usual: careful and brief. "You will tell me all about your trip," says her mother. There is no mention of Papa's notes at either end.

"For sure, Mom. Will Max be there?"

"I don't know yet. Why?"

"I don't feel very comfortable with him after what happened. I know he doesn't approve of me because I left Vancouver."

"Can you blame him? He wants the best for you."

Always the same line, Batya thinks. *Do what others think is good for you.*

"Okay, Mom. If he is there I'll try to make it bearable."

"I can hardly wait to see you," Marta says in a softer voice.

Me too, Mom, Batya says to herself, but she can't say it to her mother.

* * * * *

The next day in the afternoon, Batya sets out for the family home weighed down by a myriad of negative emotions: guilt, anxiety and regret. The same canon of feelings she had just before she crashed into the wall, when she had lost her ability to think clearly. *Stop it,* she tells herself. It has to be different this time. There has to be hope and love for Sam and Miri or she hasn't learned anything. She will face them without excuses for having left.

She gets out of the car more determined than ever to be strong. The front garden seems both familiar and strange. Only a few flowers are still blooming, mostly wild rose bushes climbing up the side fence. She has lived here for many years through ups and downs.

The children should be home soon, and she is excited at the thought of seeing them again. Her key still works and the door springs open. Misha, Sam's miniature schnauzer, barks from his bedroom and runs towards her, baring his sharp teeth. Going from room to room with the dog at her heels, she sees that everything seems the same, the house still in its unfinished state and sadly messy. She used to keep it clean and tidy; now the floor in the kitchen is filthy and the sink is filled with dishes. In the bedrooms, the beds are unmade and there is soiled laundry on the floor. She goes to work with a bucket of water, sponges and soap. Like a penitent nun kneeling on the floor, she scrubs, mops and wipes. She fixes up the bedrooms and after three hours, the house is clean and order restored.

She is emptying the dishwasher when she hears the front door open. Seconds later, Miriam walks into the kitchen. "Hi, Mom, what are you doing here?" she says. There is surprise in her voice, but she doesn't walk over to kiss her mother as she normally would.

Maybe it's natural, Batya thinks, *given the time we have been apart.* "I wanted to surprise you," she says. But when she tries to kiss her daughter on the cheek, Miriam withdraws. Batya makes an offer of tea to Miriam, quite forgetting that she is no longer the lady of the house.

"Sorry, Mom. No tea. Just a cookie. I can't stay. I have to go now to meet a friend," says Miriam quietly, avoiding her mother's eyes. For a moment she stands by the kitchen door looking uncertain.

Batya notices that she is wearing eye makeup. Discreetly, but visible. "Can we spend some time together next Saturday, go shopping and for lunch?" Batya asks.

"I'll let you know," Miriam says, quickly turning as if to leave again. The apparent rejection of her mother's invitation creates an even larger space between them.

"The house looks neat. Bye," Miriam says quickly taking a cookie from a jar and is out the door faster than the blink of an eye, leaving her astonished mother nailed to the ground.

In a while, Sam comes home.. He is taller, she thinks. Time did not stand still while she was away. "Hi, Mom," he says with a big grin, giving her an equally big hug. "I don't understand why you didn't phone from Toronto to let us know you were coming back."

Batya tries to explain. "I am not sure, Sam. I wanted to be settled before I called you. I don't want to be a burden to anyone."

If Sam feels anger towards her, he doesn't show it. As a young boy, he expressed interest in her childhood and her life in Poland. Batya was afraid to tell too much, too soon. When a troubling memory would surface, she'd tell it to Sam in fragments. He'd listen until she finished, then ask questions. He gave so much of himself, more than a child should have had to. And now he is almost an adult.

"What have you been up to, dearest?" asks Batya.

"Guess what? I made it onto the V.C. baseball team. I'm playing outfield," Sam tells her, light shining in his blue eyes. "And I want to go to law school after college and become a lawyer like your dad was."

What a happy thought. She watches his animated face and feels the gladness she has always experienced when talking to her son. But today something is different. It is a new feeling. It is as if she has been frozen all these
years, unable to unleash the love she knew she had for her children but could
not feel.

"I love you and Miri so much," she tells him. "More than I could before.
And I am so proud to have you for my son and daughter." She gets up from
the table and cradles his head in her arms.

Though Sammy is as affectionate towards her as he was before she left,
he is on guard, like Miriam. No more mush, she decides, and they start to
make plans for the birthday party.

Time passes quickly. It is almost dinner hour and Joseph will be home
soon. Her first impulse is to worry about their food. She looks in the fridge
but it is empty. She wants to tell Sam she would gladly cook for them, but is
afraid to give the impression that she intends to stay.

"It's okay. Dad is taking us out to eat," says Sam, sensing her confusion.
"Mom, are you here for good?" he asks.

"Yes, darling boy. I am in Vancouver for good."

"Miri and I think that we did something to upset you and make you
leave."

So that's it. Maybe at last an opportunity has arrived to set some of this
straight.

"No, dearest, it's not your fault. It has to do with your father and me and
my own problems. I came back to explain this to you and to try to work things
out."

Sam looks at her without his usual brightness. "I'll try to understand,
Mom," he says and kisses her on the cheek. "I've got to go now. Just came in
to get my baseball glove."

After the door closes behind Sam, the house feels empty and no longer
her own.

The next morning, she wakes up remembering that this is the day of the
lunch at her mother's. Bracing herself for blame and guilt mongering, she sets
out for Marta's place, determined not to let herself be victimized. She knew
that her mother sided with Joseph, and felt betrayed.

"Thank God you're back," says Marta at the door and kisses her daughter
warmly on both cheeks. Batya gives her mother a bear hug.

"Where are you staying?" Marta asks.

"I've rented an apartment," Batya tells her.

"Are you happy now with what you have done?" her mother snaps.

Here we go again. Will she never consider my feelings? Batya wonders.

"You should have gone back to Joseph," Max pipes up, regarding his step-daughter with contempt.

"You do not understand what I was up against," says Batya, looking at her mother.

"What problems could you possibly have had with Joseph?" asks Max. "A nice house. Great children, great husband."

"Stop it, Max," says Marta. "We have been over all this before. It's no use. Batya has had problems. That's why I decided to send her Shimon's memoir."

Max nods and is silent.

"I thank you both for that," Batya says. "But it's been hard for me to cope with all that you have managed to forget, Mama." *What the hell; the truth has to come out.*

Marta is silent for a moment. "I have already asked you to forgive me. Soon it will be your turn to ask your children to forgive you. You have hurt them deeply and if you don't repair the damage now, you may live to regret it for the rest of your life."

It's the first time her mother has said something constructive to her. Something Batya can understand and something deep they can share.

Marta suddenly bursts into tears and hides her face in a dishtowel. Max looks at his wife quizzically. There is a smell of burned onions coming from the kitchen. Batya runs in to turn off the stove then embraces her mother, who now looks pale and tired. Max, who has followed them, walks away looking disgusted.

"I am sorry," Marta says, putting her arms around her daughter. "Sorry not to have told you. Those were terrible times."

Batya hugs her mother's slight body. "It's okay, Mom, I understand. You've been through an awful lot," Batya says, stroking her mother's hair.

"I do love you, Batya," Marta says between sighs.

"I love you too, Mom."

"Let's have lunch, you two," Max calls impatiently from the dining room.

They sit down at a table already laid with salads, cold cuts and dumplings with overly fried onions. Marta recounts an anecdote about one of her neighbours. Despite all the problems between them and Mama's disapproval of her, Batya has missed her mother. After an hour and a half of small talk, Batya leaves with her mother's apple cake in a bag. The visit turned out better than she had expected and she doesn't feel guilty or blamed. Whatever the past may have been, she wants to work towards a better relationship with her mother, even if there are still far too many complex and hurt feelings to explore and to heal. And maybe Max isn't so bad after all.

Over the next few days, the phone seldom rings. She spends long stretches of time alone, but when Antonia returns from her vacation, they meet and talk over a glass of wine, happy to be together again.

"You have to understand that your reputation in this community has been compromised," Antonia tells Batya with her usual candour. "People gossip and pass judgement."

"What was I to do?" Batya says. "I had to preserve my sanity. I could no longer pretend I was the person everyone expected me to be. I heard somewhere that people's jealousies and prejudices prevent you from being yourself. They want you to be like them, or else."

"I know," says Antonia. "I knew all that before you left. You were at the point of a nervous breakdown. Tell me more about Grisha, though," she smiles wickedly, gulping down her wine.

Batya shakes her head. She really doesn't want to talk about Grisha. She is determined to focus on the present and the future.

"What are you going to do about Joseph?"

"I spoke to him briefly but haven't seen him. I'm trying hard to build up enough courage to do it. But I think it's over." They both grimace at the thought.

After Antonia leaves, Batya drinks a cup of strong coffee and musters all the energy she has left to go and see Joseph, to find out if anything besides anger could still exist between them.

She can see him through the window of his office, seated as usual at his desk. He seems to be in deep thought and is staring at something in front of him. She pauses for a moment, then opens the door and gingerly walks into the office.

On seeing her, Joseph frowns. "How are you?" he asks, not looking at her.

"Fine, thanks," Batya says in a matter-of-fact tone, then leaps in. "Would you like to go out for coffee and talk?"

"No," he shakes his head and looks about as if afraid that someone might be watching them.

Batya sits down in the chair opposite Joseph, as she did the last time, in the same room from which she had once fled in anguish. She is trying not to get upset. *But of course he is reacting to what I did to him,* she thinks.

"I'm sorry things didn't work out between us," she says bravely.

"You left," he reminds her. "Remember?"

Yes, I left, she wants to say. *I left because I felt unloved—because I was hurt, verbally, psychologically and financially. Because I was suffering and no one wanted to know. I am not saying I did the right thing, but there are bruises to prove it, even if they don't show.* She wants to tell him all this but cannot because she is afraid of sounding weak and of the tears that will make her maudlin. She chooses silence.

"I'm remodelling the house, and the children's rooms, of course," he informs her. His tone of voice warms when he speaks of the children.

"I understand you have met someone," she manages. "Do you love her?"

"Yes, and I don't want to hurt her feelings. I want a divorce."

His words cut like barbed wire. She had never until now truly entertained the finality of their relationship. Even though she embarked on an affair with Grisha, it was never with the thought of replacing Joseph and asking him for a divorce. There is nothing further to discuss. It's over, as she had told Antonia.

She feels shaky all the way to the car yet she must fight feeling helpless and powerless with all her might. Didn't she promise herself never to feel victimized again?

Her thoughts run helter skelter. *Joseph is entitled to have a life now that she lives elsewhere. Okay. Joseph. I am sorry...no hard feelings. It wasn't all your fault. How could you have understood what you have never experienced?*

Even though she has only said these words to herself, she does understand Joseph better now. Even if he didn't help much, he too was a victim of her angst. No more of that, she hopes. At least now that Joseph has found someone, she no longer needs to feel guilty about leaving him. The most important relationship for her now is with Sam and Miriam, and she will not let anything or anyone stand between her and her children.

She goes back to the hotel to pack. In a few days she will be moving again and life will start anew. There is a letter from a local college inviting her for a job interview. She is glad she had given the Sylvia as her Vancouver address. She had almost forgotten sending in her application for the position of an ESL instructor while still in Toronto. For a moment, the letter distracts her from the unhappy meeting with Joseph. She wills herself not to think about it. Nevertheless, at night, when she tries but cannot sleep, the word "divorce" goes round and round her brain, until the phone suddenly rings.

"Hello?

"Hi. Batya? Julian Karp here. Sorry to be calling so late."

"It's all right," she says, surprised. It was only yesterday Antonia had returned home and Batya had given her the new telephone number.

"I'm in Vancouver this term for the series of lectures I told you about, and I'm wondering if you would have lunch with me at the Faculty Club on Monday. I am leaving tomorrow morning for the weekend, so I wanted to speak to you before I leave. Will you come?"

"Yes, thank you," she replies without thinking. "I'll come."

"Fine. I look forward to seeing you on Monday at noon."

She is glad he called. Where would he be going away for the weekend and with whom? But why should she care? She has more important things to think about now, like Sam and Miriam coming for dinner on Sunday and her job interview on Monday morning.

It turns out the apartment had been vacated sooner than she expected. She spends Saturday moving her things and putting them away. She brightens up the rooms with flowers and sets the table, wondering whether on Sunday evening she and the children will have a serious talk about the family. She wants so badly to work on her relationship with them, but where to start? The old fear returns.

On Sunday. Sam walks in first, one arm behind his back. Miriam follows behind her brother. She seems cautious and reserved. Sam looks around approvingly. "Nice place," he says. She detects wistfulness in his voice. He must feel strange about her living here instead of at their family home. Sam's arm shoots out from behind his back and he thrusts a bouquet of red carnations into Batya's hands with such zest that Batya nearly keels over. They all laugh at the spontaneity of the moment.

It feels so good to have them here. They eat their mother's familiar food with appetite. During dessert, Batya begins to fret. She reaches for the wine on the kitchen counter. Soon the liquid seeps into her blood, warming her, making her feel less anxious. She brings the wine to the dining table. The children listen quietly while she begins to talk.

"I did love being in Europe," she begins. "It felt like home. Rome was magical, with all the ancient ruins, and Venice, a city on the water without automobiles. And Poland was beyond imagination. Someday maybe you and I will go there together.

"But what I really want to do is explain to you why I left. Why I was depressed. My past came drifting back and I could not cope with the problems it brought into my life. And this, compounded by your father's lack of understanding..."

Her voice breaks and the inevitable tears that she cannot stop roll down her cheeks. Knowing full well that she is on the wrong path, she continues her tirade of complaints and blame as if she is sitting in court as a witness in her own defence. How she hates herself at this very moment and yet she is unable to stop.

They listen, finish their Cokes in awkward silence and, after a few exchanges about Sam's birthday party the next weekend, it gets late and the children decide it's time to leave. Batya feels she is driving them away.

What a hopeless failure she is at trying to communicate with them. What a whiner—and inebriated at that! This has happened before. Will she never be able to approach them from a place of composure and courage without the booze, the goddamn tears and a lump in her throat? And she had thought she was stronger.

She must pull herself together. She must think of the next step to take. She lifts her wineglass and sees there is only a drop left so she reaches for the bottle and pours herself a bit more. As always, she thinks of her father, the love he had given her, his one gift that kept her safe—that now keeps her from drowning again. She would like to give this gift to her children, but today she has failed.

* * * * *

On the day of the job interview, the secretary at the desk takes her name. Soon Batya is shown into the office of the head of the English department. Mrs. Brown, an attractive, dark-haired woman , is seated at the desk perusing what appears to be an application form.

"Please, sit down," says the woman, motioning her to a chair.

"I see that you have an ESL certificate from George Brown College. Have you done this work before?"

"No, I haven't. My only experience is that I was an immigrant myself who didn't understand a word of English, and I know how it feels to sit in school understanding nothing, getting behind everyone else and then failing grades. And I watched my mother struggle to communicate with people in stores, on the street, anywhere where people spoke only English."

"You have good reason to want to do this," says Mrs. Brown and writes something down. She asks a few more questions, but Batya senses these are mostly formalities. She is readying herself for some hard questions about her work experience when Mrs. Brown says, "Let's try you! Welcome to the staff.

I'll send you the necessary information."

"Thank you so much," Batya says, shaking Mrs. Brown's hand, exhilarated at the outcome of the interview. "I promise to do my best for the students."

* * * * *

At the Faculty Club, Julian is already in the lounge, reading.

"Good to see you," she tells him.

"Likewise. Come sit by me," he says, stretching out his hand.

She feels shy. Time and distance have cooled some of the previous familiarity between them. She walks over to the couch and sits down next to him.

Over lunch, their conversation flows with ease.

"I'll be teaching ESL," she announces.

"Where?"

"At a college. I am looking forward to it and yet I feel a bit anxious. Will I do well?—that kind of thing."

"You will do whatever you choose to do. Remember that you have a will and lots of potential to use it well."

"Yes, Professor Karp."

"Hey. Call me Julian," he says, laughing at the formal address.

She likes his eyes. They are soft, not harsh like they were the first time she met him.

"Are you married?" she asks, unable to help herself.

"Divorced. We didn't have much in common, except food and parties," he says with slight sarcasm. "What about you?"

"My marriage is at an end," she replies, not offering an explanation. She wonders if he has heard any gossip about her.

He doesn't pry. Somehow, after this confession, she feels the space between them has contracted somewhat. They talk about the educational aspects of speaking about the Holocaust to students and writing memoirs, never mentioning her father or the war. When a pretty waitress comes with the bill, Batya follows Julian's eyes as she walks away. Grisha would never have let a pretty girl go by without ogling her, but Julian's steady gaze is fixed on Batya.

"Too bad I have to get back to work. I would love to stay and talk to you."

"Thank you for lunch."

"My pleasure. When can I see you again?"

"You can call me," she says, surprised at her nonchalance and at the fact that he wants to see her again.

In the evening, Batya phones Sam to tell him about her job. "It won't be much money, but it will help."

"It's a start, Mom," he agrees with enthusiasm. As always, he makes her feel positive about herself. *No wonder,* she thinks. *Sam has always reminded me of Papa.*

* * * * *

On the day of Sam's birthday party, she arrives in the early afternoon with a profusion of flowers. Nobody is home so she opens the door with her key. The note on the kitchen table reminds either Sam or Miriam to pick up the birthday cake at a bakery where it has been ordered. She scribbles on the note that she will get it.

Soon she is back with the sumptuous *dobosh* torte, a layered affair with chocolate cream between thin sheets of French pastry that they have always ordered for this occasion. Miriam is in the kitchen arranging flowers in crystal vases.

"Thanks for getting the cake and the flowers, Mom," she says quietly. They work together in silence, setting out the cutlery, napkins, plates and other dishes. It feels good. The house begins to look festive and ready for the party. Several helpers arrive. Joseph must have hired them to assist with serving.

Batya goes home to dress. She wraps Sam's gifts of a sport coat and a game she had bought him and then leaves again for the house.

Joseph and Sam greet her at the door, and Sam's face lights up with a grin when he sees her. Despite their bitter exchange a few days ago, she kisses Joseph on the cheek. Some of the guests have already arrived, and Batya notices Miriam talking to a young man. What a shock to see her daughter with a boy, and the boy she is talking to seems very taken with her. Has she ever really seen Miriam? Her daughter is all dressed up and has grown this past year into a lovely young woman.

Her mother and stepfather arrive and, behind them, all the members of Joseph's large family. They have always been good to her and, even now after this period of absence, they greet her with warmth. Joseph's family has meant a great deal to her. They made up for all the aunts, uncles and cousins she had lost during the Holocaust, and at their frequent gatherings, she found comfort and belonging. Although she has always liked them, she has never been fully aware of this feeling of deep appreciation she has for them until now.

Dinner is served, then the cake. Everyone sings "Happy Birthday." How wonderful it feels to be here, celebrating Sam's birthday. Just as Sam is about to cut the cake, the doorbell rings. Joseph goes to answer it and returns with a woman whose arm is hooked through his. She strides confidently into the living room with him and they stand very close together while they speak with the guests.

This must be the girlfriend! Batya freezes. She had not thought this woman would be coming to Sam's birthday party. No one introduces the girlfriend to Batya, who stands aside and watches this stranger kiss her daughter and her mother-in-law and make herself at home—the home that Batya had built and inhabited for years with Joseph. The woman acts as if she were a frequent visitor here. She walks comfortably through the rooms giving orders to the help in the kitchen and dining room. She is tall, red-haired and thin. Batya thinks her face is hard, but knows she is biased against her.

She wants to say goodbye to the children and slip out unnoticed. Why is she so surprised? She knew that Joseph had a girlfriend. This is now the new reality.

"Why are you leaving so soon, Mom?" Miri asks.

"I don't feel comfortable in this situation."

"Mom," Miri says in a defensive tone of voice, "Dad needed someone. He hates being alone. You know that."

There it is in black and white from her daughter's mouth. As if she didn't know this herself.

"Yes, of course. I do understand," Batya manages and gives Miri a hug. *Now don't you get maudlin,* she tells herself. She gives Sam his gifts, explaining she has a headache. The look in Sam's wise eyes tells her that he knows and understands. Her heart is pounding as she scurries away like a rabbit.

Though she has come a long way from who she was just a few months ago, it is still not far enough, she tells herself. But she is moving away from her life with Joseph just as she left behind her other self—Beata. Another era in her life has just ended and she ought to move on.

Chapter 29

"What a perfect apartment," says Antonia, presenting Batya with a box of chocolates and bottle of wine, both of which they waste no time opening. "Well, almost perfect. Of course, it doesn't exactly mirror your two personalities."

"Beata no longer exists, my sarcastic friend."

"I am serious. Maybe you're wrong. They might have merged into one strong woman."

"You must be kidding," says Batya, never having thought of this possibility. "Maybe you're right," she says. "I do feel stronger, although sometimes I still screw up."

"There you are."

"The apartment suits for the moment. It's central to most places and has the basics until I can get my own furniture."

"You'll soon have it the way you like it, so here's to you, kid," says Antonia, raising her glass of wine, her mouth full of chocolate.

"Some kid." Batya rolls her eyes.

After lunch, a letter arrives with a Polish address. Batya suspects that it might be from the editor of the town newspaper who promised to write about Tereska. She is afraid to open the envelope for fear of what she might find inside, but her eager fingers tear it open anyway. The editor informs her in Polish that following publication of the story and photo, a gentleman who recognized the young girl seated in the grass next to Tereska came to the office and left a number where the girl, now a physician, could be reached in the United States. He suggested that this woman might know what happened to her sister.

Once again, the door of disbelief and hope opens onto a conflicted world. Maybe this is her last chance to find closure. She has spent years thinking about her little sister either dead without a known grave or alive somewhere, growing up among strangers, not knowing her real family. And now, so many years later, is a chance to find out the truth about what happened. Yet the task at hand seems so enormous that she pushes it away for a moment. She wishes Julian or Sam were here with her while she makes the dreaded call. *Not yet,* she thinks. *After class, which starts in an hour or should I cancel it?* But she is driven to make the call. After what seems like years she hears the ring then a voice on the machine that asks to leave a message. She must go to class.

Teaching has been a healing process. There is purpose and meaning in giving one hundred percent to her students and, in turn, gaining their respect. She feels a strong connection to them, helping them explore their new language and culture, and this does much for her self-esteem. She will get on with it and do her best.

She telephones Julian. Lately, she has been turning to him more at times of anxiety and doubt.

"Can we meet after my class? I need to discuss something with you."

"Would you like to discuss it over an early dinner?" he asks, sounding surprised.

"Yes, very much," she says, annoyed with herself. Anything to delay the phone call to this unknown woman.

Julian arrives in the evening looking handsome in a black-and-white tweed jacket and crisp white shirt. She hasn't taken much care with her appearance. Her mind is elsewhere—back on the dark planet and the letter.

"My divorce will be coming through in the spring," she tells him in the car, trying to concentrate on the present. "I'm sure you've heard that I left my husband and my children. People talk."

Julian shakes his head. "No one has said anything bad to me," he replies.

She is grateful for that. Gossip and judgment in this town have been harmful, hurting more than she allows herself to feel.

"I am still trying to rebuild my relationship with my son and daughter, but without much success," she says.

"Don't blame yourself for everything," he tells her. "Even if you hadn't left home, eventually your history would still have been an issue between you, your children and your husband."

She shies away from her purpose in meeting Julian. The rotating restaurant does not seem appropriate for this conversation, particularly since they are now drinking wine and her thoughts are flying like birds going south. Here they are in the heart of Vancouver, situated on the top floor of a highrise. The necklace of lights clasping the shoreline sparkles against the midnight-blue sky, while the water and the mountains remain silent and black in the growing darkness, like her nagging problem. The waiter lights the candle and takes their order for dinner.

"How did *you* get out of the ghetto?" she asks. *It is far easier to talk about someone else,* she thinks, holding back the fear that builds up in her mind whenever the past comes calling.

Julian's fingers start twisting a napkin with such intensity that his knuckles turn white as he talks about his escape. It sounds much like her own. They have more in common than she had realized.

Batya senses how hard it is for him to speak about this time in his life. He speaks deliberately, as if in a trance and far away. She sits quietly, listening, feeling almost guilty for making him reach that faraway place in his memory.

"We were liberated by the Russians and returned to Warsaw," he says. "As you know, the city was devastated. We were petrified, paralyzed. Everything we once had was gone. Somehow, with the help of a Canadian cousin and my mother's perseverance, we were able to immigrate to Toronto." He stops and sighs, as if in relief for having reached the end of his story.

But is it the end? Batya wonders. *How long does it take to really end?* It seems, from the stories she has heard from other survivors, that the experience stays with you until you die, and perhaps it does not end even then. But one must learn to live with it and cope. If only she had understood this months ago.

"What happened to your father?" she asks.

"My father was shot by a Nazi while trying to escape the ghetto. The whole group were shot and killed, we were told, and buried in a common grave." His voice falters. The ensuing silence seems a fitting memorial to the memory of both their fathers and to the fact that both she and Julian escaped death from the same place and, in much the same way, both miraculously survived. *No more need be said,* she thinks.

"We can proceed with your testimony as soon as you feel able." Julian looks deeply into her eyes for the first time since he finished talking about the war. "I am writing a book on relationships between survivors and their children and would like you to give your testimony as a part of my research. You will have to speak in front of a camera."

"So, I am a mouse in your laboratory," Batya jokes, hoping to lighten the mood.

He laughs. "Heavens, no. Rather a fly in my web. Don't worry," he adds.

"The benefits of this will be there for you as well. You will see."

It feels so liberating to laugh with him. Here is someone who, besides being educated and wise, has the ability to be honest and open. He can get close to someone without playing games. She knows that he likes her, but in what way? Soon he will be going back to Toronto. She mustn't get too close. They finish eating and she is thankful when the dinner is finally over and he drives her home.

She invites him in. Now is the right time to tell him.

They sit down on the living-room couch and she pours each of them a liqueur. She shows him the letter and the article.

"I would ask for your confidentiality in this," she says.

Julian nods. "No question," he replies, reading the article first.

"And you have lived all this time thinking your sister could be alive?"

"Yes. I have never given up hope."

"And what now?" he asks.

"Now I have to phone this woman—the little girl in the photo who played with my sister—and we both have to time-travel back to 1943. She has no idea who I am. And I don't know if she will talk to me about Tereska."

"You must call her, now," Julian says firmly. "I will stay with you. It is still early so she won't be asleep."

Batya sits down at the desk in front of the phone and, with an unsteady hand, dials the number, her mind searching for the necessary words.

A woman answers the phone.

"Hello. May I speak with Dr. Alina Bialik?"

"This is she."

"My name is Batya Lichtenberg. I am calling from Canada. You don't know me. I have an important question to ask you."

She looks over to Julian, who nods at her, whispering, "Don't be afraid."

"Go ahead, I remember that name. Is this by any chance about Tereska?"

"Yes." Batya forges ahead sweating each word, "I am her sister, and we never really found out what happened to her. I got your telephone number from a man in Otwock who says he knows you, though I don't know his name."

"I heard about this through the newspaper article they sent me. I can tell you what happened."

Batya grips the receiver, waiting for the woman to speak. The woman seems candid and willing to unearth a difficult subject. Batya listens, afraid to breathe.

What Dr. Bialik says next is too devastating, too impossible to take in right away. The words keep coming but the horror story simply doesn't want to register.

"And on top of it all," the woman continues, "I hated my uncle, Jan Rogacki, who as you may know was my mother's brother. He was mean and greedy. When they went out in the afternoons they tied Tereska to a doorknob like a dog, so she wouldn't go anywhere or be seen by anyone. When the Gestapo found out he was hiding a Jewish child, he saved his life by giving away a cell of Polish underground fighters who had a hiding place at the edge of the forest. The next day the Nazis went there and shot them all. That's how patriotic he was."

"Thank you for this," Batya whispers into the phone.

"If you need more information and I can help you, don't hesitate to call me. Take care."

Batya puts down the phone. Hiding her face between her hands, she sits inert at the desk. No tears come. Something inside her stomach twists and a bitter taste makes its way into her mouth. The worst is the hopelessness she feels. How can anyone ever heal from such a loss? Will the world ever change, or must people go on suffering because of the chain of fear and greed, prejudice and bigotry?

Julian puts his arms around her and she lets him hold her.

"Do you want to tell me what she said?" he asks gently.

How can she speak of it? What the woman has told her is unspeakable and yet another secret that her father must have taken with him to his grave. They sit quietly for a few minutes. The warmth and closeness of Julian's arms eventually stop her body from shaking, and this terrible knowledge that she now has seeks an outlet or she will burst from it.

"My sister, who was younger than I, was also alone, hiding with Father's friends, who proved to be traitors—at least the man was, for sure. Someone had informed on her and the Nazis took Rogacki, his wife and my sister to the Gestapo headquarters. There a Nazi officer ordered a Polish policeman to shoot the Jewish child—my sister. The policeman refused, but the Nazi pulled a revolver and threatened to kill him and his family if he didn't obey, so the policeman gave in. He picked up a ball lying on the lawn and threw it down the road and told Tereska to run after it. When she started running after the ball, the policeman, under the gun pointed by the Gestapo, shot her in the back."

The look of horror on Julian's face reflects her own and the grief she is feeling. He enfolds her entire body tightly, as if protecting her from the world.

Only after she repeats the unspeakable truth to Julian, does it sink in. How will she tell mother about the murder of her daughter?

"When you are ready for my testimony, let me know. I will be ready, I hope," she murmurs into his shoulder. Her former paralysis giving way to defiance.

"I understand," he says quietly. "Let's go for a little walk," he coaxes, and helps her into her jacket.

They linger under the tree in front of her building. It's chilly and dark but the three-quarter moon brightens the night. Neither speaks. What can there be left to say? He kisses her on both cheeks, like a father at first, then softly on her lips. His tenderness and compassion coupled with the revelation of human barbarism are more than she can bear. She pulls away and stands with her back to him.

"I will call you when it's time for the videotaping," he says, still holding her hand, seemingly unfazed by her pose of rejection. "I would like to do it next week, if we can."

She nods in agreement. He lets go of her hand. "Do you want me to stay with you tonight?" he asks softly.

"I think," she says, "I would rather be alone for now. But I am grateful to you for tonight, and for being here for me."

So much hinges on trust and affection. She knows that now. She had used those words but never understood their true meaning. She could not trust Grisha, after he showed how little he cared for what she felt. Nor could she trust Joseph, whose interest in her seemed superficial through lack of understanding. But it was so different with Julian. He did not twist the truth to serve his own interests while ignoring hers.

Julian turns to walk away and is soon gone. His leaving stirs something familiar in her—the same feeling of loss she experienced when she had to let go of her father's hand, that day she escaped the ghetto. Only this time she knows that she is staying to face whatever comes.

But now there is only one thing on her mind, heavy with the burden of a terrible knowledge. Once the door closes on Julian, despite the late hour, Batya telephones her mother.

"Mom, I have something to tell you. I would like to come over but not talk about certain things while Max is there."

"Come tomorrow morning for coffee. Max will be at work."

"I will be there around ten o'clock."

* * * * *

The next day, Batya enters her mother's apartment with dread. How is she going to tell her this despicable thing about Tereska? What words can she use to describe this inhuman act to a mother about her child?

Marta greets her at the door smiling and visibly happy to see her daughter. She has changed this past year, Batya thinks, softened a little, and is not as hard on her about Joseph. Batya cringes, envisioning the look on her mother's face when she shares her new knowledge. For the first time since Papa was ill and Marta was beside herself with grief, Batya feels compassion for her mother.

"Mom, I have news about Tereska."

"What can you tell me about her that I don't already know?"

"About how she died," Batya whispers.

Marta looks at her daughter. "I know how," she says calmly. "I have known it for a long time but did not want to upset you."

"You mean about the shooting?"

Marta nods.

"But I thought Papa was never sure about her death. I grew up under the impression that she might still be alive."

"Do you think that we would have left Poland not knowing what had happened to her?"

Batya feels hot with shame at being treated like an idiot by her parents.

"Why didn't you tell me? Why do you always lie—about everything?"

"Your father took a while before he could tell me. And when he did, I told him that if you found out, you wouldn't be able to handle this information emotionally. I had a difficult enough time and I was an adult. You were only eleven years old. Besides, we didn't want to keep on filling your head with the past. We wanted you to forget it and get on with your life."

Batya is speechless. Is her mother completely out of touch with reality? Batya had already experienced horror and persecution at that young age. Her mother has never understood to what degree the past has been living inside her daughter all these years and still does. And to think she'd let her suffer, not knowing about her sister. If she was alive or dead.

"When did you find out?" Batya manages to ask, despite the rage in her belly.

"Your father found out while we were still in Warsaw. He wanted to keep it from me, but I kept searching for her, and finally he told me why there was no point in continuing and that we would never find her."

The old helplessness returns, together with all those ugly emotions she thought she had conquered. She hates both her parents at this moment. *Is there no end to family treachery? Why didn't Father write about this in his diary?*

"But all these years. Why didn't you tell me when I got older?"

"I wanted to forget."

Just like Grisha.

"But you had no right to make this decision for me."

"I am sorry. You are right. I should have told you." Marta doesn't sound convincing and her voice is hollow like it was the night Papa died. No emotion.

Does her mother even feel what she is saying? Batya wonders if she can ever trust her about anything again.

"I asked you to forgive me in the letter I wrote to you. Now I am begging." Marta starts to weep.

Forgetting her outrage, Batya puts her arms around her mother. *This woman has also suffered and has hidden it to be able to just live,* she wants so much to feel her mother's pain, not just her own.

Chapter 30

A middle-aged woman with a strained face stares back at her from the mirror. She cannot move past the phone call to Alina Bialik, nor the scene with her mother. Her hands are unsteady and her eyes are red.

The doorbell rings and she sees through the peep hole that Julian is at the door with a young man from the film school. She lets them into the room where they are to set up for the video and, excusing herself, rushes back to the washroom mirror to tidy her face and hair. She has to go ahead with her testimony today. *Be positive,* she thinks. Yes, definitely, Antonia is right. Beata and Batya have integrated. There is in her Bea's determination to go on living and Batya's need to express everything hidden and denied. She has neither her mother's nor Grisha's inclination to forget the past.

She looks to Julian for approval. "Do I look all right?"

"You look beautiful," he answers, kissing her on the forehead.

She doesn't believe him, but feels comforted.

"We are going to videotape your story as agreed," Julian tells her, and explains that his questions will be based on the information she has already given him.

"I am nervous," Batya confesses.

"No need. I am a sympathetic listener," he says. "One, I hope, who does not judge." He sounds earnest. "I will be an enlightened witness to your Holocaust experience. You must know that."

"What do you mean?"

"Someone to whom a survivor witness recounts their experience, becomes an enlightened witness to that experience and therefore has a responsibility to act whenever an injustice is being done, like bullying or an act of racism ."

But I have never spoken about this before, except for bits and pieces to my son."

"Then your son has become a witness as well. Isn't it time you talked? You told me how much hearing Doris Goldstein speak helped you. Now you too are speaking for other survivors, and for the victims." He takes her hand. "I know that this is hard for you."

She remembers only too well how drained Doris Goldstein was after her talk. In body and mind. She also remembers Signor Moller's story, and Madame Berent's. In the end, speaking to others about the Holocaust was both educational for the listener and healing for the speaker.

And I could use some healing, thinks Batya wryly. Still, these assurances don't ease her anxiety of having to speak. She sits down in front of the camera. The strong lights bother her eyes. It's like in the movies: the interrogation of a criminal by a KGB or a Nazi agent who tortures his victim with a sharp bright light.

At first, the right words don't come, but Julian's patience and kindness encourage her. "Don't think about the words. Just concentrate on the images in your mind and describe them."

Does he know what he is asking?

"What do you remember from before the war?"

"I remember a spacious apartment in Warsaw," she starts, searching for the right words and wishing she had written all this down, as it would be so much easier to read, "and my father and mother happily receiving guests who would pinch my cheeks on entering. Crystal vases filled with fruit and flowers sparkling on the tables; my newborn sister, Tereska, with big blue eyes and pink cheeks, lying in a crib, kicking her little fat legs.

"I remember French toast the cook made, using a delicious brioche, which I love to this day. The golden egg bread dipped in egg and milk and fried in butter, topped with granulated sugar or a compote of fruits. The aroma of browned butter and the vanilla taste of the bread that melted in my mouth. Whenever I eat it today, I see the kitchen in our home, smell the French toast in front of me. I see myself sitting at the wooden table delighting in the sugary taste. I also remember the drink I hated most: Ovaltine, a poor substitute for cocoa.

"On birthdays, the most precious gifts from my parents were books in which I discovered magic worlds. I loved walks with my father, trips to the park and Shirley Temple movies."

"How old were you then?"

"I was five years old."

"Did your father teach you to read?" Julian asks.

"No. My grandfather, who lived with us, he taught me. The beginning of the war put an end to a Jewish child's chances for a normal life. I had big hopes of continuing ballet, taking French lessons and starting grade one. None of it happened."

"How old were you when the war began?"

"Almost six years old. Already then I knew that all Jews were marked for death. I saw people persecuted in the streets and made to perform menial tasks. One day, while waiting for Father to come out of a store, I saw an SS man hang a Jewish man on a tree branch. His genitals were exposed and people gathered, making fun of his circumcision. I scraped my fingers against the cement wall of a building I was hanging onto.

"The day the ghetto was sealed…"

"What year was that?"

"The year 1940. We were imprisoned by a ten-foot wall, built with shards of glass inside the mortar and barbed wire all around. The sounds on the street changed. I heard harsh noises, rifle shots, slamming of doors, shouting in German and boots stomping along the pavement. We lived always frozen with fear. We were afraid all the time of being caught and taken to a concentration camp. Most of all I feared a separation from my parents. People were saying that families could not survive together."

She finds it difficult to continue, but Julian hands her a glass of water.

"You are the witness," Julian suggests. "Your testimony will help others to better understand what went on in the Warsaw ghetto."

Batya speaks more about the ghetto and tells about the events that changed her forever: her escape and the separation from her parents, life in hiding. And how she became a person with a new identity and how her former self became split into Batya and Beata. She pauses for a few moments then begins to speak about Tereska. The words don't come easily. Julian tries to calm her by stopping the video-taping and waits patiently till she is more composed. This takes some time.

"How do you feel about the policeman who shot your sister?" Julian asks gently.

"I don't hate the Polish policeman," she replies slowly, thinking of her father. "He was forced into this act and he didn't have a real choice. He only wanted his family to live. He wanted to live and I cannot make that moral judgment. But I cannot forgive the Nazi who gave the order to kill my sister…" She waves her hand in front of the camera and bows her head, choking out the words, "Sorry, I can't go on."

Julian gives a sign for the video-taping to stop. Batya gathers all the willpower she has left to collect the scattered pieces of her mind. The student with the camera looks morbidly sad. Does he empathize or hate to be forced into hearing this deadly testimony? *Maybe,* she thinks, *being able to share that terrible part of my life with others is what will give me the courage to go on.* And once again she thinks of Doris Goldstein and her courage and she tells Julian that she will go on.

Julian gives a sign for the filming to continue.

"What did your father do in the ghetto?"

She did not expect this question.

"Must I talk about my father?" she blurts out.

"So many years have passed. Your father is long gone. Don't you feel that you need to speak about him to bring this chapter to a close?"

How different he sounds from a moment ago, when he was so understanding. His last question seems sterile and insensitive. In fact, it is academic, she thinks. But is she still ashamed of her father? No, she is not. Maybe Julian is right. Maybe now, at this point, she can come to terms with the painful truth—but not yet. First she needs to be alone for a few minutes. She asks for a break and retreats to her bedroom.

There she looks at herself in the mirror again. She has come this far. Can she speak against her father? Would he want her to tell the truth? Of course, he would. By being afraid to tell the truth she is covering up for her father who wouldn't have wanted it as he had confessed it all in his memoir.

"People are so prejudiced. They will say terrible things about me and my father. They will say that I don't deserve to live, that as the daughter of a Jewish policeman I didn't deserve to survive." She tells Julian.

"No, they won't," he tells her, putting his arm around her. "And if they do, who are they to condemn? I learned this myself when I judged your father harshly. I was wrong. I know it is a perplexing and painful subject, but one that you must confront sooner or later. How can we know what we would have done in his situation? You said so yourself, even about the Polish policeman." Julian's voice deepens with emotion. "You have done much work on this. You searched for the truth, and now is the time to cast some light on this dark chapter and share it. Being the man he was, your father would have approved."

She remembers the letter the archivist at the Jewish Historical Society gave her, about how her father saved children from dying in the ghetto streets. She runs to her file box, pulls out the crumpled piece of paper and shows it to Julian.

"Perhaps you can send this letter to that woman you told me about," he says. "The woman who wrote that defamatory paragraph in her thesis. Maybe she will retract her comments to the institutions that have this statement on record."

"I tried to write to her several times," she says, "but have never heard back. So I gave up. Maybe I will try again. But now I just want to finish this testimony."

She takes the Mouth of Truth out of its pouch and places it around her neck. She will wear it in front of the camera and also show the letter. She will take her father out of his hiding place and bring him out to the light as the decent man she knew him to be, even with his dark side exposed.

When she returns to the set, the student observes the silver disk with interest. "What does this represent?" he asks, pointing at the medallion.

Julian gives the sign to begin filming.

"Tell us about the silver disk."

Batya tells the story of the Mouth of Truth. About how this object represents a deep connection between her and her father and gives her the courage to look without fear into the dark world of her past. Besides that, the silver disk symbolizes the return of memories she tried to ignore, memories that have seeped into the very marrow of her bones.

"Tell us, Batya, about your father in the ghetto."

She sweats under the blazing lights and Julian's watchful eye, telling Shimon Lichtenberg's story. "The only conclusion I have reached is that under that extreme stress, his moral judgment failed him," she says at the end. "But I feel," she adds, "that my father exonerated himself at least a little by showing his love and concern for the children of the ghetto, and here is the proof." She holds up the letter from Jerzy Konarski.

"What happened to your father?"

"He died two years after we came to Canada, of cancer. But I think that it was really the war that killed him."

"What about you, Batya? How have you felt throughout your life carrying such a burden?"

"Most of my life," she confesses, "I have felt guilty for having survived instead of my sister. If I hadn't been sick that day in the ghetto, I would have gone to Rogacki, instead of Tereska. I would have died. But instead I lived while she and one and a half million children perished. I have even felt guilt that my mother had to grieve over her baby daughter, who might have been saved if not for me. And now, when I think about my father, I feel the burden of his guilt too."

"Why have you agreed to give your testimony today?" Julian asks.

"I want this message to get out to other child survivors who may feel like I do. And to those who have experienced any kind of persecution or trauma or abuse as children. To all those children who have been bullied in their homes or in schools for being different. And to all the adults who are the abusers. And to students of history. And I want to reach all those who may think that what I have described here are ancient facts irrelevant to modern day, or that the genocide of the Jews never took place. I know that my story is relevant, because it really happened."

The student stops the video camera. The taping is over.

"What do you really think of my testimony?" Batya asks Julian afterwards. "Did I come across as self-centred and sanctimonious?"

"No," he replies emphatically. "You are far too critical of yourself. Yours are the feelings of all survivors longing for expression and understanding. How can anyone understand their present if they don't understand or remember their past? Yours is a story that needs to be told. And now you are sharing the lessons of healing you have learned. For many, the trauma continues. If you can reach just a few of those people, isn't this worth it?"

After the student leaves, Batya lies down on the couch and closes her eyes. Her thoughts gravitate to Julian, who is sitting by the window. What she secretly feels for him now is a kind of tenderness coupled with an attraction, but not the purely physical love she felt for Grisha. Julian's presence has brought her to an accounting with herself, reconciling her past and her present. He has given her courage to deal with the pain instead of sinking into self-pity or the oblivion of forgetting.

Julian comes over to the couch and sits close to her. "You were great. Thank you for today," he says, clasping her hand. He fingers the face of the silver disk resting on her chest. "Do you know that today you became the Mouth of Truth?"

He lowers his face towards hers and kisses her tenderly. She loves the nearness of him, his voice, his words, the evergreen scent of his cologne. The longer they are together the more she recognizes his psyche, his moods, his depressions, his words and his silences, and his inability to communicate at certain times. On such days, they almost whisper to each other lest the sound of words upset their equilibrium. She feels much stronger now and perhaps she, too, can help Julian through his difficult moments, because there is a sense of understanding and mutual respect between them.

Chapter 31

A few days after the taping, Julian telephones. "Good news," he says, "the testimonial videotape is ready to be shown. Why not invite your children to see it and maybe you can have that conversation you've been wanting to have?"

Batya agrees wearily. The very thought of another conversation feels scary. *What if she fails again? She has already tried and failed several times.* "Am I ready for this?" she asks him.

"Sam and Miriam, from what you tell me, are smart and kind people," Julian replies. "They are almost grown up. I am sure they love you in their own way. But your relationship with them can only thrive when it is drained of past poisons."

He is right. *This may be the final showdown,* she thinks. She will invite her children for the coming Sunday afternoon and tell them she has a surprise for them. *How can she show them her love and that her feelings for them are so much deeper now that she can feel again?*

On Sunday, everything is set for the "surprise." The children arrive and greet Julian with reserved politeness. Everyone settles down in the living room. Batya trusts Julian to be the mediator or the referee. He explains what is about to happen. The tape begins to roll and Batya begins to squirm. Instead of watching the video as it unfolds, she watches Sam, whose face is calm throughout, and Miriam, who becomes restless about halfway through and starts shifting uncomfortably on the couch.

Batya is uneasy about putting them through this and can't wait for it to end. *Better to know the truth,* she thinks, and not be left in silence, as she was by her parents. Secrets and lies are sources of misunderstandings. No truth can be more painful than a lie when it is exposed.

The videotape comes to an end. All four sit in silence until she gets up to serve refreshments. This time, she has had no wine or vodka beforehand, although a drink right now might help. But as Julian said, when helping her prepare, that would make her an escapist, less aware of everyone's feelings and less equipped to handle the situation. *What situation?* she thinks. How can she connect her testimony to her ailing relationship with her children? Her mother asked forgiveness, and so should she. Although she isn't sure she has forgiven her mother. Perhaps it will all take time.

The ice clinks in their glasses of soda. Forks strike the plates as everyone attacks the chocolate cake. They make small talk. Batya knows that Miriam wants to leave, because she is looking at her brother and almost waving her watch in front of his nose. He knowingly jokes, waving his fork back at her and grinning. She needs to spend quality time with her daughter very soon.

"What do you think of your mother's experience?" asks Julian, coming to the rescue. Three surprised faces turn towards him. Sammy looks puzzled. Miriam slumps deeply into the couch. Batya is nervous.

Sam sits up in his chair and his face is composed and serious. "I always felt that you, Mom," he turns towards his mother, speaking slowly as if searching for the right words, "couldn't really talk with us. The only times I remember you telling me about being inside the ghetto, it seemed like you felt like you were still a prisoner. That there was a wall and you couldn't get past it."

Suddenly the softness in Sam's voice turns to bitterness. "You drank a lot and, when you did that, you became a different person, not my mom."

Miriam lifts her head high. She no longer looks bored. Her eyes are lively and there is energy in her posture. She avoids her mother's eyes and turns to Julian instead. "I saw my mom," she breaks in, "as a victim. My mom was like someone who was always unhappy and always feeling persecuted by something or somebody. I didn't know much about her experience during the war. We never talked about it. My father and their friends didn't understand her. Neither did I. I didn't want to hear about the old country. I wanted her to be just a mom, like other kids' moms. She was always full of anger and it scared me."

Anger! The fire Batya had so often felt raging beneath her skin, eating away her insides. She thought she had hidden it well, but not well enough.

"It's pretty obvious your Holocaust experience had a bad effect on our family," Sam says, looking directly to her. "I think, Mom, you felt guilty about living and being happy, as if you didn't deserve to survive, and you were afraid that other people thought so too. So you created this wall to protect yourself."

So much truth in Sammy's words and Miriam's too.

"But now," Sam continues, "you have moved on. It's hard, but I respect your decisions and sort of understand them. You know, it's not all bad for us.

You've taught us to be independent. And to think about what we do and how we are living. That's not bad."

Batya is deeply moved. It's obviously her turn to say something, but the old feeling of helplessness paralyzes her throat when she tries to speak. She tells herself not to cry. This is her chance to tell the truth about what happened to the family as she sees it. She will beg them for forgiveness.

"Unlike you," she begins, not knowing what will come out of her mouth next, "I never had a chance to talk to my mother and father about the war and how it affected us. My parents didn't want to talk about the past. And I didn't want that to happen to you two. But it did. And that was wrong. There should be no family secrets. There are things you and I have never discussed regarding our own family problems and I want to talk about them now. It is time to clean up some of the baggage from our relationship."

"When you left home…" Miriam pipes up, then cuts herself off as she looks at Julian, still a stranger to her.

"Julian knows much of what we have been through," says Batya. "He is my friend."

Miriam continues, "When you left, it was hard. Dad was here for us but, you know, I may seem like I am okay, but teenagers need their mothers. I know you thought you had to go away. Because of this thing about your childhood. But why now? Isn't it time to get over your past? Because when you went away, it affected us—me and Sam. I needed you, Mom, and you weren't here for me."

"I would have been absent even if I had stayed," Batya responds. "I don't think anyone ever fully gets over being hurt, abused or persecuted in some way—or even left by their mother, like I did to you two. I've made many mistakes, trying to hide everything as if nothing was wrong. I don't want to pretend this never happened, although sometimes I wish I could. I do understand if you're not ready to forgive me."

Two sweet faces regard her intently, as if waiting for something more from her, something that would right her wrongs. "I don't blame you for feeling the way you do. When I left, I wasn't able to function as a mother and a wife should. Something broke in me. I couldn't cope and wasn't strong enough to heal myself, never mind stand up to your father."

Sam comes to the couch, sits between her and Miriam, and strokes his mother's arm. "We know, Mom," he says, reassuring her. Miriam looks as if she is about to cry.

Batya pats his hand and continues. "I know you know, but I want you and Miri to understand. None of this had to do with you. You were not to blame. These were my problems, problems between me and your father. I will always love you both, and when I was away, you were always with me in my thoughts and my heart."

"But you didn't have to leave, Mom," says Miri. "I knew you weren't happy with Dad. You fought all the time. I used to throw the covers over my ears at night so I wouldn't hear you fighting. It was better that you split up. But I missed you…" Miriam is weeping now and Batya reaches out to her little girl and hugs her. She either had no idea what her daughter had been feeling or she didn't want to know.

Sammy looks at both of them, his face serious. "Even though you and Dad fought all the time, Mom, I wanted you to stay together," he says wistfully. "I hoped you would make peace. You could at least have talked to us before you left," he adds, a note of resentment in his voice.

"You are so right, my darlings. I can only tell you that I wish things had been different. I am sorry for hurting you. Deeply, deeply sorry. I wish I could have been stronger. Can you ever, ever forgive me?"

Batya looks imploringly at her children. They are both silent. "You must both be exhausted," she says, feeling drained herself. "Are you glad we had this conversation?"

Two heads nod yes and her children stand up as if to leave. Miriam leans over to kiss her on the cheek and it feels like a little girl's kiss, the kiss of an innocent child who loves her mother. "I am here for you, Mom, if you need me," she says.

Sammy gives her another big hug. "I love you, Mom," he says. "Don't worry, things will work out."

"Next time, it will be your turn to talk," Batya says at the door. "I've said enough for now. I want to know more about you, your lives, your feelings, your thoughts. I have loved you, but not well enough. Now that I am stronger, I can love you more, with my whole heart."

Julian shakes hands with Sam and Miriam. She watches them walk down the hallway—her two dearest beings, whose goodness is the best acknowledgement of her right to live on this earth. She goes into the bedroom to be alone for a while.

All that had happened today was not just about her. It was about her children too. They have their own demons, upsets, triumphs and desires. One or even two conversations cannot erase the years of accumulated unhappiness and poor communication. But today was a start.

Papa died a guilty man. She has no right to forgive his actions on behalf of those he put into the wagons destined for death. Though he didn't kill them or want them to die, he was an accomplice. And she was carrying his guilt like a never-to-be-born child. How can she purge her father's guilt if not by telling his story and by giving her love freely and without fear, as he once gave it to her before tragedy struck? Maybe then his restless soul will finally be at peace.

I love you, Papa, she thinks, looking at her father's picture on the dresser. *In my heart I know that you are good. You never had a chance to rediscover that good in you, to repair the damage the war did to you and our family, but I still have that chance with mine. I have the chance to build on the forces of love and life left to me, no matter how damaged. I can build on the love that you had given me. You once asked me to forgive you. I now understand what you meant because I have asked my children to forgive me.*

The answer lies in the future. She thinks about Julian, whom she has forgotten for a moment. She finds him still sitting in the living room waiting for her return. He has been a witness to her deepest emotions and secrets.

"I don't know how to thank you for what you have done today," she tells him. "I still have a lot of work to do -to find that deep connection I had lost with my children and to heal their wounds."

"Don't," he says gently, as she starts to cry. "Don't let yourself succumb to guilt again. Yes, you have to turn things around with them. But you wanted their truth too. Now you know how cruel truth can be."

"Yes. I recognized the truth in what I heard from them and I know now how they, too, have suffered because of me."

"Don't you see? The process of healing has begun. Do your best with what you have now. When the little hurt girl in you heals, Batya will become even stronger than she already is." Julian's words always make sense to her.

"Let's toast the past, the present and the future," Batya says.

They pour vodka into tiny glasses.

"To the Mouth of Truth," says Julian, raising his glass.

"To the enlightened witness," says Batya, raising hers.

"And what will you do now with this video?" she asks.

"Maybe this and others like it will add to a better understanding of what a gigantic footprint the Genocide left on the human heart, mind and history."

And what a gigantic footprint it is, she thinks, watching him make supper. She feels safe in his presence. They eat, drink and talk into the night.

"It's late now and I must leave soon," Julian says, walking towards the window and turning his back to her. "I'm going back to Toronto."

Batya follows him. His words make the ground she is standing on shift a little.

"Back to Toronto? Now? This is so sudden," she manages. She cannot imagine her life without Julian. She feels bound to him by fate, by the past.

"Would you want me to stay?" he asks.

"Is it up to me?"

"Not completely. I have been offered a position here as a full professor next year, but there are also feelings involved. I have come to care a lot for you. I love you."

"And I have deep feelings for you." she answers without hesitation.

They make no promises when he leaves. She stands on the front lawn watching him walk away, his feet crunching the fallen leaves along the path. The wind's chill foretells winter, but she knows that the winter will pass, as all things must, and a new season will dawn.

Afterword

Much has been written about the inheritance of trauma, the transmission from parent to child of memories, fears, attitudes, ways of relating. Batya's father Shimon, was a thinking man who mulled over his decisions, rethought them, reconsidered, then grieved. This tendency to think and grieve over the past, Batya, the book's heroine, inherited from her father. She is always aware of how she feels but she doubts her feelings; she makes decisions, but she second guesses them; she develops insights but wonders if she is right or wrong. From her mother, Batya inherits the tendency to avoid, trying to forget the past. Batya longs for the return of the overwhelming feeling of love that she remembers having for her father. She dreams about true love; her marriage falls far short so she looks elsewhere and finds, with Grisha, a sexual awakening that she mistakes for love. With Julian she ultimately finds a love that is more reciprocal, perhaps more permanent.

All three, Shimon, Marta, and Batya, survived indescribable horrors and paid a price for having survived. Even children pay this price, though their memories are blurred, and even when no one explicitly tells them precisely what they have lived through. Very young children may be too young to remember but they are never too young to sense when something terrible is happening. A child of nine, ten and eleven, remembers.

Perhaps the most difficult aspect of the plot for the reader is Batya's (temporary) abandonment of her children, Sam and Miriam. She leaves them behind when she goes to Europe to discover the truth about her father. Is this because she considers herself unworthy of being their mother? Does she thinks they would be better off without her? Is she re-enacting her own childhood when her parents abandoned her to Bolek in order to save her from the Nazis? Batya feels guilty about abandoning her children, as her own mother must have done, especially on learning about Bolek's abuse. This is not clear because, on the surface, the mother is portrayed as unemotional, unconcerned. Batya did everything in her power to be different from her mother, to be more like the father she remembered – honest, honourable but ruthless when it came to survival.

Mouth of Truth poses the question, how is trauma passed on from parents to children? Are Sam and Miriam affected by their mother's fits of brooding, by the occasional fears, the inexplicable furies and ghosts that inhabited Batya's world. When parents are traumatized, the covert nature of the parent-child communication is itself sufficient to transmit the horror that parents try to hide. Batya tries hard to protect her children as her own parents must have tried to protect her. The reader is made aware of Batya's suffering but left to guess the fates of Sam and Miriam. This is an important parenting issue: despite the conspiracy of silence, can traumatized parents be adequate parents or will children of trauma always be scarred? Will Sam and Miriam be scarred by their mother's abandonment? Are they doomed to be forever making up for a portion of their past? Is it this hurt and scarring that Shimon asks Batya to forgive him for? Or is it that he has not told her the truth, or that he has not lived up to the idealized image she has of him, or that, by permitting her to see him as perfect, he has not sufficiently prepared her for real life? On completing the book, I was left with the unanswered question, for what act of commission or omission was he apologizing?

The effect of trauma on children can manifest itself in a variety of ways. The psychiatric literature claims that self-esteem is impaired and that the child feels pressure to become a super-achiever. This is true for Batya/Beata, with the additional burdens of needing to serve as a replacement for a sister who was lost. Research into trauma points out that children end up identifying with the role of perpetual victim. Something always seems to be done to them, something for which they think they may be responsible. This generalization characterizes Batya's marriage. Another effect of trauma are moods of anxiety and dysphoria, difficulties in intimate relationships and recurrent interpersonal conflicts. The literature talks about the pulls of dependency, looking for and finding strong people to lean on, and then being disappointed because their seeming strength turns out to be illusory. This characterizes Batya's relationship with Grisha. In many ways, Batya's life confirms the research findings. There is the vulnerability, the preoccupation with the past, the tendency to catastrophize, the feeling of deprivation and threat, and the recurrent waves of unprovoked anger and guilt, many of which, in the early parts of the novel, were fueled by alcohol. Batya originally sees herself as a victim, but tries valiantly to rid herself of this image and to heal. In Julian, she finds a soul mate who will not disappoint her and who, like her father, is someone she can respect.

The academic literature on trauma describes a deep affection for humanity in trauma survivors and a drive toward artistic contribution and image-making, motivated perhaps by wanting to transform past atrocity into art. This is exactly what the author of *Mouth of Truth* has done. She has transformed her own troubled past into a well-researched, beautifully-written and very moving story of survival in the face of death.

Mary V. Seeman OC MDCM FRCPC   March 2017

Dr. Mary Seeman, originally from Poland, grew up in Montreal, trained in psychiatry and developed an interest in serious mental illness. On the Faculty of Medicine at the University of Toronto, she has published widely, especially in the area of schizophrenia and women's mental health. She is an Officer of the Order of Canada.

Acknowledgments

I am grateful and deeply indebted to Dr. Mary Seeman, for her caring, support, and encouragement throughout the process of this novel's revision. Also, big thank you to my dear friends, who were there for me through thick and thin, and to my children, Steve, Wendy, Franci, David and my sister who cheered me on.

Special appreciation to all the readers of the novel and their comments during its various stages.

Last but not least thank you to my editor, Kathleen Fraser, who set me on the road towards completion of the manuscript.

Lillian Boraks-Nemetz
December 23rd, 2017
Vancouver, B.C.

Bibliography

Blatas, Arbit. *Olocausto: Venezia, Campo del Ghetto Nuovo.* Venice: Azienda
   Autonoma di Soggiorno e Turismo di Venezia [Tipo-Litografia Armena],
   1979.
———. *An Artist's Venice.* New York: The Vendome Press, 1997.
Dawidowicz, Lucy S. *The War against the Jews, 1933–1945.* New York: Holt,
   Rinehart & Winston, 1975.
Delbo, Charlotte. *Auschwitz and After.* Translated by Rosette C. Lamont. New
   Haven, CT: Yale University Press, 1995.
Frankl, Viktor E. *Man's Search for Meaning.* Boston: Beacon Press, 2006. First
   published 1966 by Washington Square Press.
Kafka, Franz. *Metamorphosis and Other Stories.* Aylesbury, U.K.: Penguin,
   1967.
Langer, Lawrence L. *The Holocaust and the Literary Imagination.* New Haven,
   CT: Yale University Press, 1975.
Lewin, Abraham. *A Cup of Tears: A Diary of the Warsaw Ghetto.* Edited by
   Antony Polonsky. London: Fontana, 1990.
The Living Bible Paraphrased. Carol Stream, IL: Tyndale House Publishers,
   1973.
Miller, Alice. *The Truth Will Set You Free: Overcoming Emotional Blindness
   and Finding Your True Adult Self.* New York: Basic Books, 2001.
Milosz, Czeslaw. "Campo dei Fiori." In *Holocaust Poetry.* Compiled and
   introduced by Hilda Schiff. New York: St. Martin's Press, 1995.
Ringelblum, Emmanuel. *Notes from the Warsaw Ghetto: The Journal of
   Emmanuel Ringelblum.* New York: Schocken Books, 1974.
Simonis, Daniel. *Lonely Planet Venice Condensed.* Oakland, CA: Lonely Planet
   Publications, 2002.
Tagore, Rabindranath. *Fireflies.* New York: Collier Books, 1955.

Lillian Boraks-Nemetz was born in Warsaw, Poland, and is a child survivor of the Holocaust. She escaped from the Warsaw Ghetto and spent the remainder of the war in hiding under a false identity.

Boraks-Nemetz graduated from the University of British Columbia with a Masters Degree in Comparative Literature. She is an author of an award winning novel *The Old Brown Suitcase* followed by *The Sunflower Diary* and the *Lenski File*, as well as two volumes of poetry *Ghost Children* and *Garden of Steel*. She has translated Polish Emigre poetry into English and has also co-compiled the YA anthology of Canadian Holocaust writing, *Tapestry of Hope*. She recently completed an adult novel.

Boraks-Nemetz has been working at the University of British Columbia's Writing Center from 1980 to 2016. She often speaks to students about the consequences of racism, as a member of the Holocaust Center's Outreach Program. She is a board member of the Janusz Korczak Association of Canada. She lives and works in Vancouver, BC. Canada.

Printed in February 2018
by Gauvin Press,
Gatineau, Québec